THE EYE OF MAKARIOS

THE EYE OF MAKARIOS

Ψ

DAVID CULLEN

Culpro Books

The Eye of Makarios
First published 2005
Revised and updated International Edition 2009

ISBN 13: 978-0-9559911-0-3

www.lulu.com/davidcullen

Published Culpro Books
an imprint of Cullen Productions

Then (to be brief) the foreigners
Which the king found most dangerous
Hied them off, by every way
And, in short, they went away...

But ere their journey they had started
And from Limassol had departed
The king them all did recompense
And give them gifts at his expense:
Gold and silver, silken threads
Ships and jewels *and fiery steeds...*
- from *La prise d'Alexandrie*
by Guillaume de Machaut (1300-1377)

Ψ

To be tantalised is an experience almost sensual.
Ilich Ramirov, in a written essay at the KGB
Academy Number 311 in Novosibirsk, Siberia,
April 16 1974

For Pauly - my rock, my inspiration, my life.

Ψ

Acknowledgements

For starting it all:
Pierre Rouan, who died because he told this story.

For their invaluable help:
Christina Cascianis
Mrs Margery Egginton (deceased)
Madame Sally-Anne Forêt (née Bowker)
Chief Inspector Johann Versleas (Amsterdam police)
Ms Charlotte Rapley
The ones who do not want to be identified in North America, Europe, Cyprus, Venezuela, Lebanon and Russia.

For their attempts at hindrance, and hence proving the story:
The British government
The French government

Finally my respect and admiration - but not necessarily my support - must go to the late Michael Mouskos, His Beatitude Archbishop Makarios III of Cyprus.

Ψ

Cast in order of appearance

Richard John Bingham - *7th Earl of Lucan (a patriotic fugitive)*
Commander Christou - *Cypriot Tactical Reserve Force*
Major Stavros Stavrou - *2nd In Command of EOKA*
Demetrakis Spourghitis - *3rd In Command of EOKA*
General George Grivas - *leader of EOKA*
Elizabeth O'Toole - *an Irish diversion*
Michael Mahoney - *an Irish opportunist*
Ali 'Akay' Al Khalifa - *Financial Controller of Black September*
Philomena O'Toole - *a second Irish diversion*
Khalid al-Wazir - *IRA liaison, Black September*
Ali Hassan Salameh - *Controller of Intelligence and Action, Black September*
Salah Khalef - *Consiglière, Black September*
Faisal Ibn Musaed - *PA to Ali Hassan Salameh*
Steve Graves - *an American on a quest*
Sally-Anne Bowker - *in love with Steve Graves*
Digenis – *an agent of Mossad Aliyah Beth*
Christina Cascianis - *a special lady*
Ilich Ramirov - *an itinerant terrorist*
Tony Verekelis - *a member of EOKA*
Old Mother Dimitri - *nurse to George Grivas*
Nicos Sampson - *the future President of Cyprus (however briefly)*
Raouf Denktash - *the future President of Southern Cyprus*
Takis - *a young helper*
Colonel Stanley William Egginton - *a traitor above suspicion*
Halil - *a restaurant owner*
Pan - *the spirit of nature and paganism (or just a local boy)*

Ekaterina Furtseva - *said to be Minister of Culture, USSR*
Annette Stewart - *junior executive of De Beers London*
Chaim Cohen – *Deputy Controller of the Mossad, Israeli external security service*
Nathanson – *an agent of Mossad Aliyah Beth*
The Russian Ambassador to France *(perhaps)*
Georges Pompidou - *President of France*
Albert - *Pompidou's secretary*
Jim McKane - *a manager at Gulf, Houston USA*
Bishop Michael Rigakis - *aide to the Cypriot External Affairs Minister Ioannis Christophides*
Costas - *an ogre*
Wilbur - *Air France, Houston Airport*
Sir Lovelock Armstrong - *Permanent Under Secretary, UK Ministry of Defence*
Ronald Arthur - *Security Officer MOD*
Eunice Tate - *PA to DoS MOD*
Dr Louis Thomas - *Texas Medical Centre*
Charlotte Rapley - *sculptor and artist*
Louise Petit - *fashion designer*
Claude François - *French singer*
Marcel Forêt - *friend of Claude's*
Matthew Ramm - *UK police Special Branch*
Ron Woods - *UK police Special Branch*
Don Metcalf - *UK police Special Branch*
An old Cypriot peasant
Michael Mouskos - *His Beatitude Archbishop Makarios III of Cyprus*
Andreas Papadopoulos - *a priest*
Sergei 'Hernandez' - *a Russian*
Melanie - *a masseuse*
The five Controllers of Israeli Intelligence
Alexei Nikolayevich Kosygin - *Prime Minister of the Soviet Union*
Roz - *UK police Special Branch*
Chief Inspector Johann Versleas - *Amsterdam police*

Ψ

FOREWORD

History would have judged it as a time of turbulence. A time when mankind had gone mad and the redemption of the Millennium was a quarter of a century away. But with hindsight, it is now seen as the time when innocence ended. A time when those with agendas of their own decided that they had the right to murder whomever they chose. A time when the causes - and the people - who created the horror of the early twenty-first century were in their formative years.

It was a time before the communications revolution. Mobile telephones required a battery the size of two shoeboxes, and only the select few had VCRs. 'Personal' computers were the size of a room, and Vinton Cerf was just devising the first workings of what was to become the Internet. Compact discs had yet to herald the digital age.

Germany was still divided and the Cold War showed no sign of thawing. The USSR was mighty and the cracks in communism had yet to appear. Terrorism was rife.

As far as the general public were concerned, the late summer and fall of 1974 were just like any other in that turbulent decade. The previous fall the fires of raging world-wide inflation had been stoked after the *Yom Kippur* war when the oil-producing countries had realised the power of the liquid weapon underneath their feet and had promptly trebled the price of their black gold. By September 1974 the economies of the West had assimilated this massive rise but not without the consequent affects on their 'growth' rates and retail prices. Inflation, too, was rife.

In France, Valéry Giscard d'Estaing successfully took over the Presidential mantle after the death of Georges Pompidou. In West Germany, Helmut Schmidt became Chancellor after the communist spy Gunther Guillaume caused the downfall of the affable Willi Brandt.

Indeed, it was not a year to take a bet on the security of any Head of State. Richard Milhous Nixon was finally forced to resign as President of the United States over the Watergate scandal, and Gerald Ford fell into his shoes. In Portugal, the repressive Dr Caetano was ousted and replaced by General Spinola who, in his turn, was forced to make way for Costa de Gomes. In Cyprus, the resilient Archbishop Makarios fled the island as Nicos Sampson and the Greek National Guard paved the way for Clerides and Denktash to partition Aphrodite's soil. In Greece, the seven year regime of the Colonels and General Ioannides dissolved into ashes and Constantine Karamanlis returned from an eleven year exile in Paris. In Britain Harold Wilson bounced back into power as Premier Edward Heath was defeated by a national miners' strike.

To a world-weary public, hardened by years of assassinations, terrorism and universal gloom, none of this warranted any particular attention. To them, 1974 was just another normal year in the cauldron of world affairs and the decline of their living standards...

Ψ

PROLOGUE

London, November 1974

When it came to it, the girl's head shattered easily and she was dead by the time her body hit the floor. It had been an instantaneous but very painful death, shards of skull penetrating deep into the brain. Sandra - the one person whom the police later thought might be able to name her killer for definite - never knew who her murderer was.

Richard John Bingham, 7th Earl of Lucan, looked down at the inert body and shivered. It was dark in the basement of his town house at 46 Lower Belgrave Street, but he could clearly see the dark patch which had once been the back of the nanny's head. Already there was an unpleasant smell.

His breath came fast and deep, and his hands were shaking. Strangely enough he did not feel sick, as he had thought he would. He felt somewhat relieved. Relieved that this part of it at least was over. But the worst, of course, was yet to come.

Thirty-nine year old 'Lucky' Lucan gathered himself together and got down to business. *They* had specifically instructed that everything must go according to plan. Ten minutes delay at any stage and it could all go wrong and land him in an English cell for life. He must get on with it.

Quickly he retrieved the sack from the darkened corner and began to shove the dead body into it...

Ψ

When the top of the bag was tied and the macabre bundle propped back into the corner, Lucan left the murder weapon where it could easily be found - as instructed - and rushed up the stairs two at a time. His small bag was already packed with the very few things he was allowed to take with him, and now he just had time for the cosmetics. Then would come the chat with his wife, which the police would make so much of but which the Press would virtually ignore, and his escape in the borrowed car.

Everything went according to plan and soon Richard John Bingham, without the moustache which had been his trade mark around the gaming clubs of London, was driving south out of central London towards the suburb of Croydon. The night of November 7 1974 was crisp but not necessarily cold in London, and his thick Arran jumper was ample coverage against whatever the elements had in store. It was a dry night and rain was not predicted. This time Lucky Lucan hoped that the weather forecasters would be right. He had a long way to go.

His only regret was that he had to miss his dinner date at the *Clermont* with Greville, and without a word of apology or explanation. It was damn caddish of him. A gentleman really did not do such things.

He only hoped that, if the truth were ever known, England would be grateful...

One year earlier...

Cyprus, November 1973

Dawn came at 06:00 that morning. In Limassol, the five thousand year old town on the central southern coast of the island, a normal day had begun. Normal, that is, to the populus about to rise to earn their daily crust: working in the wineries or distilleries, or in the zoo or municipal gardens, or in the shops (anxious to start selling their lace or pottery or sheepskins to the low-season tourists); normal to the hotel workers or the rich, retired resident foreigners.

But in the very smart residential area in the north-east of the town, things were far from normal. Acting on information received from an EOKA guerrilla captured after wandering too far into the wrong part of Nicosia, ten men of President Makarios' Tactical Reserve Force were closing in on two houses. Inside one of the houses - and at that stage they knew not which - was Major Stavros Stavrou, codenamed Syros, second in command to General George Grivas, the leader of the island's guerrilla movement. *[For a brief history of Cyprus, see Appendix 1.]*

Commander Christou and his men were only too fully aware of what the death or, preferably, capture of Stavrou would mean to the wily Archbishop who governed Cyprus. The EOKA movement was tottering, their leader Grivas was old and it was rumoured that he was dying. To lose his Number Two now might be a blow from which he would never recover. And the promise of Stavrou's release (which, of course, would never actually happen) might secure the freedom of Justice Minister Kristos Vakis, taken by EOKA two weeks before.

The answer to Stavrou's location lay in the head of the terrorist now being interrogated in Nicosia. Christou only hoped that the boys at HQ extracted the answer soon. As it was, the rising sun would now force him to call seven of his men back to the discreetly parked English Army lorry - for word of 'The Red Priest's Men' in this, the main stronghold of Grivas, would spread like wildfire. That would leave just the two ununiformed lads to watch on a house apiece.

Christou removed his black beret and quietly opened the cab door and climbed out. He walked the ten metres to the corner with the main road, removed a khaki handkerchief from his pocket and wiped his brow. It was the signal for the seven in uniform to disperse and separately make their way back to the lorry.

Christou turned and walked back to the vehicle. The longer the transceiver did not crackle with the answer he wanted, the more irritated he would get.

The side street was still and lifeless. Unceremoniously he undid his trousers and began to pee up against the side of somebody's villa...

As it was, it took another six hours for the terrorist in Nicosia to crack, the final breakthrough coming only after his left testicle had been crushed to a pulp.

Just before noon the transceiver bleeped once. Christou grabbed it. The voice at the other end said just three words, "The grey villa," and the transmission ended. It was enough.

The wooden door gave with one mighty kick of Christou's boot. Four members of the Tactical Reserve Force stormed inside.

In the open living area, a woman of about thirty, dressed in only the flimsiest of negligées, was setting the table for lunch. Even before she had thought about screaming, Christou had leapt across the room and had grasped her throat so tightly that any exhalation of sound or air was impossible.

"Where is Stavrou?" he snarled garlic into her face. "Syros, where is he? Tell me woman and tell me now."

The woman's tongue poked out between her purple lips. She could not have answered even if she had wanted to.

"Where is he?"

Her eyes, almost bulging from their sockets, stared fearfully yet contemptuously at the TRF leader.

"Terrorist bitch!" He rammed her into the rough brickwork of the wall, following with one mighty slap with the back of his hand across her face. Her lower lip split in two places, blood jumping over her chin and negligée.

He let her fall and turned to his men. "Upstairs. And *don't* let the bastard get away!"

The first door upstairs was a lavatory, the second some sort of clothes cupboard. The third door was locked.

Again Christou's boot made contact with wood, and this time the frame shattered, splinters flying everywhere as the door crashed inward.

A man, dressed only in white Y-fronts, stood in the centre of the room. Next to him was a metal waste bin from which smoke was rising. He glanced up as the door slammed open and a reflex action made him start to his right towards a vicious-looking machine gun resting on a chair.

"Hold it, sir!"

In the split second the man had looked away from the door and twitched towards his gun, the soldiers had entered the room. Three 9mm sub-machine guns now pointed rigidly towards his body. Stavrou took this in and immediately realised it would be folly to resist. On Christou's bark he stopped dead in his tracks. After a moment, his whole body seemed to relax and he turned towards the soldiers and smiled. His resigned shrug spoke volumes.

Christou came towards him, staring at the tall rugged man with the rough-handsome features, jet black hair just greying at the temples. His body, once obviously athletic, was still powerful, but now his stomach jutted rather severely in a combination of middle-aged spread and too much *halloumi*. He almost looked pregnant, but the equally prominent bulge in the bottom of his Y-fronts proved that this would never be possible. On recounting the episode some years later, Christou was to liken him to "A massive, proud bullock."

The Commander walked over and picked up the machine gun from the chair. He looked at it for a moment and then threw it to one of his men and turned back to Stavrou.

The captive seemed to read his thoughts, for without being asked his brown eyes sparkled with pride and what almost looked like delight as he announced, "Yes, I am Syros."

"Of course," Christou said respectfully. "You could not be anybody else, Major." He lowered his gun and felt inside a breast pocket of his camouflage shirt. He pulled out a packet of *Camel*. "Cigarette?"

Stavrou laughed softly. "Why not? I am sure cancer is now the least of my worries."

"The very least." Christou put two cigarettes into his own mouth and lit them both. He removed one, and Stavrou, being wise enough not to move his hands from their position by his sides, accepted it with his mouth.

"Anybody else here?"

"Only me and the woman."

"I see." Christou walked back towards the door. "Guard him well," he ordered the three soldiers, as much for Stavrou's benefit as their's. "If he tries *anything*, kill him. I am just going to have a look around. If you will excuse me, Major?"

Stavrou inclined his head.

There were three untried doors in the corridor. The first was another bedroom, unslept in and devoid of human presence. The second door, opposite, was a third bedroom. This one showed signs of use the previous night, the bed unmade and two empty *ouzo* bottles next to it. There was nobody in the room, but presuming Stavrou and the woman had spent the night in the first bedroom, then there must be a third person about somewhere. And there was one room unchecked.

By logical deduction, Christou figured that this last room must be the bathroom. He threw his cigarette down as he approached, listening intently for any noise from within. There was none.

And then there was.

One soft, dull thud.

Christou smiled. He was now standing next to the closed bathroom door and the smell of burning was quite distinct.

Standing to one side, he gently knocked on the door.

"Good morning, my friend - or is it afternoon? This is Commander Christou, Tactical Reserve Force. I wonder if you would oblige me? Will you come out? Or does this nasty weapon I'm holding shred the door and you with it?"

There was no reply from within.

"And don't even think about going out the back way. There are a lot of bad men out there with even bigger guns." Cautiously, Christou turned the knob, making sure he was well concealed. A gentle push made the door swing slowly open.

Crouching low, he peered round the doorway. One look and he straightened up, laughter bursting from his mouth.

Standing there, metal waste bin with smouldering contents at his feet, was a man some five years or so younger than Stavrou. He was of the same rugged physical complexion, but without the pot belly as yet. And he was completely naked. And, most curiously of all, he had a semi-erection. Either that or he was hung like Priapus.

By the side of the waste bin stood a whole pile of intriguing-looking documents which he had not a hope in hell of burning even if he had not been discovered for another hour.

To the Commander it was an hilarious sight. He pointed his gun at the man's lower stomach. "Weapon cocked, I see ? Come on, let's be having you."

Christou's sense of satisfaction turned to euphoria later that day when it was discovered that the naked man was none other than Demetrakis Spourghitis, one of Grivas' top lieutenants, suspected of being Number Three in the organisation.

To capture Numbers Two and Three of EOKA, Christou thought, was much much more than the health of General George Grivas could stand. In the last two days they - the Special Police and the Tactical Reserve Force - had captured twenty-six EOKA terrorists and over four hundred highly illuminating documents, including a detailed plan to assassinate Makarios on his daily journey from the Archbishopric to the Presidential Palace. The release by Grivas of Justice Minister Kristos Vakis must now be inevitable. Grivas had given and taken some beatings in the past but he could not, surely, ever recover from this?

As it was, Commander Christou was absolutely correct. Grivas was already consumed with a terminal heart disease, but it is still maintained by some that the shock of losing his Numbers Two and Three as well as twenty-four of his other top men was the straw that eventually broke his brave resistance to the illness.

With Stavrou gone, Grivas felt isolated from his organisation. He tried bravely to fight back, indeed the next day he issued a leaflet containing an eloquent personal attack on Makarios, 'Mr Mouskos' as he referred to him (for Grivas refused ever to recognise Makarios' title, either as Archbishop or President). In the leaflet he denied that there had been any plans to assassinate the Archbishop "That well-known arch-cook of black propaganda."

And even as the leaflets were being distributed on the streets, the remnants of Grivas' organisation were trying to ingratiate themselves with their now isolated leader by causing minor disturbances in and around Nicosia. In a pro-Grivas club in the city, a fifteen minute gun battle was waged; in a suburb a car was blown up by a crude bomb. Shots were fired at a petrol station in Larnaca, and other minor incidents occurred. But this violence was like the bite of a dog with its teeth removed.

Grivas was devastated. It was the end for him, the end of his life. By the time EOKA could blossom and grow again - as he knew he could make it do - he would be dead, and what would happen to his precious cause and followers then? *Enosis* - complete union with Greece - would probably fade away and Cyprus would be independent forever...

Had Grivas lived, the course of the 'coup' on the island the following July might have taken a turn far different from that which is now recorded historical fact. As it was, it was only a matter of weeks after the arrest of Stavrou, on January 27 1974, that General George Grivas, considered by some to be a terrorist and by others to be a hero, died.

But before his death he was to make one staggering last request. A request almost childlike in its spitefulness; for one last deeply personal victory against Makarios, to hurt Mr Mouskos for years to come. To give Grivas a triumph from beyond the grave.

And there was only one person in the world that Grivas wanted to carry out his request...

PART ONE

Ψ

OBJECTIVE

Ψ

Monday December 24 1973

"Independent Radio News, it is nine o'clock. The bombings in London. London was on full alert tonight after the bombs near Charing Cross Station and Whitehall two nights ago. Despite late-night Christmas Eve opening, Oxford Street, already a prime target for the bombers, was almost deserted by eight o'clock this evening."

Somewhere in the Irish Republic

With a bounce of her naked breasts, the girl sprang from the edge of the board and made a perfect dive into the deep end of the indoor swimming pool. Although the water was a pleasant twenty-two degrees celsius, the shock of the wetness on the naked curves of her young body made her nipples harden instantly.

Outside it was decidedly cold, as befits a Christmas Eve in Southern Ireland, but Michael Mahoney felt himself warming as he looked through the glass wall of the pool and admired the parting of the girl's legs as she crawled across the water. He smiled a wide, Irish smile and looked at the man standing next to him, heavily muffled against the chill of the two degree air.

"By golly, but she's a lovely girl."

The man nodded politely.

"I hope she… entertained you well last night?"

The man's face brightened as thoughts of last night flashed through his mind. He looked at Mahoney.

"Elizabeth was... what shall we say? Exquisite? Yes, that is the word. Purely exquisite. So charming, so... willing."

Mahoney beamed, cheeks rosy in the Atlantic breeze. He spoke quietly yet in exclamation. "Good on yer, Lizzie O'Toole. Yer a darlin' girl!" He looked at the other man. "Of course, she's available again for you tonight. And there's also a special gift for you, to mark what I hope will be the successful conclusion to our business."

The man raised an eyebrow. "Why, Mr Mahoney, I do believe you are about to offer me a bribe."

"A bribe? Me?" Mahoney's face oozed with geniality. "Heaven forfend, my dear sir. Indeed t'goodness, if it's one thing I've learned in my business it is never to offer a bribe to an Arab. Arabs are gentlemen, above that sort of thing."

The other man gave no indication that he knew the compliment was merely rhetoric sarcasm.

"No, no, listen," Mahoney continued, his breath smoking in the freezing air. "Yer've got t'stay until the twenty-sixth now before you can catch yer plane, so for the next two nights - whether our business is successful or not - I've arranged for Lizzie and her sister Philomena to entertain you in the evenings. My little Christmas present to yer. How's that?"

The bronzed skin of the Arab's face tightened as he smiled faintly. "Most... hospitable. You are the perfect host."

Behind the glass, the girl reached the side of the pool and stopped swimming. Her left hand held on to the metal bar as her right reached down between her legs. She smiled wickedly. Slowly, with circular motions, she began to rub herself...

The two men watched in silence. At the end, as the girl floated sated on top of the water, they turned away and began to walk towards the cliffs, a kilometre away.

After a while the Arab said, "And you own all this land?"

"Every last stone in the cliff." Mahoney put up his collar. "And I'd even have bought me own bit of the Atlantic Ocean if I could, but Eamonn de Valera wouldn't let me - and Childers ain't much help either."

The Arab sniffed. "I knew arms dealing was profitable, but your wealth surpasses anything I could have imagined."

Mahoney stopped in mid-stride. For just the slightest moment the guise of the simple, jolly Irishman slipped from his face and something cold and calculating was exposed. Then almost immediately the geniality was back. "Me? An arms dealer? What nonsense you do talk, Akay. I'm a businessman, that's all, and highly successful with it. Can I help it if the spirit of free enterprise has smiled on me? Painter and decorater, that's what I am." *Idiot wop.* Didn't he realise that there were such things as bugs and long-range voice detectors? Members of the Irish Special Branch, the sly boys of the *Garda*, could be listening to what they were saying from fifteen kilometres away.

The half-smile which seemed to be a permanent feature of the Arab's face did not falter at what was obviously an oblique slap across the knuckles. He gave a half-bow to his host. "Of course. Do forgive me."

Mahoney looked at him. Then he grinned and clasped Akay around the shoulders with a deceptively powerful right arm, an action which the Arab disliked intensely. "Nothin t'forgive, me ole stick," he put on his thickest brogue. "Of course, if it's business yer want t'discuss - and now's as fine a time as any, I must admit - then we'd best be getting back to the house. Constitutional over."

Mahoney steered the Arab in a tight semi-circle to take them back the way they had come.

To call Mahoney's abode a 'house' was an understatement. It was a mansion. Built from red-brick some five years before, it had cost Mahoney the best part of one hundred thousand punts, and in 1968 that had been a lot of money. It contained every domestic amenity money could buy, and included eight bedrooms *en suite*, spread across the three storeys. To any curious outsider, Mahoney would explain that he could afford such a luxury as this (and also his white Rolls-Royce Corniche, maroon Jaguar XJ6 and black and gold Mini Cooper) through sheer hard work and excellent management of his painting and decorating empire. This was only half true, the whole truth being much more sinister.

Born in County Cork in 1935, Mahoney had led a normal Irish childhood, progressing from teddy bears to toy cars to toy trains to toy soldiers to sport to books to dirty books to groping girls and finally to the ultimate anticlimax of a first sexual experience - just like any other male child in Ireland, or indeed the whole wide world. A spell in the British Army fighting the Mau-Mau in Kenya was followed by a return home and a job in a cousin's painting and decorating company. The company grew steadily and successfully.

Then one day, as they were painting the outside of someone's house, the cousin fell off the scaffolding, landed on his head and was dead before his feet had followed him to the ground. Michael was inconsolable - it could so easily have been him. The slightest wrong foot, *the slightest push,* and *he* could have been in the arms of the Lord right now. Still, his grief was not so great that it stopped him assuming full control of the company.

It was not long after when fate was to change his life and bring him money beyond even his wildest dreams.

He had been working one weekend decorating the house of a recently widowed neighbour. *God, but wasn't death everywhere?* There would be no charge, of course, as a sign of respect - and anyway what did a couple of days free labour matter when you already had over half a million in your personal account? The widow, a woman in her forties, had asked him to have a look through her late husband's things and if anything took his eye he could have it as she would no longer have any use for anything of her dear departed, God rest him. Mahoney did not really care for going through a dead man's belongings but, grimacing with distaste, he had done so just to please the woman.

Up in an unused bedroom there were shirts, suits, shoes, ties and various books packed into a large box.

The woman had gone downstairs to make some tea, and he was alone when he found the heavy brown paper bag in the bottom of the box. He had opened it cautiously. Inside, much to his astonishment, was a gun - a *Browning 1922 .32*, manufactured by *Fabrique Nationale* of Herstal, Belgium, as he was later to find out. It was in a bad condition, but he decided to keep it, smuggling it out of the house in his donkey jacket that night.

He had been an expert with arms in the army and it did not take him long to clean up the weapon and restore it to perfect working order. Casually mentioning it to an acquaintance in a bar one evening after work, he had been shocked when his drinking companion had asked him if he wanted to sell it.

"Sell it?" he had pondered. "Might as well. I've really no use for the thing."

Two days later, in his office in Duke Street off Grafton Street in Dublin, Mahoney had been visited by a rather dark-looking gentleman with a broad Belfast accent. He was keen to see the gun and, after a cursory initial inspection, he offered Mahoney one hundred punts for it. Mahoney had been staggered but, with his usual air of bluff confidence, he accepted the offer.

The visitor had asked him if he could get his hands on any more. Never one to miss a good business opportunity, Mahoney had said that indeed to goodness he probably could and would the honourable gentleman be wishing to place any orders with him? There had been no positive response, just a simple maybe. Nevertheless, Mahoney knew that he had found a way to make himself a very rich man, richer than he could ever be with his painting and decorating concerns. It was 1969 and the troubles in Northern Ireland were escalating horrendously. There was a market just sitting waiting for him, a whole new field to be conquered.

Using contacts from his army days, it had taken Mahoney six months to make the breakthrough on the supply side. Tentative feelers which had been put out in the direction of various embassies and other concerned parties - and which included two unexplained deaths and several trips to an undisclosed destination abroad - eventually paid off. Mahoney had been able to grasp the IRA and Protestants in both hands. He could supply them with arms, all sorts: big guns, small guns, bombs and bomb-making equipment and even field artillery and smaller, more sophisticated devices of death. Mostly Russian - either Russian from Russia, Russian from Libya, Russian from Africa - and, for much higher prices, arms from most other countries as well.

It had cost him all the capital he had, including three mortgages on his thriving business and two on his then semi-detached house in Howth, but in one year he was to recoup that investment ten-fold.

Now, four years later, he was considered one of the most trusted and reliable black market arms dealers in the world, and he had indeed cornered the Northern Irish market, supplying most of the needs of all the terrorist factions operating there.

His visitor that Christmas 1973 remains something of a mystery. His name was Ali Al Khalifa. At that time he was the Financial Controller, the Mister Fixit, of the military arm of the Palestine Liberation Organisation known as Black September. Apart from these few facts, nothing is known about him.

"Drink?" asked the Irishman, pulling open a drawer of the desk. They were sitting in Mahoney's office, a specially constructed windowless room in the basement of the house. In the background, air conditioning hummed with determination. "Oh no, I forgot. You don't, do you?" As he lifted the bottle of poteen, Mahoney's hand brushed against a small button in the side of the drawer. From that moment on, everything said in the room would be recorded.

Caring not for niceties, Mahoney swilled directly from the bottle. When he looked back at Al Khalifa, his manner had changed. The bluff Irishman had gone, the accent disappearing noticeably. "Now, I believe you were after something special?"

"Correct," responded the Arab. "And you have been recommended to us as being a specialist in providing what to most is unprovidable."

"God, but you're an expert in brown nosing Akay. If Kissinger was to give up his job tomorrow, you'd be his natural successor. The Belgian recommended me, so you said?"

"Yes."

"A good fellow is Jacques. Been in business far longer than I have. Knows his onions. And his Kalashnikovs. I'm surprised he has not tried to accommodate you himself."

"For Europe, he is excellent," nodded Al Khalifa. "But the event which our Operational Services is planning is to take place more to the north. We required a more local supplier and, once the Belgian had heard of our requirements, he said that you were the only possible man to help us."

"O'Connell will never let your boys into Ireland alive."

"O'Connell already knows all about it. We would not dare to approach his arms supplier without his prior permission. And we are not concerned with Ireland." The statement could not have been more blunt nor its implication more obvious.

A broad, crescent smile spread across Mahoney's face. "Well, well, well - so its The Bastards you're going for! You'll have a tough job, son, bloody tough. You were lucky to get Leila Khaled back alive, and you know it." He rubbed his nose. "And what use was she by the time they had finished with her?"

The Arab did not comment.

"Exactly what is it you want?" continued Mahoney.

"Some small arms for the personal defence of a unit of five men - "

".38 are my personal favourites. .44 magnums are quite handy little things too. I also do a nice line in the Russian Tokarev Model 30 - similar to the Browning."

"Preferably British Army issue."

Mahoney nodded. "They're yours. Actually, I can go one better than that. How about British *police* issue?"

The Arab permitted himself a full smile. "Excellent. Also we would like other personal weapons, knives and such like."

Mahoney held up his hand. "Leave it all to me. Complete personal equipment for a unit of five men. I'll give you the works." His hand came down via the bottle of poteen and he held it in his lap. "But you can get the equivalent of those items anywhere. You said you wanted something unprovidable. So hit me with it." He swilled from the bottle.

"Twelve pounds of plutonium."

The poteen sprayed backwards out of the Irishman's mouth as he shot forward in his seat.

"JEYSUS CHROIST!"

He began to cough violently, and it took a good two minutes of back-slapping by a concerned Al Khalifa to make sure that the Irishman did not pass on at that very moment. The first words Mahoney uttered when he had recovered were to do with the devil's domain and the sex act.

Ψ

Tuesday December 25 1973

"Reports are coming in from Norway of an accident involving a Hull trawler which is said to have hit the rocks in a fjord. Three trawlermen are unaccounted for."

Somewhere in the Irish Republic

Of the two men, Al Khalifa enjoyed that Christmas night the best. The pliable breasts, juddering thighs and pilose organs of the salacious sisters, Elizabeth and Philomena, had served him well. The last thing he remembered before the ever-wanting hands of sleep had dragged him forcibly away from the two Irish girls had been the lower half of Philomena's body descending onto his face.

Mahoney had slept alone - indeed, he had hardly slept at all - and he had arisen at 06:00. 'Twas Christmas Day and this afternoon his annual 24-hour party began. Some two hundred friends, relatives and simple hangers-on were expected to turn up.

But he had more important things on his mind. The staff could accommodate the thirty caterers especially employed for the party; but it was he, Michael Mary Mahoney, who had to accommodate Ali Al Khalifa and, by inference, Black September.

So, Black September was going to explode a nuclear device in Britain. The thought was outrageous, almost impossible to comprehend. Yet the idea was so simple. Just like that other simple idea the Arabs had recently discovered - the oil weapon (that had really shown the true face of most western nations when they had dropped their support of Israel almost overnight and had gone crawling to the Jews' enemies).

It is relatively simple to make a nuclear bomb. The Arabs undoubtedly had the right technical know-how, or could get hold of it (an Ivan perhaps? It was rumoured that they were behind the discovery of the oil weapon). The main ingredient required is forty pounds of enriched uranium or twelve pounds of plutonium; it will make a bomb capable of killing thousands.

And it is not all that hard for the right person to lay his hands on the right amount of the stuff. After all, Mahoney thought to himself, the Kerr-McGee Corporation in Oklahoma had at times been unable to account for upwards of sixty pounds of plutonium, and it could take as long as six months for such a loss to be discovered under the current detecting procedures of the American Atomic Energy Commission. That was just one possible source but, of course, with the inherent transportation problems he must try for a source nearer to Britain.

France perhaps? Now there was a thought. The ailing Georges Pompidou had, unknowingly, supplied him with arms on more than one occasion in the past. With the French so tetchy about world reaction to their own nuclear explosions in the Pacific, it might be possible to 'persuade' someone there to turn a blind eye whilst twelve pounds of a certain substance grew legs.

For four hours Mahoney walked about the green, rolling Irish countryside, pensive, swilling in vast lungfuls of the sharp Christmas air. It was not until 10:00 that he returned to the mansion, a much happier man.

It was about that time that Al Khalifa was waking up alone in the massive bed of one of the guest suites. He wondered if last night had been real or just a dream. There was no vestige of the sisters to be found, not even any naughty marks on the sheets, and it was only a dull soreness in a certain part of his anatomy where he had been rubbed raw that assured Akay that he had just spent one of the most pleasurable nights of his life.

Forty minutes later, as Al Khalifa walked down the stairs, fully washed, shaved and dressed (it was his custom not to breakfast), he was accosted by an ebullient Mahoney charging down the passageway,

"Akay! Akay, my dear, dear fellow. Merry Christmas to yer, and all that. God bless ye merry gentlemen!"

"Good morning, Michael."

"Yer just the person I wanted t'see. Come." Mahoney grabbed him by the arm and steered him downstairs to the office, ignoring the grimace on the Arab's face.

"Sit down, sit down," beamed Mahoney as he went around to his seat, the half-full bottle of poteen appearing in his hand as if by magic.

"You seem... happy," observed Al Khalifa, straightening his sleeve.

"Ah, indeed t'goodness," Mahoney nodded. "I had a long walk this morning, my friend. To think over your request and clear my mind."

"And?"

"Oh, I can get it, of course. I haven't contacted my friends yet - why should I worry them on Christmas Day, for God's sake?" He laughed. "For God's sake - good one, eh? But twelve pounds of the very best plutonium will be yours."

Al Khalifa nodded his approval. "That is good. Gratifying. But of course your ability to supply the item was never in doubt."

"Ah now I think there's just a touch of the old Arab camel shit there, Akay," said the Irishman warmly. "I think we can take it as read that if I could not supply the goods after what you had told me of your plans - or at least intimated even if no direct statement was made - Michael Mahoney would not have been long for this world. Not that I'm casting any nasturtiums upon the morals of your organisation, of course, heaven forbid."

"Of course."

Mahoney took a long swig from the whiskey bottle. "And now we come to the other side of this little arrangement."

"The other side?"

"My fee."

"Ah yes. We are prepared to give consideration to any reasonable quotation."

Sure and I bet you are, thought Mahoney, but you'll be surprised what I've got lined up for you, me ole stick. He asked, "Would you be wanting this... substance, within any specified time limit?"

"We have no deadline or time limit," answered the Arab. "But of course the sooner it is obtained, the less chance there is of other parties finding out about our arrangement and speculating upon its eventual use."

"True, true. Speculation can be a terrible thing. As soon as is practically possible then. Can we agree that we are talking in the middle term?"

"That is acceptable."

"After all, twelve pounds of the stuff just cannot go missing overnight - the British are not as lax about it as the Yanks are. But you need not worry on that score. That is my business." He read the question behind Al Khalifa's raised eyebrow. "Oh yes, I shall be getting it from Britain. That's the simplest answer, is it not? You want to use it there, so I obtain it there. Saves all the fuss and bother about transporting the stuff over sea - and I'm sure the British Customs would want something more than an end-user certificate for our little baby!"

Al Khalifa gave a polite quarter smile. "Of what price were you thinking?"

"Price? Two million pounds. Sterling."

The Arab was quiet, staring at a point far beyond Mahoney's head. The Irishman was able to savour two gobfuls of the wicked booze during the silence.

Then the Arab asked, "That does not include the guns or equipment?"

"Correct. Those can go on a separate account, to be finalised at a later date. Put it on the slate, as they say."

More silence. The Arab's eyes were glazed, far away. Finally he looked back at Mahoney. "Two million sterling is a highly satisfactory figure, Mr Mahoney. In fact we had estimated somewhat higher than that. Are you sure you will not be underselling yourself? Or us?"

"No, no, Akay," reassured Mahoney. "You are right, of course. It is a low amount. But I've no wish to bankrupt you - although, let's face it, I appreciate that if you were to pay me in cash the money would probably be Russian or Libyan."

"*If* we were to pay you in cash?"

"Well, I didn't say cash, my friend. You just asked me the price. I looks at it this way. I am, with all due modesty, a very rich man. What's another two million in one of my eight Swiss bank accounts? I'll probably never spend all the money I have in them already. Yes, I have undersold and I'll tell you why. I don't want your money. I want payment in kind."

"In *kind*?" The Arab looked perplexed. "And what might that be?"

Mahoney smiled. "In exchange for twelve pounds of plutonium, I want *The Star of Sierra Leone*."

Ψ

Thursday January 3 1974

"Demonstrations by Basque Nationalists continue for the second day in Spain, following yesterday's swearing-in of Señor Arais Navarro as Prime Minister. The ex-police chief takes over from Admiral Carrero Blanco who was assassinated two weeks ago."

Beirut, Lebanon

Looking back from the twenty-first century, it is hard to recall Beirut before the civil wars. Back in the early 1970s, before the madness took hold and the name of the city became synonymous with destruction and despair, Beirut was one of the most sophisticated and cosmopolitan cities, not only in the Middle East but in the whole world. Not for nothing was it called 'The Paris of the East'.

A chill winter's night had just begun, but upstairs in the *El Fateh* safe house near Sidani Street it was warm. In the dimly-lit room, five men were seated around a large oval table.

The men were: Ali Hassan Salameh, at that time controller of the intelligence and action arms; Salah Khalef (code-name Abu Ayad), co-founder of Black September and the group's *consiglière* (counsellor), and second to Arafat on the central committee of *El Fateh*; the number two of the *Fateh* intelligence agency, Jihad-al-Razd; Abu Jihad, the IRA liaison man; and Faisal Ibn Musaed, Hassan's personal assistant and protegé. *[For a brief history of Black September and* El Fateh, *see Appendix 2.]*

An atmosphere of tension, of expectancy, hung over the room. The five individual body odours were beginning to meet and meld into the stickly sweet-sour smell of humans *en masse*. It was 21:00.

"He should have been here by now." Abu Ayad, the second in command, darted his eyes from one to the other of his colleagues.

Nothing was said for a moment. Then the big, powerfully built Hassan looked up from the documents in front of him. He was chewing an item from a bowl of exotic candy on the table. He looked at his watch and grunted.

"He could have been delayed," suggested Abu Jihad, dragging on an over-stuffed cigarette which smelt distinctly of yak shit. "If he had to return via Britain he could have been delayed."

Abu Ayad turned to look at his small associate. "Yes, because of the trouble there. The 'Three Day Week' as they call it?"

"Quite."

"If only that stupid little country did not rely so much on coal." The intelligence man had spent three years at Oxford and therefore considered himself an expert on all matters Anglo. "*Oil.* That is their future power, their future prosperity. *Then* they will have no trouble with their communists."

Hassan kept his head down, but his voice was firm and definitive. "But you are forgetting, my brother. Once our operation is completed, Britain will have more, much much more, to worry about than any greedy miners or their future in oil. Indeed, if things go right - "

"Is there any reason why they should not?" snapped Abu Ayad.

Hassan looked up. The dark eyes flashed a warning. He said calmly, "Not in the execution of the operation, no. But who knows what the reaction of the British will be when thousands of them are... " He let the sentence float away. The merest trace of a frown flitted across his lined brow. He looked at his deputy. "You cause me concern, brother. You show an uncharacteristic caution." He stretched out a long, powerful left arm, extracted another candy from the bowl and crushed it between his teeth.

Abu Ayad glanced up at the leader and then looked away again. He sighed, talking to the centre of the table. "Yes, it is true. I have... a feeling that something... something..." He shrugged and raised his head. "It is nonsense, of course. It is this city. It was foolhardy to return here so soon after the murder of our brothers."

"This is, then, perhaps the safest place of all," ventured Abu Jihad.

The conversation continued for another twenty minutes. Only Musaed did not speak. He just sat there on the left of Hassan at the top of the table, taking it all in, his dark face confident, almost benign, as if he was the tolerant parent watching children at play.

It was nearing 21:30 when the door opened, flooding the room with brighter light from the staircase outside. The final guard of a six-man praetorian, each of whom were heavily armed, held the door open for Al Khalifa to enter hurriedly.

Hassan rose. "Brother!"

"I am sorry about the delay," apologised Al Khalifa after they had kissed three times. "There was some trouble at the airport here with some Christian faction."

Hassan burst out laughing and looked towards Abu Ayad. "Three Day Week, huh?" The Number Two was also smiling, his normal confidence returning with the advent of the sixth man.

Hassan motioned Al Khalifa to a vacant seat.

"How did it go?" asked Abu Jihad. "Did the Irishman prove to be to our satisfaction?"

"Oh, undoubtedly. He is the ideal man, he can supply all our needs."

"Even the most important item?"

"It would appear so."

Abu Jihad looked at Hassan in triumph. "What did I tell you, brother?"

Hassan nodded. "Indeed, your Irish contacts have served us good. We must offer our thanks and reciprocations." He turned back to Al Khalifa. "Now, my brother, what is the price involved?"

"Two million pounds."

The sounds of astonishment from the men were as one. Puzzlement flashed across each face.

"That is incredible!" exclaimed the intelligence man. "The face value of the stuff is much more than that." There were murmurs of agreement.

"Amazing indeed," nodded Hassan. "Why is he underselling?" The question was sharp and to the point.

The financier was unperturbed. He gave Mahoney's own explanation. "He tells me he has enough money. To accumulate more would be simply to make it worthless, to add more figures onto a piece of paper somewhere. He wants payment in kind."

"In kind?" asked Hassan. "What *kind*?"

"He wants a diamond."

"A diamond?"

"It is called, apparently, *The Star of Sierra Leone*."

The room was quiet again. Not even the sound of breathing could be heard as the five brains computed the news.

Outside on the stairway, the guard shuffled his feet and farted loudly.

Abu Ayad was the first to speak, shaking his head in bewilderment. "And where is this fantastic diamond that is worth two million pounds?"

Al Khalifa shrugged. "He does not know for certain. As he said to me, it is up to him to supply the goods, it is up to us to supply the payment. He has heard of this diamond and he wants it."

Hassan looked questioningly at Abu Jihad. The latter grimaced in embarrassment. "This was not something foreseen by my contacts. They said Mahoney was a cash-on-delivery man."

"This will delay the operation considerably," grumbled Abu Ayad. "*If* we should go along with it. Do we not have any other supplier?"

"Not in that part of the world," replied Abu Jihad. "It is new territory for us."

"He said it would take some months for him to obtain the substance," continued Al Khalifa. "But he can supply it *in England*. All we need is to have the diamond and our assembly team ready when the time comes. There will be no transportation problems. And the price, apart from the inconvenience, is incredibly cheap."

"In fact," suggested the intelligence man, "if we were simply to take the diamond from wherever it was, it would cost us nothing at all in cash."

Hassan nodded. His elbows were on the table, fingers steepled together in front of him. "It is an interesting proposition. One, I think, for the foreigner?" His semi-query was directed at Abu Ayad, who nodded in agreement.

Hassan helped himself to another candy and chewed it noisily.

They continued talking, slowly coming to agreement.

Only Musaed had no input. He sat silently in his place, scribbling on a scrap of paper, as if he was taking minutes. When he had finished he looked up at the other five men, once again with that curious benign expression. It was as if he was detached from the rest of the group, distrait and looking at the proceedings from afar. As if he was an observer.

Ψ

Tuesday January 22 1974

"The Dublin Court of Criminal Appeal today dismissed the appeals of Kenneth and Keith Littlejohn, who were jailed last year for their part in an armed robbery on a Dublin bank in October 1972. The Littlejohns have claimed that they were working for British Intelligence at the time."

Houston, Texas, USA

In the nineteenth century, two New York property speculators bought 6642 acres of swampland in the south at $1.40 an acre. It was their intention to build 'a great center of government and commerce'.

On January 10 1901, the first of the world's oil-gushers spewed forth just a baccy-spit away at Spindletop. There followed the building of an inland port, rising from the murky Buffalo Bayou. And in 1962 came the Lyndon B Johnson Space Center, putting the place firmly within the knowledge of most people of the western world. The great centre of government and commerce had become a reality: Houston, Texas.

It was a usual winter in Houston in 1974, mild but irritatingly damp. But, on that Tuesday, at least one person in the city had much more to concern him than the weather.

Steve Graves was a tall, powerfully built, first generation American-Greek. He wore the thick black curly hair and *Zapata* moustache that were the fashion at the time. An oceanographer with one of the 250 local firms involved in underwater activities, he had just completed a morning's session in the Public Library trying to garner research material on a particular project. *Trying* to, because frankly his mind had not been on the job.

In all fairness, he had to admit that the last three hours would have to be written-off as wasted.

And it was all the fault of that letter. That damn letter that had arrived at his apartment that morning.

Steve left the library and walked down to Lamar. This was a lunchtime for walking, for he had a lot of thinking to do. A decision had to be made.

He pondered on which way to go. Left along Lamar to find himself somewhere to eat, or right and cross over Brazo and Bragby into Sam Houston Park? The peace and solitude of the park were what he needed right now, but the hunger pangs just would not go away. He headed left into town. Four blocks down he came to the junction with Main. Just past Foley's he found a hamburger joint and ensconced himself inside.

He sat there, mechanically eating his quarter-pounder with everything, French fries and root beer, staring out unseeing at the top of the Exxon building beyond Capital National.

At precisely 12:56 he reached the decision.

It was clear what he had to do. There was no real choice. Accept that and the problem was solved.

He would have to take time out from his job. *Gulf's* exploration of the Gulf of Mexico would have to carry on without him for a while. Anyway, as a fully qualified oceanographer and saturation diver he could find work anywhere. The decision was made. He would go.

Just to ensure that his imagination was not playing tricks, that he was not suffering from a belated attack of the bends, he removed the air mail envelope from his pocket for the umpteenth time. The flap was sharp where he had ripped it open earlier.

Inside was a single ticket on the following day's *Air France 747* to Paris, and a slip of paper with a short, unsigned, printed message:

Grivas wants you.

Sally would be the problem, of course. Sally-Anne Bowker, the girl who shared his cramped downtown apartment and who had been the mainstay of Steve Graves' life for the past two years. How could he tell her that out of the blue that morning had come a letter from a terrorist leader on the other side of the world? How could he tell her that the letter requested his immediate presence? And how could he tell her that he *had* to go?

Sure, he often had trips away, sometimes at short notice. But this time, more than any of the others, he could not reveal the real reason why. No one must ever know. Indeed, it would be better that she did not know where he was going at all. But he had to tell her *something*, he could not just walk out on someone who was part of his life. He loved her, as much as any man loves his woman, but Sally had her place in the scheme of things - and her place was not within ten thousand miles of General George Grivas.

Steve left the *Gulf* offices at his usual time of 16:30 after a rather patchy and unsatisfactory afternoon's work. Forty-five minutes later he reached the apartment, as usual half an hour ahead of Sally. Quickly, he showered and changed.

At 17:45 she arrived home. She breezed through the door, her usual lively self, short cut hair in no real semblance of order, make-up on eyes only, clothes bright and attractive in flower-power style but awry. Thick-rimmed glasses gave the true school-marm effect. Balanced in her right hand were two exquisite but greasy-looking specimens from the nearby *JC's Pizza Parlor*.

"Hi, baby!" She walked over to the table by the window and plonked down her purchases on the waiting plates.

Steve was coming through the kitchen doorway, mugs in hand. "Hi, kid." He admired the taut ass underneath the bright blue skirt. "How was school today?" He kissed her lightly on the cheek, put down the mugs and grabbed two handfuls of bottom. He rubbed up against her.

She turned to him, going with the embrace. "Mmm. Steady on there, tiger. I need a shower. Let me get nice for you."

"I got some news today," he said as she walked towards the bathroom.

"Good news?" She left the door open and he watched her skirt fall to the floor.

"Well... Kid, they want me to go to the Mediterranean."

"The *Mediterranean*?" Her blouse was tossed into the laundry.

"Balaeric Islands. A new project they've just started."

She unhooked her bra but did not take it off, letting it hang, loosely cupping her small breasts. She looked at him and then smiled. Walking over, she placed her arms about his neck. "Gee, baby, that's great news. All expenses paid trip to the Med. Fantastic! Any idea when you're going? How long for?" She licked his left nostril.

Steve's arms were around her waist. Their lower halves pressed together and she could feel him growing. He looked into her eyes. "Tomorrow."

Sally's smile weakened and then recovered bravely. "Tomorrow? Gee, that's some notice. What's so important that you have to go tomorrow?"

He raised his right hand under her bra and began making circular motions with his thumb against her nipple. It needed little excuse to corrugate. Before he could tell another lie, she again asked "How long for?"

"I don't know. A month. Two months. Maybe longer."

Again the smile held bravely. "Well, that won't be too bad,

will it?"

He was relieved. The worst part was over. "No baby, no it won't."

"Listen, Graves," she pulled away. "You've got a lot of packing to do. We gotta organise things."

"Bowker..."

"Is all the laundry done? Have they delivered?"

"Bowker..."

"You must tell me exactly what you're gonna do. But first, the pizzas! Don't let 'em get cold - "

"BOWKER!"

"Yes, Graves?"

"Fuck the pizzas." He ripped her bra down off her arms, at the same time undoing his zipper. He pulled her to him, crushing her right breast with his left hand and grasping her hard bottom with the other. Their mouths touched and in a moment his tongue was down her throat.

Her glasses fell to the carpet. She made no attempt to retrieve them.

When they surfaced for air she said, "Why should the pizzas have all the fun? Fuck me, too."

For the next hour, he did.

Somewhere in the USA

He did not look like a Jew.

Which, of course, was the whole point. None of the world-wide network of Israeli Intelligence operatives – male and female – looked recognisably Jewish. The best operatives had to look like they belonged. They needed to fit in, not to stand out.

The agent known to his Controllers by the code-name Digenis was tall, but not too tall. Dark haired, but not too dark. Strongly built, but not too strong. Not too handsome, not too ugly. He *fitted in*. An ideal operative.

As night fell, he looked up at the fourth floor front left window of the apartment block. A light came on inside and he could see shadows moving about. Inside the block people would be going on with their normal, everyday lives.

And so would he.

Except he was a spy.

A new mission was starting. His subject had been identified, his instructions had been received.

He was prepared.

Ψ

Wednesday January 23 1974

"In Athens, two Arab terrorists, said to be members of Black September, have been sentenced to death for the murder of five people and the wounding of 50 others at Athens Airport last August. It is unlikely that sentence will be carried out in the immediate future."

Houston, Texas, USA
Roissy, Paris, France

"Hello, this is Sally-Anne Bowker."

"Hi kid."

"Steve? Oh, Steve honey, hi! Where are you?"

"I'm at Charles de Gaulle waiting for my connecting flight. Thought I'd ring my baby to tell her I miss her. Hope I didn't call at the wrong time. Are you in the middle of a class? It's ten at night here."

"No, honey, I was having a break. I miss you too, y'know, and its only been half a day. Seems like a lifetime already. Has your *Gulf* contact met you yet?"

"Just - he's outside the booth now, so I can't delay."

"Any more news of exactly where you're going? Which island will you be staying on?"

"Er... sorry kid, it's a bad line."

"Which island will you be on?"

"Oh, er, Minorca I think he said."

"You will write, won't you?"

"Sure I will."

"Phone if you can. And give me an address."

"The first thing I'll do when I get there."

"I love you baby."

"I love you too, kid."

"Take care of yourself for me."

"I will - and save *yourself* for me."

"Why mah deeyer sir, what*ever* do you mean?"

"I'll show you when I get back. Bye now, Bowker."

"Bye Graves - I love you!"

Steve replaced the receiver and stood looking at it for a few seconds. He did not like lying, but in the circumstances he could do nothing else. She could never know the truth.

In fact, he had not been contacted by anybody as yet, and he now found himself at a loss as to what to do. If only that damn note had been more specific. If only that damn note had given him some explanation. If only that damn note had not come at all. If only it had said something other than *Grivas wants you*. But there had been nothing, just that and the ticket to Paris.

Well, he was here, now what? One thing was for certain, he could not stay staring at the payphone all night. He had to find somewhere to go. Charles de Gaulle Airport was a big, lonely and, on the evening of January 23 1974, very cold place.

After a few minutes wandering he found a far from busy snack-stall. He bought some delicious *café* and a packet of stale cookies, and found himself a place to eat on the transfer level (the mezzanine between the arrival and departure levels here in Terminal One).

He surveyed the people. There were the usual scurrying airline reps and workers, official-looking persons in uniform and the standard sluggish cleaners, all of which were synonymous with every major airport in the world. He looked at the other persons, the travellers, the meeters, the farewellers, most of whom were obviously French. The elderly men and women, heavily but elegantly dressed against the threatened snow; the middle-aged businessman, again sartorially immaculate, greying temples an appropriate frame to a slightly worried countenance, *Gauloises* being chain-smoked; the obligatory young man in denims, possibly from university, the customary scarf flung around his neck, reading some activist newspaper; the young woman with the long, glossy hair, almost devoured by an incredibly expensive full-length fur, obviously the mistress of someone with money. It was the embodiment of France on one concourse.

The cookies were eaten and the last dregs of coffee swilled down. Moments later he noticed a shapely pair of legs approaching from his left. Their owner was a dark, Mediterranean woman in her late twenties, straight black hair parted on the right and falling to just below her shoulders. Big eyes, black and mysterious, looked out from a handsome olive-skinned face. An ample figure was covered by a short denim skirt and a denim jacket fastened to the neck against the cold.

Steve crumpled his cup and scored a direct hit into a nearby waste bin. He smiled and pulled his own leather jacket tighter against his body and looked back at the woman. This one was definitely not French and, like him, had not come prepared for a stopover, however brief, in the middle of a Parisian winter. He wondered where she was going. Obviously to somewhere where the weather was more agreeable. Just as he would be. What was she? Another mistress of some lucky bastard? An *au pair*? An *Avon* lady?

He frowned when he realised. Of course! She was coming directly towards him.

She stopped in front of him. Steve stood up. They looked each other in the eyes without speaking. The magic passed between them.

She said, "Stelios." It was a statement not a question. Her accented voice was deep, almost hoarse, and sensually feminine, but brittle, as if she was troubled by some deep emotion.

"Yes. What news? Why does he want to see me?"

"It iss not good, not good at all." A wetness rose in the two beautiful black eyes. "Come. Our flight leaves from Orly. There iss a taxi waiting."

Steve picked up his small bag and they moved off, their footsteps echoing off the synthetic flooring. "It is not good?" he queried.

She did not look at him as she spoke. "He would not send for you except for the final emergency, that wass the promise. Well, the final emergency hass arrived. Efen now it may be too late."

They reached the travelator and stepped into the totally enclosed glass tube. They stopped walking as the 'flat escalator' replaced their legs.

"So, the end is here, huh?" Steve's voice was sullen.

"We must pray that he holdz on, at least until you get there. He so badly wants you there."

Steve touched her on the arm. He looked at her, a million questions in his eyes. For a moment she seemed at a loss.

As they reached the end of the travelator, she said hurriedly "We must waste no time."

"Just a minute," he stopped her in mid stride. "What are you called?"

"*Tee?*"

"What is your name?"

"*Eh mee* Christina - Christina Cascianis."

"Christina Cascianis," he nodded.

"And you," she said softly. "You *are* Stelios."

And there, on the public concourse, she took his right hand in hers, raised it to her lips and kissed it.

Yeri, Nicosia District, Cyprus

The small lizard emerged from the cover of the long grass and froze in its tracks. It stared through the weak moonlight at the villa and outhouse a few hundred metres ahead. The place was in darkness except for the very faintest of diffused lights filtering through the shutters of an upstairs window. All was quiet and only the almost unnoticeable clicking of a group of cicadas disturbed the cool night air.

The lizard sniffed, realised there was nothing to interest it out here, and turned and scampered back into the grass.

The one softly lit room of the villa was a bedroom, but the two occupants were far from asleep. They were both nearing the ultimate ecstasy of orgasm.

The girl, the fifteen year old daughter of one of the farmers of the nearby village of Yeri, was unattractive facially and she even possessed the beginnings of a moustache. Nevertheless her body was ripe and of some substance, huge black-nippled breasts, plump but soft tummy and a down of the smoothest black fur trickling down from her navel and blossoming into a tropical forest between her legs. And big, rock hard thighs which were now spread far apart and were trembling as she thrust her pelvis up to receive the full length of the dick that was being rammed into her.

The owner of that organ was also of some substance, but in his case the body was powerful and solid, muscular without even a hint of fat. It was a body which had been trained well, in the special school at Ochakov on the edge of the Black Sea, and it was kept in perfect condition by regular and rather savage physical exercise of which the owner considered this two hour session of sex - which was just coming to a close with her sixth and his second orgasm - to be part. In contrast the face, now beaded with splashes of perspiration, was round and, to some eyes, chubby. It was a boyish face which served its purpose well by being the perfect camouflage for the power of the body underneath. The hair was short, black and wavy, pushed back.

On a table by the side of the bed were the tinted, plain glass spectacles which he always wore (except on occasions such as this), for his eyes were sensitive to the light.

The girl gave a half-scream half-sigh as she lost control as she climaxed. The man continued pushing for another fifteen strokes before he emitted a deep grunt and nearly ruptured her with a final thrust which held his organ tight inside her body until it had emptied itself.

He lay on her, his breathing fast and even. Then, abruptly, he rolled off, a job done.

The girl knew better than to talk at a time like this. She just lay there savouring the very last tingling sensations. She wondered if she would ever be able to move her legs back together again. Her anus was sore.

Ilich Ramirov put his hands behind the back of his head and brought his breath under control. His eyes were open, staring at the ceiling. He was twenty-four years of age, looked thirty-four, and had been born on October 12 1949 in Panfilovo, a village in central Russia. His mother had come from far-eastern Russia, near the borders with China, and his father, a man from Rostov in the Ukraine, had liaised with his mother just once while passing through Panfilovo, and Ilich had been the result.

Although a normal-looking child, Ilich's ability to catch weasels and stoats with his bare hands - and his obvious pleasure as he slowly twisted their necks round and around until the whole head snapped off, or hung them up by their hind legs, made the smallest of slits in their necks with his knife, and watched them bleed so very slowly to death, writhing and squealing in agony - did not go unnoticed by his local party member. Word spread up the line from the local member to the district member to the area member and ever onwards. By the time he was ten years old, Ilich was being discreetly watched by two dark and nondescript gentlemen from Moscow.

As fate would have it (and it had it a lot in the Russia of the post-war), Ilich's mother died shortly after her son's eleventh birthday. She passed away from injuries received after part of a tree had fallen on her during a walk in the woods to the north of Panfilovo. The State descended with remarkable rapidity on the orphan boy and he was whisked away into care to a suburb of the capital.

For the next seven years, Ilich underwent specialised 'schooling', the subjects upon which it would be wise not to dwell. Suffice it to say that he emerged on his eighteenth birthday not only as a super-efficient killing machine but also a master-agent, co-ordinator, organiser, tactician and executioner, the top in the field of all things subversive. The greatest – and youngest – success story of Academy Number 311.

In the early nineteen-seventies he became the first 'itinerant agent', given carte blanche by his Russian masters to give every assistance he could to any 'resistance' group which requested it. His only restriction was that he had to submit a detailed monthly report on his activities to Moscow.

Ramirov was based in this comfortable but not opulent villa on the outskirts of Yeri village, entirely supported by the KGB's vast reserve of foreign currency - in this case Cyprus pounds. He was known only to a few select leaders of 'resistance' groups: the Arabs, the Japanese and the Germans being his main clients. In early 1974, Ramirov did not yet consider the IRA and the Italians worthy of his attention. Also at this time, his presence in the form of there being just one co-ordinating force behind the increasing global terror attacks was suspected by western powers, but he was far from being known in person.

Ramirov grimaced in distaste as the girl next to him began to snore. A fart slipped softly from her distended rectum. He considered his position. A meeting with Baader-Meinhof supporters two days ago in Bavaria had ended satisfactorily with plans - his own plans - for a *Lufthansa* hijacking carefully worked out down to the last detail. That would please Furtseva in the monthly report. Something would be said about the fact that he had failed to kill Sieff in London at the end of December, but he could gloss over that. Apart from that one little incident, things were going well.

So why couldn't he sleep?

It was not the noise of the girl or the insidious odour of her gas. It was nothing external. Something was going to happen, he knew. He had inherited this sixth sense from his mother and it rarely let him down.

It was not until 11:00 the following morning that he was to receive the first signs. A visit to the *poste restante* in Nicosia revealed three letters waiting for him under the name of Martinez. Two of the letters were of little consequence but the third, postmarked Roma, looked of great interest. Ramirov, always cautious, waited until he was back in his villa before giving the letter further attention.

He knew already what the Rome letter would contain, nevertheless he still opened it, inclining his head to one side as he did so, a curious habit of his. Inside was the expected blank sheet of sepia A4 parchment.

A letter from Rome was the signal that the Arabs wished to see him. The place would be one of three newly vetted safe houses in Beirut, dependent upon the value of the stamp furthest to the right on the envelope. It was 300 lire, therefore it would be the third of the three addresses he had. The date would be twenty-eight days from the date of the postmark, January 11. So the appointment would take place on Friday February 8 at the house in the district of Borj El Barajneh, Beirut. The time was always 21:00.

Ramirov permitted himself an inner smile. Good, he was glad

action was planned. He did not like periods of inactivity. The Arabs only called when one of their own men could not handle the job, when they needed his expertise. Therefore, as always, it would not be easy. But those were the sort of jobs he liked best.

So, his feeling of the night before had been correct.

And, without further thought that his sixth sense was ever wrong, not even in the slightest, Ramirov began to formulate his travel plans.

Ψ

Thursday January 24 1974

"There have been more bombs in London this evening. Three bombs exploded in Chelsea, causing extensive damage. There are no reports of any casualties at this time. Earlier today, a parcel bomb was thrown into an Israeli bank in the City, slightly injuring a typist."

Above the Mediterranean

The Olympic Airways DC10 was twenty minutes away from touchdown at Nicosia Airport. In the rear seats on the left side, the young couple smiled at each other, their hands brushing as they reached for their drinks.

His questions had started just after take-off. "So, tell me about Christina."

He had learnt of the Cypriot girl who had longed to get away from her native island and see the world; who had great hopes as a singer, performing in all the clubs in Famagusta, Nicosia and the other main towns. She was a popular attraction in concerts given for the British troops who, fourteen years after independence, still maintained a presence on the island. Ten years ago, when she was nineteen, she had been offered club work in Athens. She had been about to leave the island when her father had been taken by Makarios's soldiers.

Although a hardened supporter of Grivas and EOKA, Christina's father had never actively indulged in any form of 'resistance' against the Makarios regime - but this had not stopped the Archbishop's men from torturing him for non-existent information and then summarily killing him. She had thought he was being held somewhere in Nicosia; she had not heard of his death until three months after he had been killed. Her mother had been shattered by the news, and Christina vowed to stay with her on the island and fight, in any way she could, for the overthrow of the black-clad priest and for *Enosis*, union with Greece, the cause for which her father had been murdered.

She had started off running local messages for Grivas sympathisers and helpers. Slowly, over the years, she had been drawn into the web of the organisation. With Makarios inflicting defeat upon defeat on the General, annihilating or arresting his top men, she became closer and closer to the old man. He tended to confide in her a lot, treating her as a daughter, and he began to seek her opinions on his various plans and strategies.

When Syros and Spourghitis had been captured last autumn, she had realised that there was nobody left above her in line of personal contact with the General. By the process of elimination by Makarios, she had become the person closest to her leader, his only trusted contact with the outside world now that the disease had confined him to bed for the last time.

Steve had listened to the story. On the one hand she was virtually a mouthpiece for the ailing leader of EOKA - a tough, uncompromising job for anybody. And on the other hand she was a woman, interested enough in the subject of life in the States to have interrogated him at length, and cheeky enough to have asked him "And what about girlz? Are there plenty of those in America? You haf a girl?"

He had grinned. "Yes, there are plenty of girls." He looked at her teasingly, saying nothing else, making her re-ask the question.

"Do you..." She hesitated. "Do you haf a girl?"

"Yes," he smiled gently. "I do have a girl."

Christina's face did not move a muscle, but he could sense the struggle within. She did not want to ask but she just *had* to. "And… and this girl off yourz… she iss good looking?"

"She's okay, as good looking as any other girl… Just as you are."

She looked away, reddening, but with that coy, satisfied grin that is taught to every female at birth. Then with a sudden coldness that shocked him, she said "You may haf to forget her. I do not know what he wantz you to do, but he said it would be tough and would not be done quickly. You may be here for some time."

Steve looked out of the airplane window into the nothingness of night.

"You will not disappoint him?"

He turned back. "Of course not, not under any circumstances. How could I? If it has to be, then it has to be."

Now the seat belts sign flashed on as they approached Nicosia, and they both finished their third drink and obeyed the notice.

"What happens when we land?" Steve asked. "Will you be safe?"

"Oh yes. The Priest's men know I am with Grivas, but they do not know exactly what I do. They probably do not consider me worthy of picking up."

He smiled. "On the contrary, baby, on the contrary."

She tried to pretend to ignore the remark, but that grin crept across her face again. "There will be a car waiting for us. It will be a journey of one hour and a half into the mountains. Do not be afraid to be seen with us, they will find out about you eventually anyway. There should be no danger at this time. But iff you could try to control your American accent a little, it would help with our own people. They haf a distrust off anyone they haf not known for years, especially foreigners." It was her turn to smile. "But then, you are not a foreigner, are you? You are Stelios."

Steve made a show of quickly hiding his hands in his pockets before she could reach them, and they both laughed softly.

She placed her hand on his thigh, lent over and lightly kissed his cheek.

Troodos Mountains, Cyprus

The room, normally so bright in the scented early morning, was in shadows. A pair of heavy black curtains barred the entrance of the sun.

Tony Verekelis, a short, thick Cypriot, heavily Greek, entered the room quietly and looked at the small, grey, emaciated figure on the bed. He had survived the night, that was good, but his breath was harsh and irregular. It would not be long now. Soon he would be no more. Tony shook his head. It was distressing to see a great man die.

Tony walked softly across to the small bedside table. He deposited the fresh glass of water, with lid and special drinking lip, ready for old mother Dimitri to give on request.

Tony turned, and as he did so Grivas opened his eyes. They were clear and bright, and seemed so big against the wasted face. They were the only sign of life on the otherwise exanimate island of his small body. He was looking straight at Tony.

"They... they are here?" The voice was only a whisper but it was clear enough to be heard in the silent room.

Tony hesitated in case the eyes closed and he drifted back again. They did not, and so he answered. "No sir, not yet. But we have word that they have arrived safely and are now on their way."

"They come..."

"Yes."

"They come…" The eyes closed.

Tony walked silently out of the room, passing old black-clad mother Dimitri as she shuffled her way in.

They came at 09:00, travelling by jeep. As they wound up the tracks into the mountain, Steve's body registered tiredness for the first time. It surprised him to calculate that he had not slept since the flight from Houston yesterday. The flight from Orly to Nicosia had been completely taken up with Christina.

But he relegated fatigue to the back of his mind as he savoured the sheer pleasure of early morning in the Troodos Mountains. It was winter but there was still plenty of green about, and the temperature could only have been three or four degrees. There would be snow higher up, Christina had told him. The air was crisp, clean and fresh, and the smell of the pine trees was exhilarating.

Soon they turned between the trees into a discreet narrow road. About a kilometre along they came upon the house.

They climbed out of the vehicle, shaking their stiff legs. For a moment Steve paused to take in the place, the small clearing, the white stucco walls of the two storey house. Then he said sadly, "So, this is where it will all end."

Christina looked at him but did not speak. Behind them the driver of the jeep reversed, turned around and quickly drove off the way they had come. Nearby, two other vehicles were parked, a Land Rover and a battered old Ford Consul of the early sixties.

As they reached the front door, Tony Verekelis appeared. He looked at Steve in silence, staring intently at his face. After a moment he nodded and said, "My God…" Then he reached out and with an iron grip pumped the American's right hand in greeting. "Stelios, *kahloss*."

"Hi."

"Stelios, this iss Tony, Tony Verekelis," introduced Christina.

"Tony helps out here - in fact I do nott know what we would do without him most off the time."

"I do my best," shrugged the Cypriot. "What with the departure of Syros and Demetrakis, and now… this." He shook his head. "But come, come."

The front door led into a spacious, white-walled room, bright and warm with that pervading smell of fresh pine.

"Should we see him now?" asked Christina. "How iss he?"

"He fades. But yes, you must see him as soon as you can. He has been asking for you."

"This way Stelios."

Steve followed the girl over to the stairs at the far corner of the room. Her tread was swift but soft on the unadorned boards.

Upstairs, seven doors led off the passageway which stretched from the front to the back of the house. Christina headed for the door at the end to the left, the room looking out front, to the south. She tapped gently and entered.

Old mother Dimitri looked up from her knitting. Quickly, she rose to her feet and scurried out of the room, pausing to look long and hard at Steve as she passed. She crossed herself and then closed the door softly behind them as they looked at the pathetic object on the bed.

After a moment Steve said lowly, "My God. This… this is the man?"

"This iss he."

On the bed, Grivas' eyes sprang open. "Stelios!" For a second the voice was loud and clear, as it always had been. Quickly Steve moved into view at the side of the bed.

"I'm here."

The pain in the body was so great now, Grivas could not even turn his head. But his eyes, the sole vestige of the once great life, sparkled with excitement as they met the American's.

It was a traumatic experience for both men. Their eyes filled with tears as they looked at each other. Steve sat down on the bed and gripped the grey, wizened left hand. For a full two minutes neither of them spoke. Then, swallowing hard, Steve greeted him in faltering Greek.

Grivas' cheeks twitched infinitesimally in what was probably the best he could do for a smile. When he spoke his voice was again a mere whisper. "Stelios... well... a fine man..." It was a great, almost superhuman effort for him to form the words. Steve leaned forward to hear. "What... voice - accent... after... these... years... underst... ble... course... Thank... you... coming... You will... stay now...?"

Steve gently squeezed the old man's hand. "Sure I'll stay. This is my home - even if I do have a foreign accent!" His laugh was sad.

Grivas' head nodded ever so slightly. "Help... however you can... Christi... good girl... good girl... my girl..."

Steve looked behind, but Christina's head was turned away as she sobbed quietly into her hands.

Suddenly Grivas' fingers tightened with surprising strength. "Stelios!" The whisper was urgent. "Listen... in case... there is no further chance... You came... for me... get something..."

Steve leaned closer as the voice grew weaker and weaker. His left ear was close up against the dry old lips.

"When... Grivas gone... get it for me... you must get... from Mouskos... get it... you must, you must!"

"What is it? What do you want me to get?"

The voice was only just audible now and the eyes had closed. "From Mouskos... you, must be you... get it... get... The Eye of Makarios!"

Grivas exhaled violently and the hand grew limp.

"Christina!" Steve span round, but she was already up to the bed and pushing him out of the way.

She grabbed the limp wrist and put her right ear to his chest. After a while she straightened up. "He iss still here - but only just."

"Jesus Christ." Tears fell unashamedly down Steve's face. He shook his head. "Why must it be like this? Why can't he just go in peace without pain?"

She sighed. "Death iss never easy, Stelios."

"Don't I know that," he said.

In fact Grivas had fallen into his last coma and he was never to regain consciousness. But life was to remain in his body for another two and a half days before his heart gave out and the excruciating pain stopped forever. It was ironic and, in some ways, tragic that the last word he ever said was "Makarios".

PART TWO

Ψ

OBJECTIVE TRACED

Ψ

Tuesday January 29 1974

"In California, a Los Angeles Superior Court today ordered President Nixon to appear in person to testify at the trial of his former Domestic Affairs assistant, Mr John Ehrlichman. It is reported that the President, who tomorrow delivers his State of the Union address, will not obey the order."

Troodos Mountains, Cyprus

Makarios had forbidden Bishop Gennadios of Paphos from holding the funeral in Limassol Cathedral, therefore it had been decided to bury Grivas in the grounds of the house in Limassol where the body had been transported the day before. Thousands were expected to pay their respects.

The attack therefore was completely unexpected, and most of the occupants of the house in the mountains were still in their beds when it started at 06:30.

No stealth had been employed this time. Three lorries had pulled up on the main road, blocking the route from all directions, and thirty members of Makarios's Tactical Reserve Force had spilled out and immediately vanished into the trees. They had their orders, they knew what to do. The house and everything and everybody in it were to be razed. Now Grivas was dead, it was thought this final assault would eradicate the core of the EOKA movement forever.

The soldiers ran through the trees, sub-machine guns poised, ready to shoot anything that was not wearing the camouflage uniform of the TRF. Their Commander, Christou, was among the front-runners. It was he who fired the first blast, shattering the downstairs windows of the house, glass and stucco shrapnel flying in all directions. At the first sound of shooting, the soldiers began to roar, almost as one, a wall of horrific sound from the vectors of death.

A face appeared at an upstairs window and was immediately disintegrated by a shower of bullets and glass.

Christou reached the already bullet-ridden front door and sprayed the heavy locks. Three kicks of his right boot and the door crashed inwards noisily.

A young girl who had been preparing breakfast ran in from the kitchen and was peremptorily executed by the Commander, the impact of the bullets spinning her around, mouth spraying blood like some obscene fountain. Old mother Dimitri also appeared from the kitchen and she suffered a similar fate, her old apron being ripped from her body by the burning lead.

The soldiers gushed into the house, some charging upstairs, others moving through the ground floor to take up positions outside at the back.

There were a few shouts from up above, ominously cut short by the gun-fire as the iron-tipped boots thundered through the building. Downstairs, the ceiling shook.

It had only been ten seconds since the first burst from the Commander's gun, and the young couple were still in bed together upstairs. They sat up staring in shock and horror as two of the TRF burst into the room. The girl's breasts turned into deep red pulp and the man's face dissolved as their lives were sprayed away with no more concern than a child would have in treading on an insect.

Tony Verekelis had awoken five minutes earlier and was just

putting on his pants when the invasion started. His feet and top were naked. He knew what was happening and he did not hang around to make sure his suspicions were correct. His room faced out the back, towards the mountain. Without thought for physical safety, he wrenched up the window and jumped the seven metres onto the grass below.

He felt his left ankle turn horribly as he landed, but it was a few seconds before the pain seared up his leg. He staggered upright, tried to run and fell, and he knew that the ankle was broken.

At that moment the first of the TRF charged through the kitchen and out into the garden. Tony was lying to the side of the door, not immediately visible. By the time the soldier spotted him, Tony's knife (which he always kept in a sheath around the waistband of his pants) was coming upwards from where he lay. It was rammed into the soldier's genitals, yanked sideways and pulled out again. The soldier screamed in agony, and his trousers were immediately stained by a spreading patch of dark maroon. He looked as if he had pissed blood.

Tony caught the gun as it fell and turned it on his attacker and a second soldier who was just bounding through the doorway. The first man was already dropping with his castration, and the second man fell like lead.

With a supreme effort, Tony forced himself to rise and run towards the far fence. God, his ankle! He couldn't do it, he just couldn't do it. But he must. He must! His run was nothing more than a hobble, a fast hop, but he had to reach them, to warn them.

He looked around and fired as another soldier came through the kitchen door. The first burst missed but a second chopped the soldier's legs from under him.

Beads of perspiration, of pain, of effort, broke from Tony's brow, and he forced himself forward. He reached the low fence and flung himself onto it.

He was just about to drop down the other side when the back of his head exploded.

He never even heard the burst of gunfire. One moment he was alive, the next moment all was blackness. He did not even have time to realise he was dead.

He stayed upright for a moment and then fell, the right leg caught over the top of the fence. The body dangled like some grotesque sacrifice with its brains dripping out.

In the doorway, Commander Christou sniffed in satisfaction. *Murderer! Murdering terrorist pig!* Two of his men dead and another losing blood at an alarming rate. *Murdering EOKA bastard!*

And again Christou was to have the satisfaction of a job well done. Nobody in the house was spared and soon, with some strategically placed charges, the house was blown up, bodies and all.

Six minutes and forty-two seconds after the attack had begun, the TRF men were walking back through the trees towards their lorries, leaving behind them a burning pile of rubble and an old, shot-up Ford Consul car.

The dead bodies, all except that of Tony Verekelis, were cremated where they had died.

They had risen at five that morning and had left the house while it was still dark, climbing into the Land Rover and driving off as quietly as they could. Their destination was the area higher up the mountain. They would not attend the public spectacle of the funeral. They had said their goodbyes to the body before it left the house yesterday. Now their objective was solitude amongst the pines, somewhere to think things out.

It had only been two days since Grivas' death but already the pressure was on from the remaining EOKA members for Steve to step into the old man's shoes. Present at dinner the previous evening had been Steve, Christina, Tony and three men from

Nicosia: Raouf, Nicos and Lefteris.

"We need a man who is not only a leader but a person whom all the people can respect," Tony Verekelis had urged. "And they respect you, Stelios. They know about you and, in some ways, they fear you. You are a myth that has proved to be a truth. You have their respect sight unseen. If you do not step into his shoes, nobody else can. You will be the public face of EOKA."

The others nodded in agreement.

"This is all very hard for me to accept," reasoned Steve. "It is all so incredible. Just a few days ago I was an oceanographer in Houston, Texas - "

"But you were always aware of your background," put in Nicos softly.

"Sure. But now here I am being asked to take over an army of resistance in a country whose internal politics I don't really know too much about. It was part of The Agreement that he would not pull me into Cypriot affairs whatever happened. You must know that."

"Yes, but you are back and he has gone," argued Raouf. "This island is born into you, Stelios. Think what a figurehead you would be."

The pressure had been tough. The debate had lasted all evening, ending with discordance. The five EOKA members had pleaded, begged and cajoled, but Steve was not to be committed. Not in the best of humour, the three men from Nicosia had left for Limassol at 22:00.

As Steve, Christina and Tony were going upstairs, having bidden the others farewell, Tony asked, "Are you going back then, Stelios?"

Steve tried to sound reasonable. "I have another life to live - my own. I *cannot* step into his shoes. *He* knew that. He did not bring me here for that."

"When will you go?"

"Sometime. Indefinite. But not just yet, there is something I must do first."

Tony looked at the girl pleadingly. He knew she and Stelios had been lovers since the first night. "Christina? Can you not persuade him?"

She shrugged. "I haf no power over him, Verekelis. It iss hiss life as he says. My own opinion hass no bearing in this." She looked at the American. "What iss it that you must do first, Stelios?"

Steve hesitated at the top of the stairs, uncertain whether he should mention it. Had it been just the rambling of an old man on the point of death? Would they think he was a fool to give any credence to the request? Nevertheless, if he was to get anywhere, he had to talk to - and trust in - somebody.

He looked from Christina to Tony. "Tony, would you come inside? I think this must be said in private." He was aware that the young helper, Takis, was in a nearby room with his girl.

Once inside the room, Christina sat down on the edge of the bed, Tony remained standing by the closed door. Steve stood by the window, facing them.

"I didn't want to say anything in front of the others..."

"You have upset them, you know. They were looking to you. They will probably now arrange something by themselves."

"Sure Tony, I know, and I'm sorry to have to disappoint them. But I am *not* here to take over, and I will *not* be persuaded otherwise. Now listen," Tony opened his mouth to argue but shut it again when he saw the look in the other man's eyes. "Please! I want no further discussion on the subject. Lefteris seems a fine leader to me."

Tony shrugged in resignation. "They will not like it, you know, not one bit. Especially if you stay on the island. It *is* your place, you know - yes, yes, yes, I know. We have been over this a thousand times this evening. Anyway, what was it you were going to say?"

Steve looked at both of them long and hard. "Just before he slipped into the last coma, he whispered something into my ear."

"Yes, I saw that," nodded Christina.

"It was a request. He wanted me to get something. I might not even have been hearing right. Anyway, his exact words, as far as I could make out, were… 'Get The Eye of Makarios'."

He waited for any reaction. There was none.

"Get *what?*" said Christina.

"The Eye of Makarios."

Christina and Tony made puzzled faces.

"The eye of Makarios?" Mused the girl. "Eye as in eye - ?" She tapped her right temple.

"I guess so. Do you know what it means?"

"Apart from the obvious," said Tony. "No."

"The obvious being that he wanted me to kill the President? A sort of John the Baptist? 'Bring me the eye of Michael Mouskos'? Could be… Grivas *would* understand what he was saying, I presume? He seemed coherent enough. It would not be an old man's ramblings?"

"Never!" said Tony sharply. "Grivas would not 'ramble', *never!*" The two men looked at each other, a tension rising then falling again just as quickly. "Did he say anything else, give you any indication?"

Steve turned to the window, thinking. He gazed unseeingly at the diamante Mediterranean sky. "He talked generally for a few moments about the usual things," he turned back to face them. "About my accent! And then he became urgent, as if he knew the end had come. He said there was something he wanted me to get for him when he had gone."

"When he had *gone?*" repeated Tony incredulously.

"Yep, that's what he said. 'When Grivas gone'. He said that only I could get it for him, from Mouskos… The Eye of Makarios."

"When he had gone..." Tony pondered. "He wanted you to get this eye of Makarios for him when he had died..."

"A final hit against the hated priest from beyond the grave," concluded Christina softly. "That would be typical of the General, to get the last word. At least we know now he was not rambling. Only he could haf thought off something like this. And to ask *you*, Stelios, to do it. Don't you see? It iss a master stroke. A master stroke! *You* of all people to deliver Grivas' final snipe from beyond the grave." Her eyes shone and yet at the same time were clouded in memory of the General. "Oh brilliant, *brilliant!*"

They were quiet. Then Tony nodded slowly and chuckled. "It is good, yes. So, the General is not dead, even now. And it is *you*," he pointed at Steve, "who are to carry on his work. He has decided."

Steve's face erupted into a bright purple. "Dammit, yes, yes, yes, it's *me*, I know! Damn all of you crazy people. I will do as he has asked and no more. He had no right to expect anything else of me, no right at all. He knew that. The Agreement. By Christ, I will get this fucking eye of Makarios, I will get it and personally take it to his grave. And then as soon as I can I will return to the States, to my *home*, to live *my* life, and leave the lot of you feuding madmen to go on killing each other, which is what you seem to like doing best..." He realised what he was saying and forced himself to stop. Then he said, "I will *not* lead EOKA, but I *will* get The Eye of Makarios."

Tony looked at him without expression. The girl was staring at him intently. Then she smiled. She nodded slowly. "Ah ha, so there it iss. There at last iss the fire, eh Tony? The fire that shows he iss truly Stelios."

"Yes," grinned Tony. "Yes, indeed."

"And Stelios, my love," continued the girl. "I will help you. Whatever it iss, I will help you find 'The Eye of Makarios'..."

Ψ

Now Steve and Christina were on the plateau high above the house, wrapped up against the chill morning air, watching the beautiful sunrise. They could see the snow on the slopes and peak higher up the mountain. People would be skiing up there later on.

"The thing is," remarked Steve as he surveyed the landscape, "we must find out what The Eye of Makarios is, otherwise we are thwarted before we start. Don't you have *any* ideas?"

"No," sighed Christina, drawing on the cigar she held between her lips. It was quite normal for women in this part of the world to smoke cigars or pipes. "But we shall find out, we must. Someone somewhere will know what it iss and, most importantly, *where* it iss."

"But you and Tony have been the closest to Grivas these last weeks. If you don't know, who in EOKA will?"

"I am nott saying anybody in EOKA will - and really Stelios, you upset them last night. We will be lucky to gett any help from them at all. Mouskos knows, and presumably some of hiss followers know. It iss just a matter off persuading someone to tell uss."

"That's all, huh?" Steve reached out to stroke her soft olive face. "Any idea what it can be?"

"No, none at all. It must be important - to Mouskos at any rate - for the General to want to take it from him, to warrant this last action. It probably hass to hurt Mouskos, almost like a slap in face. What more could it do?"

"But why, what is the point?"

"Haf you efer been slapped in the face by a dead man? An unbelievable surprise, I yam sure. And that iss why *you* haf to do it. Word will spread and Mouskos will know who sent you. Once you have The Eye of Makarios we will make sure that word spreads about who obtained it."

"Once I have it! You make it sound so easy, Christy - and perhaps it could be if I was trained in these things, in fighting, in tactics. But I'm a humble oceanographer, that's all, not a... a guerrilla." He knew it was a lie. She did not.

Christina gripped his arm tightly. "But it iss there, Stelios, it iss there. We saw it last night. Just remember who you are. It wass born into you. You are no stranger to danger. When you are under the water, you are in constant danger there."

"Yes, but..."

"You haf to haf your wits about you. Supposing you are attacked by a shark or some other predator, you know how to defend yourself and counter-attack."

"That is the world I know, under the water, I can handle those situations - in fact I can handle any situation, because I'm trained for it. This is different."

"*Why?* Why iss it? Iss it so different? Mouskos' men are the sharks, the barracudas, the moray eels. Cyprus iss your ocean. You haf to make it your world, just ass you would do the seabed. Efen iff you will nott stay, this island iss your world until you find what Grivas asked."

He leaned back on the grass and smiled gently. "Christy, you really do have a way of making it all sound so easy. Yes, and giving me confidence too, I like that. You are nice people."

She frowned. "I... I yam people?"

Steve found her confusion totally charming. "Yes, you are nice people, dear singer Christina, dear terrorist Christina. It is an expression, that's all. Means you're a nice person. That I like you. I like you a lot."

She smiled, shivering in the chill air, and leant down next to him, her face not far from his. "You, Stelios, you are... nice people, too."

She bent forward, cigar thrown aside, and they kissed.

"And do you know something?" he complained as he pulled out of the clinch. "I haven't heard you sing yet."

She grinned, the wide, lovely grin. "Well, maybe sometime soon you will."

At that moment the gunfire started from far below.

It was followed by the horrible, inhuman roaring.

"My God!" exclaimed the girl.

Steve dashed to the edge of the plateau and lay down. Christina grabbed some binoculars from the vehicle and threw herself down beside him, focusing quickly.

"It's the house!" cried Steve. "Jesus Christ, they're attacking the house! We must get back."

He was halfway to his feet before she peremptorily pulled him back down.

"Do not be a fool," her voice was hard and cold. "There iss nothing you or I can do. You do nott fight a shark unarmed."

The sound of gunfire thundered up the side of the mountain.

"But there must be *something* we can do! Surely to God!"

Christina lay on her elbows, not speaking, watching the devastation below. She saw Tony Verekelis jump out of the upstairs back window and try to run. It was obvious what was going to happen. Oh, Tony... Tony... She swallowed hard as she saw him die, and the tears filled her eyes. *The bastards!* The evil, evil bastards!

Steve snatched the glasses from her. It did not take him a second to recognise the body hanging from the fence. "Oh no, no...." His head shook in dismay. "Why?"

The girl had been resting her head on her forearms, and now she looked up, tears streaking her face. "The final blow," she said hoarsely. "Why did we nott think? We should haf expected it. Mouskos' final thrust against EOKA. Against hiss one-time comrades. He wass part of EOKA and fought side by side with Grivas and the others against the British. And now... now look what he hass done. He iss shit." She spat viciously over the edge of the ridge.

Gathering control of herself, she retook the binoculars. Down below, the firing had stopped. She looked for a moment and then said, "They are going to blow it up. The final insult.

Bastards!" She looked at the American, her nostrils flared and mouth tight. "Yes Stelios, there iss something that you can do. Do what iss your destiny. Get it for him, Stelios. For Grivas. Get The Eye of Makarios."

Limassol, Cyprus

They had expected thousands to attend the funeral. In fact, tens of thousands turned up.

Limassol was at a standstill.

And one of those in the crowd – just another anonymous local male, *fitting in* – was agent Digenis of the Israeli external security service.

$$\Psi$$

Thursday February 7 1974

"There is to be a general election on February 28th, the Prime Minister announced in the Commons this afternoon. At the same time he appealed to the miners to postpone their national strike over pay, which is due to start at midnight on Saturday, at least for the duration of the election campaign."

London, England

It snowed that month in London, the first time the capital had seen snow for two years. At the window of the second floor of Stuart House in the south-east corner of Soho Square, Colonel Stanley William Egginton CBE stood gazing at the large flakes as they drifted slowly downwards, adding to the patina of white covering the trees of the Square. Inside the conference room it was warm, perhaps too warm, giving the lie to the weather outside. Egginton thought about the miners and how every decent man in Britain must despise this forthcoming strike.

At that time, the newly formed United Kingdom Standing Committee on Arms Sales Support (these were the days before witty acronyms) consisted of twelve permanent members. These were the Directors of the Service branches of the Ministry of Defence. Three of these men were suspect and their files were under scrutiny by the British Internal Security Service. Colonel Egginton, fifty-four, stout, with a veritable mop of iron grey-to-white hair, was not one of them. His bi-annual positive vetting was always quite thorough and showed him to be a man of the utmost integrity and loyalty, his trustworthiness never in doubt.

The morning session of the meeting of the Standing Committee had finished and the ten attending members now stretched their legs in preparation for lunch (a cold buffet set out in the room directly above) in five minutes.

Colonel Egginton puffed at his pipe contentedly as he looked out of the window (these were the days when smoking was permitted everywhere), his thoughts transferring from the miners to his daughter's forthcoming wedding.

"Sir, Colonel Egginton?"

The Colonel turned around. It was one of the ADCs who acted as receptionists at these meetings. In his hand he held one of the standard two-tone grey telephones, its wire dangling unconnected from the back.

"Mm?"

"Telephone call for you, sir. Gentleman wouldn't give his name, said it was personal. Shall I plug it in?"

"Damn and blast, just at lunchtime as always. Okay son, plug it in."

The young man plugged the wire into a socket in the floor under the radiator, presented the phone to the older man and retired. Egginton placed the phone on the windowsill and picked up the receiver, removing his pipe with his right hand.

There was a click as the switchboard responded.

"Egginton here."

"Just one moment please sir." Click, buzz, the noise of a camel breaking wind, and then, "Go ahead please."

"Hello, Egginton speaking."

"Stanley William me ole dahlin', and how are yer?" said the Irish voice.

The Colonel stiffened. He turned his back to the rest of the room and spoke lowly. "What the hell do you want? How dare you ring me here!"

"Now, now, is that the way t' treat an ole friend? I was over here on business an' oi taught how noice it would be if I took me ole friend the Colonel to lunch."

"Impossible, can't make it, engaged."

"This business is *profitable*, lunch will be on me an' all that. Make it a late lunch if yer busy right now."

"No - er - I have appointments for the rest of the day." Blustering.

"Break them." Joviality gone.

A pause, then resolution. "When?"

"Ah now, ain't that good t' hear, knew yer wouldn't refuse an ole pal. Any toime yer like. I'm just downstairs. Hurry if yer can, it's bloody freezin'."

"I'll be down shortly." Phone replaced brusquely.

Egginton had turned as white as the snow outside. He remained looking out of the window, trying to regain his composure before he turned around.

"Stan? Stan! Coming upstairs?" A gentleman almost identical to Egginton was calling from a metre or two away.

"Er, no... no," Egginton turned and tried to smile. "Something's just come up, have to see to it. About me girl's wedding. You go on, Douglas, I'll be back later. Sorry." He made a beeline for the door, leaving his pipe on the windowsill.

At that same moment, Michael Mahoney appeared in the Square having just left the telephone box in nearby Carlisle Street...

Egginton, dressed in a heavy grey overcoat, silk scarf and trilby hat, turned left, treading gingerly in the settling snow. Through the falling white feathers he could see Mahoney approaching from the south side of the Square.

There was no pretence of stealth from the Irishman. He raised his gloved hand and roared greetings.

"Stanley! Stanley, me ole bum-stroker! An' how are yer?"

Their paths merged and they began to walk down Greek Street. There was no shaking of hands.

"Do you have to?" snarled Egginton. "I know you for what you are, remember? You can drop the brainless Irishman routine."

Mahoney was undaunted. "Sure an' yer bein' very unkind t' me today, Colonel. Anyone'd think yer weren't pleased to see me!"

"The only place I want to see you is in hell."

Egginton stumbled in the snow, and the Irishman's hand came out to steady him. Brusquely, Egginton pulled himself away. "Get your bloody hands off me!"

Mahoney smiled, a big Cheshire Cat smile. But when he spoke his voice held the merest nuance of malice. "Such aggression, my friend. Especially when I've got a five card trick and you're payin' on seventeen."

"Crap."

"What?"

Egginton controlled the rage within. He snarled. "I prefer baccarat."

Mahoney frowned and then, slowly, the smile returned. "Ah, a little joke then, was it? A little play on words. Now, isn't that grand? Isn't that more like the Colonel we love and admire! Where d' you want to eat?"

"What do you want with me?"

They turned right into Old Compton Street, past the then Casino Cinema.

"What d' you fancy? French, Italian, Chinese?"

"What do you *want*?"

"All in good time, my friend, all in good time. Y' know, I fancy some seafood. Are oysters in season, d' you know? Worked wonders for me last time." Mahoney manoeuvred the Colonel across the road to the southern side. "But first I've got to go somewhere. Does the cold affect you that way, Colonel? Goes straight to me kidneys. I find myself weeing all the time. Any public bogs around here?"

Ψ

Friday February 8 1974

"Skylab 3 returned safely to earth today after a record eighty-five days in orbit. Splashdown was in the Pacific."

Beirut, Lebanon

In the district of Borj El Barajneh, the foreigner – Ilich Ramirov – met with Ali Hassan Salameh and the other core members of Black September, as planned.

Kyrenia, Cyprus

Early evening, the darkening sky stained a violet red. The sun was a gigantic, burning orb to the west, slowly descending to fizzle out its fire in the calm water of the Mediterranean.

In Kyrenia Harbour, a normal evening's festivities were getting under way in *Halil's Kebab Restaurant*. The huge Cypriot-Turk Halil was up to his usual tricks, striding between the already full candlelit tables, a metre-long kebab skewer in each mighty hand. At every table, he attempted to guess the nationality of the persons sitting there and address them in their own language, his eyes meanwhile drinking in the ladies. Apart from everything else that was big about him, Halil had a sexual appetite of mammoth and insatiable proportions.

A coach-load of thirty early-season English tourists occupied a long table down one side of the restaurant, and Halil entertained them with his 'dumb Cypriot' act, shouting "Cheers!" and "Thomas Cook!" as often and as loudly as he could. In fact his English was excellent, if heavily accented, but he wasn't going to let them know this. He had made some of his best conquests of the ladies by appearing to be the big, dumb, beautiful oaf. After all, not many foreign women knew how to say no in Turkish.

Steve and Christina sat at a table in a far corner. Far enough away so as not to get embroiled with the tourists and yet not so far as to be conspicuously separated from the other diners. They were enjoying the finest kebabs they had ever tasted.

After five more minutes of entertaining, Halil left his audience and lumbered over to where the couple sat. With a great fuss and bustle, he sat down and swiped one of the three bottles of wine on the table, a black *Mavro*. A full third of the litre bottle disappeared down his throat in one swill.

Christina was dressed in a blue cotton dress, a lilac garland (purchased on their way to the restaurant from a local urchin on a bicycle) in her hair. "Well?" she queried expectantly.

Another mouthful of *Mavro* was swallowed before Halil spoke. His voice was quiet, serious. "Why should I help you? I! Halil! Why should I help a Greek?"

Christina looked heavenward. He was in one of those moods! "Do not be stupid, Halil. And do not play games with me. This iss Christina, remember. Your old friend."

"You have sung for me at times, yes…"

"And other things."

Steve raised his eyebrows. Halil looked abashed, and then a smile of memory crept across his craggy face.

"So stop playing games," scolded the girl.

The Turk looked uneasy. "My darling, it is not easy…" He squirmed on the seat in discomfort and downed another gullet-full of wine.

Steve leaned forward impatiently. "Buddy, I think we're wasting our time here. Your food is excellent, but your loyalty is something else."

"Loyalty?" The tanned brow creased. "Loyalty? You can tell me nothing about loyalty, my friend. I am a Turk. Christina, she is a Greek. Loyalty does not - cannot - enter into it. It has been that way for centuries. It will be that way forever. You are welcome in my restaurant. You may stay. Enjoy. Are these not the finest kebabs in the world? Is this not the finest wine? And you will eat and drink free." A giant hand was raised to quell Christina's protestations. "I insist. But loyalty? That simply cannot be. There are some things you cannot understand."

As Halil swilled again, a trickle of the black wine rolling down his chin, Steve suggested "Then what about friendship?"

The empty bottle was returned to the table. Halil contemplated the flickering flame of the candle between them. He looked up and then frowned. The candle cast a very faint shadow across the American's face. He reminded him of somebody.

He asked quietly, "Who *are* you, Mr American?"

"I am - "

"A friend," interrupted Christina. "A close and loyal friend. It iss better that that iss all you know, my dear Halil."

The Turk looked at her questioningly. Her dark eyes and that low voice had lost none of their seductiveness. And none of their insularity either. She was her own woman, was Christina, and he knew that she was hiding something. He also knew that he would never get it out of her, whatever it was, unless she wanted to tell him.

Halil decided. "Okay!" He slapped the table. "He is a friend. You are a friend. I am a friend! In friendship then. But I must tell you this," he leant forward, his faintly sour breath wafting across into the American's face. "I am a simple restaurant owner. Okay, so I know people. I have many friends. But I

cannot become so involved. You will understand, Christina."
The girl nodded to the plea in his eyes. "Certain of my friends...
they may be able to help. I can promise nothing. Just maybe. I
will make enquiries. This is for you Christina, because I love
you. And for you my friend, because I like you."

"How long?" asked the girl.

Halil shrugged the mighty shoulders. In the background,
three men began to play Turkish folk music on pipes and
tambourines. "A week. Maybe two..."

"We will return in a week then."

"No! You must not return. Not for a long time. Not until at
least the summer. It must not be thought I was involved."

The music insinuated, growing in insistence.

"Then where?" asked Christina.

Halil thought. "Be at Salamis. In *ten* days. At dusk. Someone
will come."

The girl nodded.

Halil stood up. "And now I must see to my customers." He
waved an all-embracing hand, joviality back. "My other friends,
they need Halil!"

"Just one more thing," Christina grabbed his hand. Her eyes
softened. "Be careful."

For the briefest of moments the Turk looked at her in silence.
Then a broad grin split his face in two. "Careful..." His raised
his left leg off the ground. "As my British friends would say, I
will be discretion itself!" He twisted around and gyrated his
hands and hips in time with the music. "Cheers! Enjoy!" His
mighty feet crashed down onto the floor as he stomped off
boisterously and was immediately swallowed by the throng.

As they left the restaurant a couple of hours later, heading for
their make-do living quarters in an old house on the outskirts of
the town, Steve asked "Why didn't you tell him who I was?"

"It wass not necessary, my darling." Christina slipped her

hand in his. The evening was mild, balmy. The waters of Kyrenia Harbour were totally still, not a boat bobbed.

"Maybe he'd have been more keen to help us."

"And maybe he would have slit your throat."

He put his arm around her as they walked. Considering the time, the place and the woman, he was not really interested in maybes, but he asked "Do you really think so?"

"Oh yes." She leant her head on his shoulder. The soft black hair smelt fresh. "You must understand the Turks, Stelios. Like us, they are proud. Like us, they have long memories."

He pulled her up and raised her head, cupping her chin in his right hand. "Talking of which, my lady, what was that about you and he, hm?"

"Mm?"

"Well...? Did you...?"

Her smile revealed the perfect white teeth. "You would like to know, yes?" Coyly. "Well, I will tell you..." She walked a couple of paces away from him. "Maybe!" With a giggle she ran off along the harbour's edge.

"Why, you little..." Steve set off after her.

Taking Halil's advice, that night they enjoyed like they had never enjoyed before.

As if there was no tomorrow.

Ψ

Monday February 18 1974

"An army helicopter crash-landed on the lawn of the White House earlier today after being chased and fired on by two police helicopters. The pilot, a young army mechanic, has been taken under armed guard to a nearby hospital where he is being treated for gunshot wounds."

Tel Aviv, Israel

Chaim Cohen, Deputy Controller of the Mossad, the Israeli external security service, sat at his desk in the office in the nondescript building somewhere in northern Tel Aviv. Unlike his network of agents worldwide, Cohen was obviously Jewish – from his distinctive, hawk-like features, the hint of sibilance in his voice, right down to the fact that he wore a skull cap on his bald pate. He bore a distinct resemblance to the Director of *Mossad Aliyah Beth*, Zvi Zamir.

Cohen looked at agent Nathanson sitting in the chair on the other side of the desk. "They are planning something," he said. "Salameh and company. They have been meeting together too often and they would not present us with such a target unless they had something important to discuss. They think the house in Beirut is safe, that we don't know about it. The fools," his laugh held contempt. "The last meeting was ten days ago. And there was someone else present, someone we do not know. Not one of them. Possibly a freelance."

"Why would they want a freelance?" Nathanson smoked

through a small, golden cigarette holder.

Cohen shrugged. "Why indeed. A freelance usually means one of three things. They need more man power – but the Arabs never employ mercenaries, they detest them as unclean. Or they are planning something with which they don't want to be identified - "

"Which would defeat their own object."

"Absolutely. Or thirdly, they need the freelance to do something they cannot do themselves."

Nathanson blew two perfect smoke rings. "And what might that be?"

"That's what I want you to find out."

"W-M-P?"

"Whatever means possible, yes. Discreetly."

"On my own?"

"Always better, don't you think? Especially with Hassan."

"Okay. Any links or fail safe?"

"All depends where you have to go. Digenis is back in the area if you need him."

Nathanson nodded.

"Find out what these fuckers are planning," scowled Cohen.

Salamis, Cyprus

Darkness. A deadly quiet, still, eerie darkness. High up in the bespeckled night sky, a quarter-moon shone lamely, casting barely enough light to see by.

Steve and Christina sat side by side in the centre of the third row of the Salamis amphitheatre, like the sole members of an audience come to watch the last performance of a closing play.

The amphitheatre dated from Roman times or even before. Behind the couple, the tiered, semi-circular seating area rose up to meet the stars. In front was the stone stage area behind a proscenium of air.

A torch sat patiently on the seat next to Christina, switched off to preserve its life. Steve hoped that it was the only life that would need preserving this chill, sinister evening. He sat on her left, his hand absent-mindedly rubbing the smooth surface of the centuries-old stone beneath him.

He sniffed. "Are you sure he'll come?"

"Halil? No. But he said someone would come." There was an edge to her husky voice.

"I don't like this." His eyes darted around what little of the stage he could see. "I don't like this one little bit. What a godawful place to pick for a meet."

"I think the theatre iss beautiful."

"Sure, but there is a time and a place, kid... And who the hell are we supposed to be waiting for? Suppose he tipped off Makarios's men?"

"He would not. Halil would *neffer*. Whatever else he may be, he iss not a traitor. He iss a Turk, remember?"

"Okay, okay, you're right. It's just that gradually I'm becoming aware of who I am and just what I might mean on this crazy island of yours."

"That iss good, my Stelios." A kiss was planted on his right cheek.

"And it scares me shitless." A dry chuckle came from his throat. "Jeesus... Got any chocolate left?"

"Yes." From a canvas shoulder bag resting at her feet, Christina produced some puce-wrapped offering.

Steve was not overstruck on Turkish chocolate, but he was quickly getting used to it. It was that or nothing in the confectionery line. Not a patch on *Hershey's*.

He bit into the over-hard candy and stared out into the darkness. "I wish to hell they'd show."

As if on cue a voice said "Hello."

They both span round. Christina grabbed the torch.

Three tiers above them stood a youth of no more than thirteen. He had a mop of tousled hair and wore a sleeveless pullover with no shirt underneath, dark shorts, no socks and local leather sandals. In his right hand he carried a small musical pipe. On his face was the most disarming of smiles.

"I am sorry if I startled you," he spoke in perfect English. "It was not my intention."

Christina frowned. "What do you want?"

The boy's smile did not waiver. "They sent me."

"Who?"

"They. You are expecting a message, no?"

"Jees buddy," said Steve. "You sure have a way of approaching people."

"What iss the message?" snapped Christina.

"They cannot help you," replied the boy, a respectful trace in his voice but the smile still radiating full blast. Was he laughing at them? "You will have to try elsewhere."

Steve stood up. "They can't help us at all?"

"That is all I was told to tell you. They cannot help you."

"But didn't Halil say anything - ?"

"They cannot help you. That is all. You must not contact them again."

"Yes, but - "

"I must go now. The others get worried. Goodbye!"

"Hey now, just a minute fella - "

But the boy had clomped lightly up the steps and was enveloped by the darkness.

"Hey - !" called Steve.

Christina touched his arm. "Let him go, Stelios."

"But..."

"He iss only a messenger."

"Shit." He relaxed. "Yeh, I suppose you're right."

Christina picked up the bag. "More chocolate?"

"What? No, no thanks. So, what do we do now?"

"Now? Now we haf to try somewhere else." Resiliently. "Tomorrow we move on." The bag was slung over her shoulder. "Tonight we rest."

"We must be careful," cautioned Steve as they moved away. "The more people we ask, the more chance there is of Makarios finding out about our quest. Or even finding out about me - us. And that could be fatal."

She handed him the torch. "Yes, we must be very careful Stelios. Very careful. That was a warning."

As they reached the edge of the amphitheatre, Christina looked back to where they had been, to where the boy had been standing. It was a stupid thing to imagine, she knew, but she could not help the involuntary shiver that ran the full length of her spine. The tousled, closely curled hair of the youth; the pipe in his hand; the noise his feet made, almost like hooves…

If she had even an ounce of belief in her, she would have said that the boy reminded her of someone. Someone from mythology. But that was preposterous and ridiculous. Totally and utterly ridiculous. And she did not believe.

Did she?

And this was Cyprus. This was 1974.

Wasn't it?

[Not wishing to get involved, Halil has since admitted that he never did make the enquiries. Until the author's interview with him he had never mentioned The Eye of Makarios to any living soul, or even tacitly acknowledged that it existed. Who the boy was who spoke to Steve and Christina on the night of February 18 1974 is not known.]

Ψ

Saturday February 23 1974

"Reports are coming in of a robbery at Kenwood House on Hampstead Heath, London. Preliminary reports say that a painting - The Guitar Player *by Vermeer, said to be worth over one million pounds - is missing. In Lahore, the Islamic summit conference, attended by the kings, presidents and prime ministers of the Moslem world, has opened. Items on the agenda include a discussion on how oil revenue should be used."*

Moscow, USSR

To the western world she was known as the Soviet Union's most powerful woman politician. For several years she sat on the all-powerful Praesidium of the Soviet Communist Party, a feat seldom emulated by a woman in the *Soyuz Sovyetskikh Sotsialisticheskikh Respublik.* Her name was Mrs Ekaterina Furtseva, and at that time in 1974 she was presumed to be Russia's Minister of Culture, a post which she was supposed to have held for the last fourteen years.

In fact she was nothing of the sort. The Soviet authorities have always denied her true position, for it was considered not *kulturny* for a woman in the Union to rise to such a powerful and dominant rank. For this very same reason, western journalists have never bothered to question her status. Even the mighty American CIA is not aware of what she truly did.

For the last five years of her life *[she resigned on October 24*

1974 and died in her sleep that same night, ostensibly from a heart attack] Ekaterina Furtseva was none other than the overall head of a very special, self-governing division of the Committee of State Security, the KGB. Such was her division's autonomy that it was tantamount to a KGB within the KGB, and Furtseva reported direct to only Premier Kosygin himself (some said the division was his brainchild), by-passing even Shelepin and his cohorts. Furtseva was in total charge of her division, taking full praise for its successes - and full responsibility for its failures (which were very few).

At 09:00 that morning the temperature in snow-driven Moscow was a mild zero degrees, and by that time Furtseva had been in her office for an hour and a half.

She looked up as Ramirov entered, shown in by a minion. Ramirov was dressed in a floor-length coat with an incredibly thick fur collar, and a fur hat. The face, so young and chubby, was bright red with the cold. It would crack and chip if he was not careful.

Without saying anything, Ramirov slowly removed the coat and hat and went over to the blazing fire in the grate in the wall to the left. Thick fur mittens had completely covered his hands, but on removal he noticed that his fingers had still turned that almost translucent red, and they ached as they began to thaw in the heat of the flames. Even after the *déshabille*, he was still wearing a thick woollen jacket, heavy pants and two polo-necked sweaters. And he was freezing.

He looked over at the woman. She was dressed in a man's military uniform of indistinguishable, but very high, rank *[it has never been ascertained for certain what rank the woman held. Not that military rank at her level of the KGB was of particular worth, it was political rank that counted]*. It was buttoned to the neck, the colour a basic KGB green but with a stirring of brown, grey and khaki. Her grey hair was cut short above the ears and parted on the left. When, after a minute or so, she stood up to greet him, he could see that her pants fell over rugged leather knee-high military boots of at least a size 44. Ramirov grinned to himself; he always marvelled at the size of her feet.

Her voice was deep and totally masculine. "My God, Ilich, anyone would think you were not used to Russian winters. Is your body forgetting your motherland?"

Ramirov smiled, out of respect more than out of amusement. He had been back in Russia for almost twelve hours now and his mind had promptly adjusted to thinking and talking in Russian. "It could never forget its true home, Comrade Furtseva. It is just that these western climes are ruinous to the skin."

She laughed heartily and clapped him on the back. "Come! Some wodka?"

"Thank you."

She extracted a bottle of *Osoboya* and two tumblers from a tall cabinet behind her desk. She filled one tumbler to the brim and put it down on the front of her desk, then she proceeded to fill her own to a similar level. "Come! Pull up a chair Major and sit down."

Ramirov hated the stupid title and he inwardly winced, but he did as he was told, draping his wet coat over the back of the plain wooden chair. He sample the wodka. It was good.

"Saw that stuttering idiot Philby on the way in."

"Oh?" Furtseva sat down and lit herself a cigarette from a box on the desk. She pushed the box towards Ramirov.

"Thought he was supposed to be redefecting last year?" Ramirov shook his head at the cigarette box.

The woman raised an eyebrow at his impudence, like a mother with a naughty son. She said curtly, "Something went wrong."

"Oh." Ramirov knew better than to press the point. Changing his mind, he leant forward and took a cigarette and Furtseva's expensive lighter from the table. Immediately he lit the cigarette he wished he hadn't. Good God, what did they put in them nowadays? Peasant shit?

"And to what do we owe this unexpected but entirely welcome pleasure?" asked Furtseva, and before Ramirov could reply she went on, "Your monthly reports have been illuminating, most illuminating. Your success has been astonishing, greater than we could have hoped for. You are to be congratulated."

He inclined his head in that curious fashion of his as an acceptance of the praise.

"Even though you missed Sieff." The sting in the tail. "However, I presume some outstanding exigency brought you here into my office?"

"In some ways, yes." Ramirov, *even Ramirov*, felt intimidated by the woman - no, the *person*, the *hermaphrodite* - sitting opposite him. But he was damned if he was going to show it. "I am in need of your directions. As you know, the kidnapping of the British Princess Anne is scheduled for 20th March, three and a half weeks time."

"Yes, how is that coming along?"

"All the plans have been made, it is simply now a matter of execution. She and her husband are going to a film show that evening, they will be returning around 19:45. Our man intends to strike as they near Buckingham Palace."

"He is reliable, this 'man'?"

"I am satisfied. No one is completely as reliable as oneself, naturally, but he suffices. His name is Ball. I think perhaps he is… shall we be kind and say an idealist? Of course, it is my intention to leave Britain immediately I have disposed of the princess, her husband and Ball. The bodies should not be found for several days in the house in Kent, longer if I am lucky."

"Good."

"However, the Arabs have asked me to assist them in a little scheme they have cooking at the present time."

"They still do not know you belong to the Committee?"

"Oh no, not at all, no one does. My cover as Martinez/Ramirez is concrete."

"Good. Keep it that way."

"Naturally, Comrade. Anyway, I should assist the Arabs if I possibly can, but if I do it will mean my staying on in Britain, possibly for sometime after the kidnapping. I am confident that I am covered anyhow, Ball does not really know who I am. He considers me to be a fellow idealist, from South America of course."

Furtseva nodded her satisfaction.

"Nevertheless, I feel that I should have your concurrence before I agree to the Arabs' request, as there may be just the slightest risk of danger if I stay on in the country."

"What is it that the Arabs are asking?"

Ramirov explained in full detail what he had learnt at the meeting in Beirut two weeks previously. How the Arabs planned to explode a nuclear device in Britain and how their supplier, an eccentric Irishman, wanted a two million pound diamond in exchange for enough plutonium to make the bang. It all sounded so ludicrous now, sitting in an office in the middle of freezing Moscow.

The woman listened patiently, gradually finishing her tumbler of wodka and refilling the glass. Ramirov's was still half full. At the end of his expatiation, she was grinning sardonically.

"They will never succeed, of course." (Ramirov inclined his head but did not comment.) "They have not a hope in hell. To try it in Britain of all places! It is almost impossible to commit a major act of significant terrorism there [history was, of course, to prove her wrong] they just won't have it - as we have discovered previously. The kidnapping and murder of a royal princess is one thing - she is of no consequence or political importance. But to set off a nuclear explosion, perhaps close enough to an atomic plant to cause a major disaster - HAH!" The cavern of her mouth revealed rotting teeth amongst the cheap single dentures. "It is ludicrous. They will probably all die of radiation before they even move the stuff."

Ramirov nodded. "Maybe, and I have no doubt that you are correct Comrade. I did not enquire of their exact *modus operandi*, whether they have the appropriate technicians available and such like, because it was none of my business, and it is not within my jurisdiction to ask such things. The Arabs are confident enough, therefore it must be left to them. What they want is for me to get this 'Star of Sierra Leone' for them."

"Tell me about this. It is a diamond, you say?"

"Yes, I have been doing some research. Apparently it was found not long ago - just one moment please." He turned in the chair and extracted a folded but crumpled sheet of paper from an inside pocket of his overcoat. He read from it. "It was found in the Diminico Mine in Yengema, Sierra Leone, which is state-owned. It weighs 969.8 carats and is the third largest uncut diamond ever found - larger even than our own *Orloff* - estimated value two million pounds sterling. Measures... let me see... two and a half inches long by one and a half inches wide. The Sierra Leone government asked *De Beers*, the mining company, to sell it for them. The transaction took place through their London offices. Whom it was sold to will never be revealed publicly." Ramirov refolded the piece of paper. "Should you agree to me giving my assistance to the Arabs, it would be my task to find out who bought the diamond, to ascertain whether it has been cut or not and, if not, to take it."

Furtseva breathed in deeply. "Hmm... and what if this diamond has been cut? What then?"

Ramirov shrugged. "I do not know. Presumably the Arabs will come to some other arrangement with the Irishman. It is really a strange affair all round. They tell me that their supplier is well aware that the cash price for the amount of merchandise they require far exceeds two million pounds, but he has enough money, so he says, and wants this diamond. Almost like a child wanting a toy."

"Ardent Communists might call that the product of capitalism gone mad," commented the woman. She downed the remnants of the second tumbler of wodka and lit her third cigarette. "Well, Ilich," she ruminated. "You know that your brief is to help in whatever way possible. I suggest that you do that."

"Yes, Comrade."

"In fact on reflection, I like the Arab idea. I like it very much. It is amusing. Impossible, of course. But just supposing it did succeed, eh? Just supposing… I think we must help them in whatever way we can, Ilich, even to the extent of abandoning the royal princess plan. The very slim chance of the Arabs' plot coming off is worth much more than the simple assassination of a puppet."

Quickly Ramirov reached for his wodka and poured it down his throat to stifle his natural spontaneous reaction. The princess murder was his idea, his entirely. How *could* she expect him just to relinquish it? She had been so keen on the plan originally. The bitch.

But, of course, he knew better than to argue. It was literally more than his life was worth. He just replied "Comrade," acquiescently.

Furtseva pursed her lips, satisfied with her decision. "Let this man Ball continue against the princess if he so wishes. You will not contact him again. All your energy must be devoted to getting this diamond, if it is still in existence. Report back to me when you have succeeded."

"Comrade."

Ψ

Monday March 4 1974

"Mr Heath has resigned as Prime Minister. The fourteen new Liberal MPs this afternoon rejected Mr Heath's offer to form a Conservative-Liberal coalition government, and the Prime Minister travelled to Buckingham Palace almost immediately to formally tender his resignation to the Queen. Shortly after a subdued Mr Heath left the Palace, Mr Harold Wilson arrived to be invited to form a government. In France, it has been confirmed that all 345 persons aboard the Turkish Airline DC10, which crashed in the forest of Ermenonville near Paris yesterday, were killed. At least 200 of them were British. It is the world's worst-ever air disaster."

London, England

At that time *De Beers'* registered office in London was at 40 Holborn Viaduct. It was a round, eight-storey, typically depressing example of 1950's architecture. But *De Beers'* London business is of such a size and volume that this monolith could not contain all the necessary staff, and in nearby Hatton Garden (London's diamond centre) was a wide old building known as The Annex.

In the small office on the second floor of The Annex, Annette Stewart sat tapping figures onto a small mains calculator. Annette was a tall, well-built young woman in her mid-twenties, smart brunette hair cut to just below the ears, a pretty almost delicate face nearly smothered by a huge pair of spectacles, and make-up applied with taste although perhaps a bit too thinly on the lips. That day she wore a high-collared maroon dress, pinched in at the waist and falling to just above her knees.

After contemplating the answers given by the machine, Annette transferred the data onto a sheet of paper in front of her. It was part of her junior executive responsibilities to write a report of each Friday's bourse and to give detailed accounts of each deal involving *De Beers'* merchandise.

She was so absorbed in her work that she did not notice the time passing. When the telephone rang at 10:55 she visibly jumped and nearly dropped the short holder in which burned her *St Moritz* cigarette.

She put the cigarette holder between her teeth and mumbled into the mouthpiece. "Yes, Annette Stewart?"

It was General Reception downstairs. "Miss Stewart, your eleven o'clock appointment is here."

"Eleven o'clock! God, is that the time?" Her left wrist snapped up to her eyes and down again. "Okay, have him shown up will you please?" She replaced the receiver and hurriedly set about tidying up her desk. The calculator was unplugged and stuffed into a drawer, telephone straightened, papers assembled into two almost orderly piles and cigarette disposed of into an ashtray which also found its way into a drawer. She patted her hair and sucked her lips inwards. She wanted a pee but there was no time now. Why on earth hadn't she kept an eye on the clock?

There came a short tap on the door and it opened to reveal a tall, well-built man, wearing a rather out of fashion double-breasted two-piece striped grey suit, and carrying a small document case. His Latin face had a warm, permanent suntan and the jet black hair with shocks of grey at each temple was pushed straight back. A pair of golden-framed spectacles, tinted a pale brown, covered dark eyes.

"Mister Garcia," announced a voice from behind, and a hand reached out to pull the door closed as Garcia walked quickly into the room.

Annette rose. The hand that took hers was warm and the skin was hard, the grip powerful, the contact prolonged an iota longer than the norm.

"Good morning Mr Garcia, Annette Stewart."

"Miss Stewart, it ees my pleasure." He grinned, as if the last thing he was expecting was such a good-looking young woman. "Indeed, my pleasure."

"Won't you sit down?"

"I thank you." As he said it he inclined his head gently to the right and back up again.

"Now then, Mr Garcia," Annette pulled the chair in under her. "What can I do for you? Your secretary said you wished to talk about diamonds - any aspect in particular?"

"Perhaps I had better explain, Miss Stewart," an attractive, toothy smile added to the warm, accented voice. "Basically I would like to put myself in your hands." He opened his case and took out a small rectangle of cardboard. "My card."

Annette read: *Raimondo Garcia Martinez, President, Martinez Shipping, Cadiz, España,* together with telephone and telex numbers and the company crest, a golden filigreed M.

"Miss Stewart, the situation is that I own my own fleet of ships - in fact I will be truthful with you, I inherited the concern some ten years ago from my father. We manage a fairly lucrative business with cruise ships in the Mediterranean and cargo ships world-wide. I have nothing at all to do with diamonds. Frankly I possess no knowledge of them. I have some money - my own money - to invest, and I thought that in this age of uncertainty and inflation, diamonds would be - how do you say? - the best bet. I would like to use your good services, if it is at all permissible." He felt into his pocket and pulled out a packet of *Marlborough*. "Do you smoke?"

Annette smiled. "I do but not at the moment, thank you."

"It ees permitted?"

"Of course, please go ahead." She opened her drawer, surreptitiously tipped her own ash onto some important papers, and then withdrew the ashtray and passed it over to Garcia.

"I thank you."

She waited for a moment, looking at him light up (and noticing the crested lighter which looked as if it was 24-carat gold) and then she said, "Well, Mr Garcia, we can certainly help you. How much were you thinking of investing?"

His right hand flicked into the air. "Oh, that does not worry me. It ees all dependent upon what you have to offer me. I will be guided by your recommendations." Again the head inclined to one side.

Annette raised a mental eyebrow and went into her spiel. "You will find no better investment than diamonds - in the long term, that is. Prices are rising continuously, and quite sharply nowadays. But the retail mark-up is quite considerable and it will be years before a diamond will sell for what you paid for it. A good quality diamond - weighing a carat or over - is a good long-term investment.

"*De Beers Consolidated* owns and/or controls most of the diggings in southern Africa, mining some £91,000-worth of rough diamonds each day. Eighty percent of the diamonds aren't good enough to be gems and are used in industry. Our mines supply thirty-five percent of the world's new gem diamonds *[Russia supplied twenty-five per cent – a fact of which Garcia was well aware.]* Eighty percent of all diamonds mined are sent here to the Syndicate - the Central Selling Organisation. Here diamonds are sorted by weight, shape, colour and clarity.

"Now, I will be perfectly honest with you, we do not usually deal direct with customers in such a manner as this - we have our own list of 250 buyers who come to our five-weekly sights. However, your references *were* impeccable."

"Thank you." The head inclined. "Tell me, you mentioned that I should invest in diamonds of at least one carat. One hears of carats in diamonds and gold and such," he waived his cigarette, "but I am afraid that I do not completely understand their significance."

She smiled, her mouth wide and, beneath the formal British exterior, somewhat inviting. "Of course, please excuse me. Dealing with these things everyday one often forgets that the whole world does not know every facet of one's trade."

"No, no," Garcia's voice had become softer, even more friendly. The eyes smiled. "It ees I who must apologise for my ignorance."

She cleared her throat. "A carat is basically a unit of weight. Measured in points, there are one hundred points to a carat and one hundred and forty-two to an ounce *avoirdupois*. To give you an idea, most normal common or garden engagement ring diamonds average anything up to point five of a carat. Other rings with just one big diamond," she made a little figure of the size over a finger on her right hand, "are usually in the region of up to five carats."

"Intriguing. And to think that I have been living in ignorance all these years!" He chuckled and lifted his spectacles once off the bridge of his nose and then replaced them. He stubbed out the half-smoked cigarette. "Tell me more, Miss Stewart. Tell me how diamonds are discovered."

And so she told him, everything a layman would be able to understand about diamonds, their formation from carbon, discovery in the rough in kimberlite rock, the processing and reprocessing, the sorting at the Central Selling Organisation, the sights, the sawing and cleaving, the deals, the *mazel* and *brocha* (luck and blessing), the not so scrupulous activities of some members of the retail trade.

She found it easy to talk to this man with his intelligent questions and humorous interjections, and she found herself liking him more and more as the morning went on. Before she knew it, it had passed midday; a quick look at his watch made Garcia aware of this also.

Annette had just completed her lecture about the retail trade when Garcia asked, "Miss Stewart, please do not think it presumptuous of me, but I have taken up a lot of your time with my silly questions, and you are obviously a very busy lady. Would you do me the honour of allowing me to buy you lunch? Apart from an exquisite meal - which I can promise you - we can conclude our business and I need not take up any more of your time this afternoon." He suddenly looked abashed at his own audacity, and added quickly "Or perhaps you have another engagement?"

She had not and she hesitated only a moment. "Oh! Well, no, no, I have nothing on - I mean... yes, I'd love to! Thank you."

Outside, London was cold and grey and very windy, the pedestrians of Hatton Garden struggling bravely to keep their composure in the face of a wicked north-wester.

Garcia hailed a taxi which had just dropped a Jew in a large floppy overcoat outside number 87, the London Diamond Club, three premises up. They travelled not too smoothly through the lunchtime traffic, eventually coming to a halt opposite the *Warner* cinema complex in Leicester Square. Garcia led the way into the *Trota Blu* restaurant.

Annette felt relaxed with the man and conversation flowed smoothly and easily. His occasionally stilted English added even more to his charm.

Garcia chose the meal: *Zuppa di datteri, Biscetta alla fiorentina con melanzane al funghetto,* followed, of course, by *tiramisu.*

They downed aperitifs of Martini, and went through two bottles of red *Lacrima Christi* during the meal. At the end, Annette had to firmly refuse his near insistence on another bottle of wine, compromising instead with a small brandy, the mellow *Hennessey*. Her head was spinning lightly but she felt good, and the food had been excellent.

Garcia had talked a lot during the meal, about his businesses in Spain and of his inherited wealth - which, Annette formed the impression, was immense indeed. Then he had asked about her, and she had heard herself telling him all about her private life, about Simon her fiancé, about where she lived, everything.

With the brandy downed and coffee being served, Garcia finally reverted to business. "Now, if I may, about my investment. Gem stones are, of course, beautiful but - and I must be honest with you - my investment will be purely for, er, how you say… financial expediency."

"I un'stand," Annette heard the faint slur in her voice and she quickly dragged on her cigarette. Garcia seemed unaffected by the alcohol, he was still his charming *good looking* self. Oh, that accent!

"So, from what you have told me, I was wondering if I should invest in rough diamonds rather than the finished article?" He smiled. "As you have explained, of course, a large rough could be worth several times its original price when cut - and, therefore, I presume the buying of rough diamonds is very much a closed shop. Quite simply, I would like to enter that shop." His head inclined to the left and the dim light of the restaurant reflected off his spectacles.

As the brandy's final assault on her system began to take effect, Annette's head became more and more fuddled. Garcia's voice was so deep, loud yet soft, as if it was only for her ears and her ears alone. She felt as if she wanted to go to sleep, to go to bed. She forced herself to pay attention, her eyes dreamily holding his.

"What I was thinking of," he continued, well aware of her state, "was that I should buy just one big rough diamond as my initial investment and then review the situation sometime afterwards. I would be prepared to spend in the region of five million pounds to start with."

That awoke Annette like a plunge into iced water. As with anyone being shot out of a near narcosis, she felt confused at the sudden alertness and she wondered if she had heard correctly. To cover her confusion and embarrassment, she blurted "We had a stone in not so long ago."

"You did?"

"It would have suited you perfectly. A 970 carat beauty. In fact, the third largest rough ever found. Sold for over two million."

"Pah!" Garcia slapped the heel of his hand against his forehead. He showed no sign of noticing her confusion. "And I have missed eet? Eet would have been perfect! Tell me, tell me who bought it. Please. Do you think they would sell?"

Annette giggled, a little girl with a secret. She leant forward. "Actually, I'm not supposed to tell, that information is s-strictly con-con-confidenshul."

His lips puckered. "But dear Miss Stewart, *please.*" He also came forward, taking her right hand in both of his. "It ees just what I want. Perhaps I can persuade them to sell."

She shook her head, giggling. The booze spoke. "No chance, my dear Raimondo, no chance. It was sold..." She placed her left hand over her face in a wasted effort to contain a burp. "It was sold to the P-President of France."

Which was exactly what Ramirov wanted to know.

That night a terrible fire completely devastated Annette Stewart's home in Orpington, Kent. Her parents were away in Portugal, and only one charred body was found in the place the next morning. It was later identified (by the teeth) as Annette. So badly burnt was the corpse that the head just snapped off when the forensics attempted to bundle it into a plastic bodybag. Nobody ever detected the single needle mark on her chest where a full syringe of air had been injected directly into her heart.

Ψ

Wednesday March 20 1974

"Two British soldiers were killed and another seriously wounded in Ulster earlier today when members of the Royal Ulster Constabulary opened fire on them on the border with the Republic. Exactly what happened is not known at this stage but an official source has described the incident as 'a tragic accident'."

London, England

The attempted kidnapping of Princess Anne Elizabeth Alice Louise, GCVO, Chief Commandant Women's Royal Naval Service, Colonel-in-Chief 14th/20th King's Hussars, the Worcestershire and Sherwood Foresters' Regiment, 8th Canadian Hussars, Commandant-in-Chief Ambulance and Nursing Cadets, and only daughter of Her Majesty Queen Elizabeth II of the United Kingdom of Great Britain and Northern Ireland, took place at 19:45 that evening. What happened is a matter of historical fact, the Princess and her husband being saved by their solitary bodyguard, an Inspector in the police, who was shot three times and eventually awarded the George Cross, Britain's highest honour for peacetime gallantry.

Peter Sydney 'Ian' Ball was overpowered a few hundred metres away in St James's Park and was taken into custody to a cellar underneath the premises of the old police headquarters just off Whitehall. Despite harsh and stringent questioning, intimidation and plain torture, the police could glean no information from him as to their being an accomplice - although at one point, after a thin electrode had been inserted into the urethra of his penis, another into his anus and the current switched on, he did start rambling about the foreigner, the Peruvian who had helped him, who had set up the whole operation. However, no credence was given to this as the precipitate electric current had been greater than intended and, still tied to the chair, Ball had been flung across the room with the shock, his head landing with a terrible thud against the concrete floor.

Ian Ball was tried at the No 1 Court at the Old Bailey (the Central Criminal Court) on May 22 1974 and pleaded guilty to charges of attempted murder, wounding and 'attempting to steal and carry away Her Royal Highness Princess Anne'. It was ordered that he be detained in a special hospital under the Mental Health Act (in fact the top security Rampton Hospital in Nottinghamshire) 'without limit of time'.

That very same evening, and not a kilometre away from the incident in The Mall, Stanley William Egginton lay naked face down on the leather-topped massage table and cringed as the masseur's fingers gouged into his pectorals with what he considered unnecessary brutality. He was in his Club in Pall Mall.

In fact, the cringe was not only caused by the masseur's vicious administrations, but also by what was going on in Egginton's head. For over a month now he had lived on tenterhooks wondering what the Irishman wanted. The meeting on February 7 had been a pure and simple softening-up job. Mahoney had been as nice as pie, treating him to an expensive meal, wine and spirits, and an exquisite Cuban cigar, and only occasionally mentioning that he was after something big this time - a fact which Egginton had already worked out, as it was very rare for Mahoney to set foot out of Ireland to do business, let alone poach on another person's territory (and London was Bilbeisi's territory).

After the lunch with the Irishman, Egginton had made a brief appearance back at his meeting in the afternoon but had left after forty minutes giving 'a bloody migraine' as an excuse. Ten minutes walk away in Leicester Square, Mahoney had been waiting, and the rest of the afternoon had been spent driving around London, the Irishman marvelling with glee at the various sights. "Look, there's Westminster Cathedral, haven't been in dhere fr' ages - which remoinds me, oi must go t' confession. My God, Victoria Street's in a mess, hope all this rebuildin' is worthwhile."

And, in between the marvelling, Mahoney had been checking, asking Egginton if things were the same. How was his daughter? Getting married? Getaway! Did his wife Margery still have that very weak heart? ("Marvellous how she's lasted this long Stanley, me ole son of a donkey.") And did he remember those lovely and totally obscene photographs Mahoney had, locked away somewhere safe, of Egginton and two thirteen year old schoolgirls? And what a great pity it would be if they were accidentally to fall into the hands of Mrs Egginton ("I'm not sure her ole heart would stand it, yer know."). But that would never happen, of course, because Mahoney would look after them. And wouldn't it be possible for Stanley to supply him with an especial item he wanted at some unspecified date in the future? And sure, wasn't he a co-operative little Colonel to say of course he would get anything he was able to and sure didn't Mahoney know that indeed he was able to get *anything*? And wasn't the Colonel happy to know that this time, as the item required was extra-special, Mahoney would truly give him all the photographs and negatives and also a quarter of a million pounds.

Yes, he had heard right. A quarter of a million pounds. The

item, you see, could not go missing overnight. It would have to disappear slowly, and subsequent investigations would be bound to point the finger if not directly at Egginton then at least in his general direction. The quarter million would enable him to get out, to save his neck, to spend his last remaining twenty years or so living as he had always wanted, anywhere in the world that suited him (except Britain). And think of all the thirteen year olds he could have then, all those ripe cheeky-pink bottoms and what was beneath them.

In his somewhat inebriated state (Mahoney supplying a bottle of whiskey on his guided tour of old London town), Egginton did indeed find the idea attractive. To get those photographs alone would be worth everything, for he loved his wife, deeply and dearly, and he would rather die (and even risk social disgrace) before he would let any shock or harm come to her. He would have to get what Mahoney wanted anyway, so he might as well relish the prospect of his rewards.

That night, Mahoney had treated him to a *VIP Special* at a certain well-known establishment in Kensington Church Street, and Egginton had spent the night, not with thirteen year olds this time, but with two of the juiciest whores West London had to offer.

And he had heard nothing from the Irishman since. Not a bloody word. And that was why on the evening of March 20 1974, Stanley Egginton had plenty to cringe about. Just when would that damn mick contact him again with details of his intended 'purchase'? It must be something colossal to warrant a payment of a quarter million. A brace of tanks, perhaps? A *Harrier* jump-jet?

He cursed roughly as the masseur dug a knuckle just a fraction of a centimetre too deep into his buttock, and he forced himself to fart sharply in retaliation.

Ψ

Wednesday March 27 1974

"The new Labour government announced today that it was suspending technical aid to Chile and no new arms deals would be made with the ruling military junta."

Paphos District, Cyprus

The waves came charging in towards the shore like wild fluorescent eels, laying end to end and stretching sideways on to the beach, threatening, only to peter out at the last moment with the weakest of liquid thunderclaps. The eels caressed the smooth white sand softly, like fingers on a body. Up above, the night sky was cloudless and the myriad stars shone like neon bulbs in the heavens. It was a full moon.

The situation was a kilometre or so to the north of the port of Paphos on the west coast, near the Tombs of the Kings.

The couple walked along the beach, arms around each other, like lovers do or wished they did the world over. They were lovers physically, and had it been another time, another place, another century, another planet, they might have been lovers in the full and true sense of the word: physically, mentally and spiritually. But this was Cyprus 1974. She was one of the remnants of a once powerful resistance organisation and he was a man with a mission. A mission that was proving most frustrating at that present time.

Her head was resting against his left shoulder, and they

walked slowly, at a half-pace.

"I just can't understand it," Steve's voice contained neither resignation nor determination, he was simply stating a fact. "Two months. Two goddamn months. And no trace. Not a damn mention of this 'Eye of Makarios'. It's incredible. Nobody seems to have heard of it except Grivas - and he can't help us now."

Christina sighed. "I am forced to agree with your sentiments, dear Stelios. It iss not, how do they say, for the want off trying? We haf tried both EOKA and Mouskos people, both Greek and Turk," at that word she spat once, softly, onto the sand, "but nobody knows what it iss. I fear that it does not exist, this Eye iss not real. We haf discussed before about the General speaking in - what was the word you used?"

"Metaphor."

"Metaphor, yes. But he could not. He would haf known that his death-bed was not the place for riddles - especially for you. If you consider the search to be worthless continuing, Stelios, I will understand. Even Grivas in heaven would not hold it against you."

And they *had* searched. They had made surreptitious enquiry of nearly every person they had met; they had put out feelers, other persons had discreetly asked other persons, Greek had even asked Turk before slitting his throat. But everything had been met with a negative response. The only Eye of Makarios that was known were the two things on either side of the Archbishop's nose.

Apart from the frustrating quest, Steve and Christina had had to keep continually on the move after they had left Kyrenia. Word was out amongst Mouskos' followers that Cascianis and a male had escaped the final inferno of EOKA. And they, the final sperm of the movement, must be caught before they could fertilise a new generation.

The belief that EOKA was moribund was encouraged by the

three gentlemen who split their time between Nicosia and Limassol - Nicos, Raouf and Lefteris. For it suited their purpose very well to have Makarios believe this. Little did the Archbishop know that EOKA was regrouping, without Cascianis and the male, and gaining strength day by day in preparation for something terrible that summer.

Steve and Christina had not stayed in one place more than three or four nights, and Christina had argued that even that was too long. But the followers of Grivas were still plentiful, and the couple had not as yet had to forego shelter when darkness fell. Washing facilities, food and clean clothes (sometimes badly fitting, usually on the larger side) had been provided when necessary.

For the first few days after leaving Kyrenia they had travelled around in the Land Rover which they had taken with them into the mountains on the morning of the attack. But they had decided that it was getting too well-known as word about them spread. The vehicle had had to be abandoned. Now their way was made in vehicles either borrowed or 'borrowed' or, for short distances, on foot. At that time they were lodging in a room in a house near the Church of St Kendias in Paphos.

They came upon some boulders separating the dry inland shrub from the beach, and they sat down. The noise of the waves made soporific musak.

Christina, rather fetching in a white billowing cotton top and a simple three-quarter length black skirt with a red and yellow flowered hem, sat open legged and withdrew a vicious-looking knife from a sheath around her left thigh. She did not lower her skirt but left it where it was, balanced at the top of her leg, plain white cotton pants showing a few centimetres away. Absentmindedly she began to churn the stones and sand with the knife.

Steve, who was wearing his own denim jeans and bomber-jacket with a borrowed black cotton shirt underneath, sat to her right and at an angle facing her. His listened to the rolling tide and the gentle patting of the girl's knife on the sand. He thought.

After five minutes he said, "No."

Christina looked at him. "Stelios?"

He smiled. "No Christy, I don't think continuing the search would be worthless. If the information will not come to us, then I - "

"We."

" - must go to *it*. It is time to look fate square in its goddamn face, kid. After all, that is the reason I am here. This…" he spread his arms wide to embrace the whole of Cyprus, " - is my destiny, the reason for my existence. I see it. It can be no other way. We *shall* find out what The Eye of Makarios is, even if we have to ask Mouskos himself."

He reached out and touched her soft black hair. "It's good of you to say you'll understand if I no longer wish to carry on, but I *must*. He would not want me to quit now. Grivas *will* have The Eye of Makarios - even if it kills me." He looked into her eyes as he said, "The least I can do after all these years is to obey my father's last request."

Ψ

Friday March 29 1974

"In Washington, President Nixon has agreed to hand over tapes and documents subpoenaed by the Watergate Special prosecutor Mr Leon Jaworski. Also in Washington, Dr Henry Kissinger today met the Israeli Defence Minister General Moshe Dayan to discuss troop disengagement from the Golan Heights."

Paris, France

Born July 5 1911 at Montboudif in the Auvergne

1934 military service

1935 teacher of classics in Marseille, married

1938 moved to Paris to teach at *Henry IV Lycée*

1939 40 Alpine Infantry regiment

1940 returned to *Henry IV Lycée*

1944 liaison work with the Education Ministry

1946 resignation of De Gaulle, stayed on in position but gradually became De Gaulle's close collaborator, became Treasurer of the *Anne De Gaulle Foundation*

1948 made head of the shadow cabinet by De Gaulle

1954 employed by Guy de Rothschild

1956 made director of Rothschild bank

1958 chief of staff to De Gaulle who emerged from retirement

1961 entrusted to join the broken threads of the Algeria negotiations

1962 nominated as Prime Minister, April 16

1968   resigned as Prime Minister
1969   elected President of France

Georges Pompidou became noticeably ill in the winter of 1972, Elysée spokesmen putting the President's sickness down to influenza and relapses. In May 1973 he appeared on television with Richard Nixon, the then American President. The whole world noticed the Frenchman's puffy features, hesitant manner and difficulty in expressing himself clearly.

By March 29 1974 his condition had worsened and his features had swollen to balloon-like proportions. Although his speech retained its hesitancy, his mind - as any of his doctors would attest - was as alert as ever. The disease would, of course, eventually prove fatal but no one that day imagined that the President would be dead in four days time - at least, not of his illness.

For the last year, Pompidou had spent whatever time he could in the modern (some would say futuristic) rooms in the east wing of the Elysée Palace, rooms he and his wife had personally decorated. There were four rooms, each brilliantly and beautifully layed out with modern furniture, *avant garde* ceiling and wall coverings and pictures by the time's top artists. *Les quartres salles* were completely out of place with the rest of the eighteenth century palace, but they were a magnificent anachronism.

At 11:45 that morning, the Russian Ambassador to France and his aide, a chubby-faced, curly-haired, Latin-looking fellow, were shown into the drawing room. They were keeping an appointment made at their behest some days previously. The President would not keep them a moment, they were told, and the private messenger scurried off, leaving them alone.

Neither man spoke, for they were well aware that even here there might be concealed microphones or hidden cameras. Instead they busied themselves admiring the paintings on the synthetic resin walls, offerings from Kupka, Delaunay and Matisse.

They were kept waiting only three minutes before the President arrived, wheeled in by his personal private secretary, a neat and thin fellow who had the aura of a mother hen.

Both the Ambassador and his aide were shocked as they looked at the grotesquely swollen facial features and the distended hands gaping out from the sleeves of the expensive dressing-gown. But it was the eyes that the Ambassador's aide noticed most. Yes, the eyes said everything. The eyes said there was still life in the President, a tenacious wonderful life that would not be relinquished easily.

The Ambassador recovered his composure quickly and smiled politely, speaking in French. *"Cher Monsieur le Président,* how nice it is to see you." He went to offer his hand in greeting but then thought better of it. Could Pompidou move his limbs?

The swollen face wobbled, and the President said, *"Messieurs, bonjour.* It has been... a long time since I have seen you, Mr Ambassador." The voice was deep, coherent without being clear, and held just an intermittent trace of hesitancy.

"The President cannot be troubled for too long, gentlemen," put in the secretary tartly. "He is unwell and has been advised to rest."

"Pah, do shut up Albert, for God's sake!" Pompidou half turned his head and slung the words over his shoulder. "Anyone would think I was a senile old man on his... death-bed. I am all right and I will probably see you in your grave. Now leave us."

Albert bridled and left. The three of them were left alone in the room, but the Russians were only too well aware that no more than a few metres away outside were guards with enough firepower to blow the flesh off their bones without even an effort. And they had, naturally, been discreetly screened before being admitted to the Palace.

Pompidou spoke. "You said the subject was of some... urgency. So, what is so urgent that the Russian Ambassador himself comes to visit me?"

The Ambassador smiled solicitously. *"Monsieur le Président,* may I present Alexei Mirzoff, my aide."

Pompidou looked at the younger man, who inclined his head in greeting.

Pompidou's head nodded gently as he said, "Please gentlemen... sit down." The right hand twitched in indication of the chairs. There were four in the room: two brown bucket divans to sit three apiece against two of the walls under the Matisse paintings, and two single chairs of the same design. The Ambassador sat on one of the divans, just a couple of metres away from the President. After a moment's hesitation, Mirzoff sat next to him.

The Ambassador looked uncomfortable. "Actually sir, it is about a diamond."

"A diamond...?"

"Oui monsieur, if you will excuse? It is a rather delicate matter," he leant forward in his seat, hands together, an unconscious supplication. "Recently my country's diamond, the *Orloff,* was stolen. This news has been kept secret, even from some members of the Praesidium, and you are certainly the first westerner to have been told about it. The persons who stole this diamond were members of a Ukrainian nationalist organisation known as OUM. They have since been captured and have been dealt with. However," he grimaced, displaying a definitely non-socialist gold filling in one of his left molars. "The diamond has not been recovered."

Mirzoff had remained silent and he now stood up and, with hands in pockets, strolled over to admire the Kupka and Delaunay paintings on the lateral wall.

"We managed to glean from the criminals that the diamond had been smuggled out of the Soviet Union," continued the

Ambassador, "travelling via a *sympathique* captain on a Black Sea vessel, through contacts in Turkey, and eventually down to South Africa. Our agents suspect that the South African Security Service, the BOSS, then took a hand, but that is not a matter to concern us at this moment. Truthfully, we have not been able to trace *le diamant* further. However, we have strong suspicions that it was 're-processed' - by that I mean a large diamond was claimed to have been discovered, it was processed in the usual way and then sent as normal to *De Beers* in London. The history of it being concrete enough to fool that establishment, they took their proper action. Eventually the diamond was sold.

"This is only suspicion, of course. But it is very strong suspicion."

Pompidou's head wobbled. *"Très intéressant Monsieur l'Ambassadeur*, but what has this got to do with me?"

"Sources tell us that at the same time as the *Orloff* might have reached *De Beers*, they did in fact start negotiations on a large diamond. It was named 'The Star of Sierra Leone'. And we are told it was purchased by you."

"Ah!" There was amusement now in the President's eyes and the jowls wobbled some more. "Now I see." He looked towards Mirzoff, who was now standing in front of a Matisse two metres to his right. "I am indeed grateful for your prudence. Obviously you wish to ascertain whether The Star of Sierra Leone... and your *Orloff* are one and the same stone."

"My government has asked me to make discreet enquiries."

"And what do you propose to do if it is, *hein?* No, no, do not worry... I make fun." He stopped for a moment, thinking. Then he said, "Unfortunately I do not... have the diamond."

Both the Ambassador and Mirzoff looked up sharply.

"Monsieur le Président?"

"You see, my dear friend, I did indeed buy The Star of Sierra Leone - or the *Orloff* or whatever... I bought it in good faith with my own private and personal funds... and I bought it as a gift."

"The *Orloff* would make a very expensive gift."

"That is… my business."

"*Mais naturellement.*"

"It was a gift for a friend. If you… want to see whether it is the *Orloff*, I suggest you ask him."

"I certainly shall, *Monsieur le Président, merci.* May I ask the name of your friend?"

"The President of Cyprus, Archbishop Makarios."

The Ambassador and Mirzoff looked at one another. Mirzoff inclined his head slightly and smiled. The Ambassador looked back towards Pompidou and stood up.

"*Monsieur le Président* you have been most helpful, I thank you…"

Mirzoff, just out of range of Pompidou's vision, removed a pen from his pocket.

"Naturally we will both treat this conversation in the strictest confidence," assured the Ambassador. "And, of course, the story of the *Orloff* will go no further than these walls."

"Of… course."

Pompidou did not notice the pen next to his right ear, neither did he have any heed of the two cubic centimetres of colourless, odourless, slow-acting cyanide gas that was squirted from the end of it. *[A more potent and immediate-acting form of this gas was used to kill Dr Lev Rebet in Munich on October 12 1952. The gas induces heart failure and is virtually untraceable upon post mortem examination.]* Pompidou felt no different from normal as Albert returned, and he bade the Ambassador and his aide goodbye.

Under one hundred hours later Georges Pompidou was dead.

Subsequent checks have shown that the Russian Ambassador did not visit Georges Pompidou at 11:45 that day. Neither did the Russian Embassy employ an aide named Alexei Mirzoff. It is suspected that immediately after the interview, the exact double of the Russian Ambassador was hastily driven into Belgium and from there onwards into the Soviet Union. It is a fact that he was seen in a suburb of Moscow on Sunday March 31. 'Alexei Mirzoff' was also seen in Moscow on the same day.

As for the link between Pompidou and Makarios, this has never been fully discovered. To this day, close family and friends believe their only affinity was that of two heads of two dissimilar republics. However, it is probable that in late 1973 Makarios struck up a friendship with the Frenchman during clandestine discussions on arms and agricultural sales, completely without the knowledge of France's EEC partners. It is also probable that the Archbishop was instrumental in obtaining the services of two Turkish and one Yugoslav specialist medical consultants who visited Pompidou in early February 1974. No allegory concerning a future French President and diamonds from an African 'republic' is to be drawn.

Ψ

Monday April 8 1974

"The joint Egyptian-British-American operation to clear the Suez Canal of debris from the Yom Kippur War starts tomorrow. Three Royal Navy minesweepers and one support vessel have today arrived at Port Said ready to commence operation."

Houston, Texas, USA

"Hi, this is Jim McKane."

"Ah, hello Mr McKane, you don't know me, my name is Sally-Anne Bowker and I'm a friend of Steve Graves?"

"Why Miss Bowker, of course, I recognise the name. Steve spoke a lot about you. What can I do for you, ma'm?"

"Well, actually, it was about Steve that I rang. He hasn't written or called me since he went off to the Mediterranean nearly three months ago. I kinda wondered if you could tell me how he was getting on and when he will be coming back...?"

"Well, I would if I could Miss Bowker, but how should I know?"

"Well, I - "

"Y' know it's strange the way Steve went off like that."

"Went off?"

"Without any notice or anything. Okay, he only worked for us on an assignment basis."

"An *assignment* basis?"

"Contract, you know. He was not on the payroll as an

employee. Well, he just came back from lunch one day, a Toosday I think it was, did his afternoon's work and then announced that he could no longer complete his current contract and that he would be leaving immediately. He wouldn't explain further and none of us could understand it. He was brilliant at his work and he'd never complained about contract rates... So, he went off to the Med, eh? It would have been nice to receive a card or somethin' from him. But if he hasn't written to you well then I guess there's no chance of him writing to us, eh? Heh, heh. We *would* like to know why he left, though - hope it wasn't somethin' we said, heh, heh, heh. So I really can't help you on that score ma'm... Hello?... Hello, Miss Bowker?... Hello?... Well! And a Happy Easter to you too, you stupid broad...!"

Ψ

Friday April 19 1974

"The state of Bihar in north-east India was on full alert tonight after yesterday's dismissal of thirty-five government ministers by Mrs Gandhi. This followed the state government's formal resignation nine days ago over allegations of corruption. A new fourteen member cabinet has been formed."

Nicosia District, Cyprus

April in Cyprus is beautiful. It is a month of clear skies and a perfect temperature averaging twenty degrees. The citrus trees are in full blossom in preparation for the harvest of the summer, and the sweet, tempting, gorgeous smell of the orchards pervades the countryside. The tourist season is not yet fully under way, and it is a time of peace, a time to relax, a time when languor can be forgiven.

It is not a time for violence.

The Mercedes arrived at the house in Eylenja, south-east of Nicosia, at precisely 08:30, as it did every morning. The official government chauffeur did not alight or give any indication of his arrival, but nevertheless just fifteen seconds later the heavy wooden door in the side wall opened and the figure stepped out. He was dressed as usual in the long black flowing robes of a bishop of the Greek Orthodox Church.

Bishop Michael Rigakis was not an official Minister of State but an aide of External Affairs Minister Ioannis Christophides, and a close friend and confidant of the President.

Settling down in the back of the car, the Bishop closed his eyes and began to pray silently, as was his custom every day. Between his hands he held a silver crucifix which was tied on to a leather thong around his waist. The journey to the House of Representatives on Leophorus Omirou just outside the south-west walls of the old city of Nicosia would take twenty minutes.

Without a word, the driver engaged gear and pulled away. The roads were always quite clear at that hour of the morning, and he expected a short, uncomplicated drive.

They had been travelling for eight minutes and were on the main road to Nicosia when the attack happened.

It was the sound of the windscreen splintering that made the bishop open his eyes, just a split second before something hot and wet splashed onto his face. He screamed before realising he had not been hit, and he looked up to see that the left side of the driver's face had disintegrated into a ruby-coloured pulp. Only then did he hear the blast of gunfire.

The chauffeur leaned against the door, as if tired. The car swerved wildly as the dead hands fell from the steering wheel. The Bishop instinctively wiped his hands across his face and then pulled them away, covered with the driver's blood and brains.

The Mercedes thundered off the road, jumping madly up and down as it ploughed through the long grass. The chauffeur's body jogged up and down, almost hitting the roof, his flopping head painting firm, thick strokes of gore onto the closed side window.

The Bishop made to lean forward to grab the wheel but before he could do so the car came to an abrupt halt with an almighty *bang* from underneath as something broke and the undercarriage hit the hard, rocky ground. He fell forward and then sideways, cracking his head on the door. Dazed but conscious, he was aware of the door opening and then hands were dragging him out, His cassock caught on something, and for some stupid and irrelevant reason he found himself thinking that he would have to ask his housekeeper to stitch it for him later.

Then he was sitting on the dry, dusty ground, propped up against the side of the vehicle and facing away from the road. Any passing motorist would not have seen him.

An iron hand was clamped hard around his bearded jaw, puckering his features. The grip was so hard that he thought his jaw was going to be crushed. He winced in agony.

The owner of the hand was a huge beast of a man, totally bald but with a thick black moustache which contained various items that had fallen from his nose. His eyes were black and full of hatred, the one hatred that is worse than that of Greek and Turk: Greek and Greek. His breath was disgusting, and the Bishop would have turned his head away if it had been within his power.

In the extreme right of his vision, Bishop Rigakis could see another man. He was similar to the ogre, but this time not so fat and with more hair. A relative, possibly his son.

The Bishop made a noise, trying to ask the question, but he simply could not move his jaw within the grip.

"I'm glad you want to talk." A pair of blue-denimed legs entered his vision and their owner crouched down so that he was next to the ogre. "Because you've got something to tell me, fella."

It was a young face underneath a mop of tight, curly black hair. The face possibly looked older than it was because of a drooping moustache. The skin was tanned, but only recently so, as if the man had not been in Cyprus for long - which was really self-evident by his accent: it was American.

The priest's fearful eyes turned towards Steve.

The American's face was hard, yet it held none of the hatred of the ogre. "Don't worry, I'm not going to hurt you - providing you tell me what I want to know. Do you understand?"

The Bishop said nothing, he just looked scared.

"Do you understand?" The voice colder this time, menacing.

To help the Bishop's powers of speech, the ogre bashed the aching head hard against the side of the vehicle, then he released the jaw from the terrible grip.

The Bishop thought that two of his teeth had become locked together from the sheer pressure of the ogre's hand. He was vaguely aware that he had pissed himself with fear. "I... I understand," he managed to stutter.

"Good. Now tell me, Father: what is The Eye of Makarios?"

A dazed look came into the Bishop's eyes and his head twitched involuntarily. For a moment Steve thought he was going to pass out.

"The Eye of Makarios, Father. What is it?"

From behind the American a girl appeared, dressed in peasant clothes. Rigakis thought that her face was vaguely familiar. In her hands she held a rifle. So, it had been *she* who had killed the chauffeur.

He was about to speak when, without warning, the ogre's hand came down sharply across his face. He felt a nail rip the corner of his mouth.

"We don't want to have to use force," the young man sounded as if he meant it. "But we will if necessary. Tell me - please. We know you know. What is The Eye of Makarios?"

The Bishop's mouth moved in silence for a few seconds and then sound came out. "It... it... is that all? There is no need for all this - "

Again the hand across the face, blood in his beard.

"Please." The American.

"It... it is carried on his person at all times... in a pouch around his waist... I do not know where he got it... said it was a gift... I think it is a safe place for his money." He was finding it even more difficult to talk as his lips puffed and turned a wicked shade of purple. "He has not had it long..."

"Yes Father, but what *is* it?"

Rigakis managed to frown. Surely everybody knew what it was? "It is his name for it. It is a diamond... a big diamond."

Steve and Christina exchanged glances. Then he ordered, "All right, let him go."

Ogre and relative relinquished their intimidating positions and disappeared from view. Rigakis watched as the American stood up, said "Thank you, Father," and turned towards the girl.

"At last" he said. "Okay, let's go." He moved off.

The girl remained where she was for a moment, looking at the dishevelled, bloody figure on the ground, all the pride and dignity of his ecclesiastical rank ground into the dust. She lowered the gun and fumbled in the folds of her skirt. She bent down and gently wiped the Bishop's forehead.

"Th - thank you." He noticed what deep, dark eyes she had.

She stared at him. Then Rigakis' eyes widened in total terror as he saw what was in her other hand. He tried to move but his limbs would not respond.

The finely sharpened meat skewer was inserted into the head behind the Bishop's right ear. It was pushed easily up into the brain. He died instantly with just the briefest flash of pain.

She arose and followed just twenty paces behind the American.

Half a minute later, a vehicle pulled out from behind the bushes and sped of down the road, away from Nicosia.

Back by the Mercedes, the Bishop's nervous system gave its final, convulsive twitch and he lay still forever. A fly landed on the swollen upper lip and began exploring the lower nostril hairs...

Ψ

Saturday 20 April 1974

"In Israel, it is now almost certain that the Labour Party will elect General Yitshak Rabin to succeed Mrs Golda Meir when it meets on Monday. Mrs Meir resigned ten days ago. Meanwhile in Greece, preparations are under way for the celebrations to mark tomorrow's anniversary of the colonels' military coup seven years ago."

Yeri, Nicosia District, Cyprus

The villa had been empty for over a month now - a fact which had not gone unnoticed by the locals of Yeri village. The businessman who owned the place must be off on one of his jaunts somewhere. Sometimes he had been known to disappear for up to half a year before arriving back out of the blue. He would stay for anything from ten days to ten months, and then he would be off again. One rumour had it that he was some sort of rich recluse who owned shipping lines. But the elders of the village knew better. They knew for a fact that his money came from crime. He was one of the leaders of the *Mafia* or the *Union Corse* and, they stated categorically, his periods away were on Family business.

Whether the people of Yeri village believed this to be true or not, they kept their distance from the house without actually isolating it, only speaking to the owner when spoken to and supplying the occasional domestic. They let him be and he let them be. It was an amicable, tacit understanding.

So far this time he had been absent for nearly two months. Whether it was by coincidence or design, he usually went away at this time of the year just when the tourist season was starting. If the past was anything to go by, he would not be back until September or October.

When the two Grivas people arrived unexpectedly two days ago, the idea had been discussed by the village elders. The couple were looking for a safe house while they planned some operation. The villa was perfect, isolated and well away from the village, empty and secluded. Why not? The man would not be back until the late summer, he never was.

Earlier that evening, a village elder had contacted Christina at the farm of Costas, the ogre. Suggestions had been made, heads nodded sagely. Not only did the place seem ideal but, in view of recent events, it also got them out of the village's hair.

Nobody in the village had spoken about what had happened yesterday, but the news of the Bishop's hijacking and murder had spread like wildfire throughout the island. Makarios had ordered a full alert, and three hundred members of the Tactical Reserve Force had swarmed into the area south of Nicosia.

The TRF expected to find nothing. The unit Commander, a man called Christou, reckoned that the murderers would be long gone, to a far part of the island if not to the mainland all together. It was this that Christina and Steve were banking on, that the centre of the storm was the safest place.

Their hypothesis had proved correct. The TRF had saturated the area, asked a few peremptory questions and had received well-rehearsed and totally false answers. Yes, people had seen them. Witnesses estimations of the number of persons involved ranging from ten to fifty, their escape route being towards Kyrenia, towards Larnaca, towards Morphou and towards Famagusta, all at one and the same time. Against this wall of well-prepared confusion, the TRF had withdrawn after just one day from saturation level to just a 'presence'.

Now Christina expertly picked the lock on the door of the villa. They entered by torchlight, not daring to try any of the light switches to see if the power was still on. These places usually had their own generator somewhere out back, and it would have been turned off by the owner before he went away.

The villa was cold inside, the windows closed and shuttered for the past two months.

Steve's torch played around the room. It was a big, split-level living area, tastefully furnished in contemporary Mediterranean style, tiled floor, honey-coloured stucco walls. At the far end was a door which would lead to the kitchen and thence to the back entrance and out into the grounds and outhouse.

"We shall explore more in the morning by natural light," said Christina, whispering even though they knew they were alone in the place.

"Sure," agreed Steve, his voice also instinctively subdued. "I think the best thing we can do now is find somewhere to lay our heads. C'mon, let's have a look upstairs."

On the floor above were three bedrooms and two bathrooms. A quick look in all the rooms revealed that the first one, on the southern side, was the one probably most used. The bed was stripped, as it would be if its usual occupant expected to be away for some time, but a convenient cupboard revealed sheets and pillows for the use of.

They prepared the bed together in the twilight of the torchbeam.

"God, I'm looking forward to a proper bed," said Steve. "Especially after that meal of old mother Makouri's. I've never tasted *stifatho* like that before."

"Haf you *effer* tasted *stifatho* before, Stelios?" Fold, flap, tuck.

"I have indeed, my child!" Indignant. "I'm not a complete freshman to the delights of things Cypriot, you know." He strained his eyes to see the curves beneath the blouse and skirt. "Especially women."

Christina straightened up. "I hope you arse miling when you say that, Stelios."

In the darkness he was in fact smiling broadly. As she went round to the other side of the bed, he stretched out and whacked the firm right cheek of her bottom. She squealed and ran out of reach of further discipline.

He chuckled, then changed the subject, "Y' know I'm surprised at all the help we're getting. EOKA seems to be more alive than ever, at least in support."

"In support yes, and in members too. Remember Nicos, Raouf and Lefteris? They are alive and active. We could haf been with them but we chose not to. But around here people know what Mouskos can do. And they are kind because you are who you are. The myth of Stelios, Grivas' long lost son, precedes you. Haf you not noticed the way they look at you, scrutinising and comparing?"

"Yes, I have."

"We should be thankful that it hass not got back to the TRF or Mouskos yet that Grivas' American son is one off the people they are looking for, or else we would stand no chance. Think what a pretty prize *you* would make for the Priest. The area iss crowded enough as it iss since yesterday."

The bed finished, she came over to him. He put his hands on her shoulders, looking down into her eyes. "And what a prize *you* are, beautiful lady. Now we must rest, for tomorrow we've got a lot of planning to do. Buddy Makarios carries that diamond around his waist. *That* is not going to be easy. I think I'm gonna need to take a few trips into Nicosia. Will Costas let me have the car?"

"There should be no problem."

"Good. This is gonna take some time, kid."

"But you will succeed."

"Oh yes, I will succeed. For my father."

"And then you will go away?"

"I don't know. Honestly, *I* cannot lead EOKA. I guess I will go back to the States."

"And to your woman - Sallyan?"

"Sally-Anne. Possibly. She's probably forgotten about me by now. But that's in the future, Christy. Think only of now. Think of what has to be done." His lips gently brushed against hers. "Think of us."

Her arms went around his neck and she pulled his head down firmly, her strong wet tongue forcing its way into his mouth.

Ψ

Monday May 6 1974

"Chancellor Willi Brandt of West Germany has resigned. Announcing his resignation this afternoon, he said that it was the only proper course open to him as he was politically responsible for negligence in the espionage affair concerning his former personal assistant Gunther Guillaume, who has admitted spying for East Germany. At home, the million-pound Vermeer painting The Guitar Player, *stolen from Kenwood House Hampstead on 23rd February, has been found in St Bartholomew's Churchyard in the City of London. It was wrapped in a newspaper."*

Houston, Texas, USA

Sally-Anne Bowker had spent a fretful weekend. The fact that it was her time of the month did not help, but she was well aware that the cause of her fretfulness was purely emotional, not physical. It had been a month since she had heard the earth-shattering news from that stupid man McKane. A month since she had been told that Steve, *her* Steve, had not gone off to the Balearics for *Gulf* as he had told her.

Just to confirm that McKane hadn't been lying, she had phoned *Gulf's* Personnel Manager a few days after phoning McKane. She too confirmed that Steve Graves had simply upped and went that afternoon in January, breaking his assignment contract.

Sally was perplexed. She just could not understand it.

Perhaps both the *Gulf* people were mistaken? No, stop fooling yourself sister. And what was this about him being on contract only? She thought he was a permanent employee. Something was obviously going on. Maybe it was national defense work and the 'quitting the job' story was just a cover? Steve had mentioned to her once that *Gulf* undertook certain undersea assignments for Washington (or for Langley, to be exact). Then again, maybe it was the old, old story - another woman. But Steve would not just load a pack of lies onto her and then walk out, it was not in his character. And anyway, it was not as if they were married. If he wanted to call it a day as far as their relationship was concerned, he would only have to say so, and he knew that. The fact that she was crazy about him would not enter into it.

What *had* happened to him? Had he met with some unearthly accident?

These thoughts had plagued her since her calls to *Gulf*. Up until a few days ago she had resigned herself to the fact that there was little or nothing she could do. However, her period depression had now instilled more determination into her, and she had gone into school that morning with her mind made up.

That lunchtime she dismissed her class immediately on time. What she had planned would take more than her allotted hour and twenty, but it just couldn't be helped. She jumped into her ancient Ford and quickly drove out to the airport, thanking God that the traffic was not too heavy.

It took her a while to find a place to park and then a further while to find what she was looking for. The middle-aged guy with the toupée behind the *Air France* desk smiled pleasantly as she approached the counter.

"Afternoon ma'm," he was a local, not French as she had expected. "My name is Wilbur, I represent *Air France*, what can I do for you?"

"Hi, er... I wonder if I could ask you a question?" Like a lot of her countrymen, Sally spoke in continual question-marks. "It's a friend of mine? Well, basically, to tell the truth, he went off to Europe a few months ago and I haven't heard from him since, And, well, really..."

"You want to check whether he did in fact go?" Wilbur nodded knowledgeably.

"You got it."

"Well I think we may be able to assist you there. You have any details? Day, time, flight number an' all?"

"Hold on." She rummaged in her purse, coming up with a scrap of paper. "He went January 23rd, in the morning, on the direct flight to Paris?"

"Ah ha." Wilbur hastily scribbled down the details. "And he has a name?"

"Oh, sorry, yeh. Graves. Steven Graves?"

"Steven Graves... right. I can certainly check that for you. If you would like to wait over there ma'm?... Shirley, can you take over for a second please?"

A big-breasted, uniformed blonde squeezed out of a room behind as Wilbur went in. She gave a half-smile to Sally and then turned to attend to an elderly couple who, by the look on the wife's face, had something to gripe about.

It seemed like ages, but Wilbur was back in two minutes, a computer printout in his hand. He looked pensive. "Well ma'm, I'm afraid we had no Steven Graves on our morning flight to Paris on that day, it *was* January 23rd? Uh-huh... Oh, hold on... oh no, I guess not. The nearest we come to Graves is a guy called Grivas," he pronounced it Grivers. "Apart from that..." He shrugged his shoulders regretfully.

"Do you think I may just have a look at that list?" Sally smiled sweetly, pushed her specs up with a finger, and held out a tentative hand.

"Well, really I'm not supposed to, but..." He made a show of being circumspect. "I guess just a peek wouldn't hurt." He placed the sheet on the counter top and turned it in her direction.

She ran her finger down the column. He was right, of course, there was no Steven Graves, only this Grivas person. Stelios Grivas. Her eyes travelled down the other two hundred names. Nothing...

Hey now, just one minute... SG... Steve Graves - Stelios Grivas... it could be... No, could it?... Yes, it must be, it was too much of a coincidence. But why on earth...?

"Ma'm?"

She became aware that she was staring abstractedly into space. "Oh, er, oh, sorry."

"I said have you finished with the list?"

"Oh yes, thanks, yes."

"No Steven Graves, I'm afraid." The paper was taken back and slipped under the counter.

"No, no I guess not." She gave a false laugh. "Oh well, thanks for your help anyway."

"You're welcome ma'm. Thank you for enquiring of *Air France,* and you have a nice day."

"Mm."

PART THREE

Ψ

OBJECTIVE OBTAINED

Ψ

Thursday May 16 1974

"The stoppages in Ulster go on. Shops and offices, factories, public houses, clubs and hotels were closed today because of the Protestant Ulster Workers' Council Strike. Public transport in Belfast has been completely withdrawn. The strike is against the Sunningdale Agreement. In West Germany, the Bundestag *today elected Herr Helmut Schmidt as the new Chancellor following the resignation of Willi Brandt ten days ago."*

London, England

"And how are yer, me little piece of English mutton?"

"Oh it's you. At last. It's about bloody time you rang. Where in God's name have you been?"

"Ah, I have more important things to attend to than you, Stanley William me ole son. *The Bloomsbury* at one o'clock. Be there."

The Bloomsbury Wine Lodge was in New Oxford Street at the intersection with the southern half of Museum Street. It was a respectable single-bar establishment, rated as one of the best in the district by its clientele, many of whom were denizens of the nearby Ministry of Defence buildings.

Egginton arrived a little before 13:00 to find Michael Mahoney already seated at one of the tables against the wall, tucking into a large helping of shepherd's pie. The Irishman looked up as the shadow filled the doorway. He waved his hand, beckoning the Colonel over.

"Afternoon, Colonel. The usual?" Mahoney put his knife and fork down and felt in his pocket for money.

"I'll buy my own."

"Ah, t' hell with yer and don't be such a miserable sod. Hold it a minute." Mahoney slid off his seat and went over to the bar, returning two minutes later with a pint of bitter. "Place is filling up. That's good. The more people here, the less we are noticed. And we wouldn't want to compromise your distinguished position by having people see you talking to a mick now, would we ole son?"

Egginton mumbled something which came out like a growl. Mahoney attacked his food once more, deliberately stringing the Englishman along with silence. But Egginton was not to be baited. He had known Mahoney long enough to be wise to his tactics. Notice the imperiousness in the voice today, the dominance? That was a sign he was ready to make his wants known, to drop the bombshell. He was a fisherman at the point of heaving his catch from the water: it had been teased, played with and given line long enough.

It took a few minutes for Mahoney to finish eating, during which time Egginton sipped his beer and said nothing. You can make the running, you bastard, he said to himself, I'm not going to cue you one iota.

Mahoney downed half the contents of his pint glass of Guinness and then belched unnecessarily.

"Now then Stanley, t' business. Are yer game to my proposition?" He lowered his voice. "Remuneration as I stated. Quarter of a million and the negatives and all existing prints of the photographs."

"And you off my back forever?" asked Egginton too quickly. He must not seem eager.

Mahoney feigned hurt. "Well now, ain't that a nice t'ing to say! After all the good toimes oi've given yer, the women and children oi've paid for. That's gratitude for yer!"

Egginton sneered. "Stop pissing about you Irish bastard and get on with it, I haven't got all day. This is to be the last one."

Mahoney stared at him, all traces of geniality extinguished. "It's to be the last one when I say it is. But if you used yer brains you would realise that with the photographs in your possession I would no longer have a bargaining position, would I? And anyway, would you really stay around with a quarter of a million under your bed?"

"*If* I get a quarter of a million, *if* I get the negatives."

"I'm a man of my word, Colonel, you know that."

"Hmph, but I suspect the - "

Suddenly Mahoney leant forward, eyes slitting. "I don't give a fuck for your suspicions Egginton, okay? *I'm* fed up with *your* pissing about. Are you in or does your wife get the photos?"

"Damn you, you bastard."

Mahoney leant back. He smiled. "Great, well at least we've got that settled." The remainder of the Guinness was downed in one. "Come, walk with me."

Oxford Street, London's famous two and a half kilometres of every shop under the sun, is always at its busiest on a Thursday. With the anarchic shopping hours operating in Britain at that time, Thursday was the one day when all the shops stayed open to the unearthly hour of 20:00. The mass of beings ever eager to spend, spend, spend - and only the minority of whom were English - began to build up well before lunchtime, ready to observe the luxury of 'late opening'. Mahoney and Egginton were soon lost in the crowds.

For the first few hundred metres until they reached the intersection with Soho Street, the Irishman was silent. Then he said, "It's twelve pounds of plutonium."

At that very second a number 73 bus chose to thunder past, and the drama of the moment was lost. Egginton said "What?" brusquely.

"Twelve pounds of plutonium."

Egginton heard it this time and, on balance, he took it very well. He turned a nasty shade of grey, certainly; his hands started to tremble and his power of speech left him, without doubt; but he carried on walking with not a falter in his step. His eyes took on a strange, glazed appearance.

Mahoney smiled, recognising the symptoms he himself had experienced five months before. "I know, it's horrible, ain't it me ole fella? I felt like it too. Don't worry, you'll soon get used to it. Twelve pounds of the beautiful stuff it is. Not an ounce less, not an ounce more. And as soon as possible - although my clients appreciate that such an amount just cannot disappear into thin air. Shall we say three months? Three months and you'll have a quarter of a million quid and the photos, and me off yer back forever. Don't worry about transportation, just let me know where the stuff is and when it is available, and I will arrange collection. Make it in Britain, of course. Here," an envelope was removed from his jacket and placed into one of Egginton's pockets, "a little something as a sign of good faith. I'll be in touch."

It was a full five minutes before Egginton realised that Mahoney was gone, and by that time he had walked as far as Argyll Street, next to Oxford Circus, the halfway point of Oxford Street at the junction with Regent Street. Egginton's brain was too numb to give his body anything but the most simple of commands, and it was certainly in no condition to think or evaluate.

He found himself entering *The Argyll* pub, and then he was at the bar and a voice which sounded like his own was ordering two triple brandies.

With the first triple inside him, his hands were sufficiently recovered to be able to reach into his pocket and extract the envelope the Irishman had deposited there. He knew what it felt like but it was not until he was in a cab travelling back along Oxford Street that he risked looking inside.

Mahoney's 'good faith' consisted of two thousand pounds and a print and a single negative of Egginton doing something particularly dreadful to a young person's nether regions.

Ψ

Sunday May 19 1974

"Preliminary statistics from yesterday's general election in Australia indicate that Mr Gough Whitlam's Labour Party has achieved a narrow victory over the Liberal opposition. And in France the final round of the French Presidential elections has been taking place. It has been a closely-fought contest between the two candidates: Monsieur François Mitterand and Monsieur Valéry Giscard d'Estaing."

Crimea, USSR

The villa was between the towns of Feodosiya and Yalta on the south-eastern coast of the Crimea, the mountainous part of the Russian Riviera. It was an official *datcha* reserved for the exclusive use of Very Important Members of the Party down for short spells from the capital. The villa itself was some thirty years old, but regular decoration and refurbishment made sure that it remained in prime condition for its honourable guests.

Ramirov had been at the villa for three weeks now, by order, and he was getting irritable. His mind and body were yearning for action again. He was not trained for a life of ease.

The first week of the current visit to Russia had been spent in Moscow with Comrade Furtseva. Ramirov had arrived direct from Paris under the guise of 'Alexei Mirzoff', and Furtseva had been deeply interested in what he had learnt from the French President. *[She did not know, nor would she ever know, about the incident with the cyanide gas. That was Ramirov's own doing. The only other witness, the look-alike Ambassador, had tragically had his skull caved in by a mugger in the Moscow metro two days after his return.]* After Furtseva had made a telephone call and then visited Someone, she had recalled Ramirov to her office and in no uncertain terms made him aware that he should be deeply honoured to be a party to what she was about to reveal.

Something was brewing in Cyprus, and as usual the *Komitet Gosudarstvennoi Bezopasnasti* was more than a little involved. An opportunity might arise soon when he could secure the diamond without any overt, singular attack on Makarios. Until she could give him more detail, he was to remain in the Soviet Union.

That had been nearly two months ago.

Three weeks at the secret KGB Academy Number 311 at Novosibirsk had followed, an enjoyable time for Ramirov who had to be warned about his zeal on the unarmed combat after a junior officer had had three ribs broken and had required no less than sixty-eight stitches in a head wound. There had followed another week in Moscow and then, on May 5, he had been told that the *datcha* on the riviera was available for him.

The weather had not been over-good (he would be getting more sun now back 'home' in Cyprus) and even this party palace was beginning to pall now that he was into his third week.

The one consolation, of course, was Natasha. To be very cruel, she could be described as an official whore supplied by the masters in Moscow for the privileged use of the *datcha* occupants (male or female). To be very kind, she could be described as a pretty local girl of some twenty summers, charming, always cheerful and an expert at all things carnal. She visited every third day, and Ramirov had to admit that he looked forward to her coming. She was due today.

Ramirov lay on his front on the grass feeling a welcomingly warm sun on his vested back. He listened to the soft, soporific sound of the sea mating with the beach not too far over the back wall. He smiled as he heard a vehicle pull up outside. She was right on time, as always. The key turned in the giant front door, and then the footsteps echoed across the tiled floor of the living-room.

Ramirov's head snapped up. Something was wrong. Something was not quite right. The weight of the tread was the same but the timbre of the echo was just the minutest bit different from usual. Only an expert would have picked it up. The shoes were not the usual ones. A state employee in Natasha's position would possess only one pair, so it followed that the person who had just entered was not her.

It took only a few seconds, but by the time the woman reached the patio Ramirov was up, gun in hand, and standing to one side of the door.

As the woman came through he seized her from behind, the barrel of the Polish *Radom .35* pointing straight into her left ear.

Then he let her go immediately.

"Comrade Furtseva!" He stood rigid, almost to attention.

The grey face looked at him without expression. "I see three weeks at the Academy have done you good, Ilich. I am pleased. A little refresher now and again hurts no one. Not even you. And," she moved her head up and down ruefully, "I am pleased that you are on our side."

"Thank you Comrade, and my apologies if I caused you any distress. Would you like a drink? Shall we sit inside?" The gun was tucked into the waistband of his slacks.

"No, let us walk in the garden, it is a lovely day." Furtseva was not dressed in her usual KGB uniform but in a grey dress of expensive material and probably of western manufacture. It was complemented by a light blue cardigan. The clothing was her attempt at looking casual, and with the short masculine grey hair and the hard features she looked utterly ridiculous.

They walked slowly, Fursteva observing the blooming bougainvillaea without interest. She spoke. "Have you been enjoying your rest here, Ilich?"

"To be honest Comrade, it has made a peaceful change but I cannot say that it has been enjoyable."

"Hnn! Always the man of action, eh? Always wanting to be in the thick of things!" She patted his arm, an almost maternal gesture. "Well, shortly you will champ at the bit no longer. I mentioned in Moscow about certain plans that were being formulated regarding Cyprus - of course, this will go no further than ourselves."

Ramirov inclined his head in agreement.

"Well, now I can tell you. You are aware of the organisation EOKA?"

"Naturally."

"Certain arrangements have been made between them and our own interest, the Akel Communist Party, on a little 'joint effort'. Sometime within the next two months there will be a coup on the island. Makarios will be killed. Your services have been offered. Neither EOKA nor Akel know fully what you are or who you represent, and I have no intention of them finding out. But I have told them that when the coup takes place we will have our own man on the island and his one specific task will be the President. Nothing, absolutely nothing, else."

"Is there anybody else involved?"

"Anybody else?" She smiled, looking like a harridan-coquette. She knew exactly what he was talking about.

"Any other... interested parties?"

She guffawed and slapped him mightily on the back. "I think that Academy is too good, Ilich. You will be wanting my shoes next!" Behind her laughter, her eyes gave him a piercing glance. Ramirov deliberately did not look at her.

"Yes," she continued. "There are other interests involved. Our comrades, the rulers of Greece. As you know, they have a presence on the island in the form of the National Guard. At a given date and time - which I do not yet know - they too will turn against Makarios. It is to be a concerted effort between EOKA and the National Guard, together with our interest."

Ramirov thought what an unholy, treacherous, potentially volatile alliance that would be, but like the good comrade he was he said nothing.

"The Colonels in Greece have leapt at the opportunity of your services. They still have some trepidation about liquidating the charmed person of the Archbishop. They are content to leave that up to you."

They had reached the wall at the end of the garden, and they turned to retrace their steps to the house.

"You *really* want me to kill him?"

The lips wrinkled. "Yes. In fact, Comrade Kosygin has expressly ordered it. Makarios has been a thorn in everyone's side for long enough. But get the diamond first. That is your priority. If it is at all possible to removed Makarios, then do so. But take no undue risks for his sake. There is excitement in the Praesidium over the Arab's plan. Let us not spoil our part of it."

"But if Comrade Kosygin has - "

"*I* will worry about him." She said tersely.

"Yes, Comrade."

A bird landed on the grass in front of them, looked around, crapped and then flew off again.

"When I have the diamond, should I report back?"

"No. You are not to contact me at all until the diamond is safely delivered and your part in this business is over. It must *never* be suspected that the Soviet Union was in any way involved with the detonation of a nuclear device in Britain. We must be grateful that your cover as a South American is so strong. If even the merest hint of Soviet involvement was ever made..." She looked at him stonily. "Then heaven help us *all*."

Ramirov returned the look. "I understand, Comrade."

They reached the villa.

"Now, Comrade Ilich, I think I will have that drink. You have wodka, of course."

"Certainly comrade. You wish anything with it?"

"Pah! Of course not. Perhaps some ice on this fine day, that is all. Natasha will not be visiting today," Furtseva continued as she sat down upon a well-upholstered leather couch and splayed her legs out in front of her. "So, after the wodka, we will see if we can improvise without her. Then afterwards you may cook me a delicious meal. Come, sit down here next to me and relax. I am in no hurry."

Ψ

Monday May 20 1974

"Five hundred more troops were flown into Northern Ireland today, the first full day of the Ulster Workers' Council strike. So far, two-thirds of the province is without electricity, and the delivery of essential food supplies has stopped."

Houston, Texas, USA

It had been another depressing weekend for Sally-Anne Bowker. And this time it could not be blamed on a period. This time it was purely the fault of Steve Graves.

Why oh why hadn't he written like he had promised? Had something happened to him when he had reached Paris? Had he, in fact, reached Paris at all? He had telephoned her, but that could have been from anywhere. What *was* going on? He tells her that *Gulf* are sending him on a project to the Balearic islands. *Gulf* say he just upped and left. Indeed she finds out that he didn't even work permanently for them. He phones her and says he will write. *That was four months ago and she had not heard a thing since.*

These thoughts and many others had been playing around in her head for so long now that it seemed they had made permanent camp there. They nagged at her as she drove to school that morning, windows open, arm resting on the side of her car, on a particularly warm May Monday.

Goddammit, she and Steve had lived together for two years so she should know a bit about the guy's character. It was not in his make-up just to leave her like that. But... there had been no contact.

Sally beeped her horn at an innocuous convertible and shouted "Bastard!" as her battered but powerful Ford thundered past. Most un-school-marmy. She felt aggressive to day.

Today was a day when she would be teaching the etymology of English sayings to some of her younger students. Well there was one that fitted perfectly the situation she was in now. *If the mountain will not come to Mohammed...*

Steve Graves was the mountain and he would not (or could not) come to or contact Sally-Anne Mohammed. So she must take things into her own hands. Two weeks ago she had checked that flight list at the airport, and the name Stelios Grivas had stuck firmly in her mind.

If she was going to play at all, she must play a hunch - and Graves/Grivas was the only hunch she had. It had taken a fortnight for her to reason it out and, if she were truthful, to pluck up the courage. After all, it took guts just to up and go off. At least she thought it did, but Steve Graves – whoever he was - seemed to have done it coolly enough.

Today was the day. Her summer break did not start until the middle of June, but with the sudden death of her favourite aunt up in Boston - no, make that her grandmother (or had she used that one before? No bother, it was her other grandmother if she had) she had to rush up to Mass immediately.

It would be frowned upon, of course. She would be called upon to explain to the Principal (miserable old sonbitch) how she *had* to go to arrange her grandmother's funeral and look after her estate, how her grandmother had brought her up since she was a bitty child and been like a mother to her, how she was deeply upset by Granny's sudden and unexpected death from a heart attack at the age of a hundred and twenty (now now kid, don't get frivolous) and how she was broken up and couldn't teach right now anyway if she was forced to stay.

She would be allowed to go, of course. Probably unpaid, but what the hell?

Her right foot eased fractionally off the accelerator as she neared her turning off the freeway…

It was the other driver's fault, of that there was never any doubt. But had Sally been concentrating more on her driving and less on her private thoughts, it was reckoned by the police afterwards that she could have swerved and saved herself.

Without warning, the other vehicle slewed across from the southbound lanes, crashed through the central barrier, and headed straight for the old Ford like a missile homing in on target.

Sally never even saw it. All she was aware of was the world outside suddenly spinning around. Then a horrible metallic crunching sound. The road above her where the sky should be. The edge of the seat belt gouging her chest like a knife into cooked cheese. A great splurge of something red and gooey on the cracked windscreen. A miasma of lights.

And then no lights at all…

Ψ

Thursday May 23 1974

"In India the railway strike continues into its thirteenth day. During violent clashes in many parts of the country, it is reported that up to forty-thousand railwaymen have been arrested."

Yeri, Nicosia District, Cyprus

Costas, the ogre who had helped in the attack on the Bishop's car, had brought round supplies that afternoon. It was enough to last for quite a while, paid for or stolen by local EOKA sympathisers. That evening Christina had cooked Steve a magnificent meze of *talattouri, taramosolata, dolmas, tavas, keftedes* and unbelievably delicious *lokmades* (hot doughnuts in syrup).

Now, with a half-bottle of *ouzo* inside him, Steve sat back on the comfortable couch and listened to an album by *Aphrodite's Child* playing on the old mono record player.

But, exquisite as the meal had been, beautiful as the music was, and contented as he felt thanks to the *ouzo*, he was also feeling edgy. For they had been here too long.

The hue and cry for the Bishop's murderers had long died off, but a month was a long time. And more and more people were beginning to know of their existence. Word was spreading that Grivas' son had come home to lead them to their glorious union with Greece, *Enosis*. It was a rumour that had been encouraged by the three men in Limassol.

Costas was the only person outside of Yeri village, to their knowledge, who knew of their presence in the villa. And that was the way Steve wanted it to stay. But tongues wagged, and if the TRF ever got even the slightest inkling that they were in the area it would not take long for them to 'persuade' a villager to reveal all.

A month had passed, they knew exactly where The Eye of Makarios was, and they still had to come up with a viable plan to get it. They had formulated and dismissed many theories. Excursions to the Presidential Palace (Steve as an American tourist) and to Makarios' home - the Archbishop's Palace - had produced many ideas on how Makarios could be intercepted. But it was the matter of physically getting the diamond from him without being blown to pieces by his guards that was the problem.

"You are looking worried again, my Stelios," observed Christina as she came though from the kitchen. "It iss the usual?"

"The usual," he nodded. "Shit, I simply can't see how I can do it Christy. Short of suicide."

But she wasn't going to listen. "Enough!" she snapped, and Steve looked up. "Get up!"

"What?"

"Come! Do not argue!"

She grabbed his arm tightly and heaved him from the couch. Deliberately, he fell against her, his face nuzzling into her soft and lightly scented neck.

"Will you get off me!" she scolded. "Come along." Drag. "And be unbuttoning your clothes... it would be futile to resist!"

"Yes ma'm. Whatever you say, ma'm."

Steve was dragged upstairs behind her (contriving to bump his face more than once into her bottom), and she pushed him into the bathroom. She stripped him and pushed him into the shower. Through the tingling water he watched her disrobe. She stepped in with him, kissed him firmly and then reached for the soap. She began to wash him, her hands tickling into the very crevices of his being. Then it was into the bedroom for a complete body massage.

An hour later she was just finishing. Steve, as relaxed as a rag doll, was both sleepy and aroused by her ministrations despite being attended to twice in that area.

She took her hands from him and hummed a tune from her half-forgotten repertoire as she wiped her mouth. Languidly, Steve leant over and rummaged in a drawer of the bedside cabinet. He produced a wrapped package which Costas had smuggled into the villa earlier.

Christina frowned as he offered it to her. "What iss this please, my darling?"

"C'mon, take it."

Like a child on Christmas morning, she proceeded to rip off the cheap paper. "A *komboloi!*" She grasped the amber beads of the rosary-like object between her fingers. "Oh Stelios, darling. Thank you, thank you so much."

His lips came down on hers and he pushed her backwards, pushing his way between her legs…

Three times a charm.

Afterwards they slept the wonderful cashmere-coated sleep that succeeds sex. By midnight they were both deeply gone. Christina was on her back with her arms above her head, provocative lips slightly parted. Steve was face down on her right, his right arm flung over her body and his face resting on her soft right breast, the warm breeze of his breath keeping the nipple erect.

They both dreamt of Makarios, but in different ways. Steve was on a long, dusty road with the Archbishop walking alone in front of him, a small bulging pouch on a rope around his waist. Every time Steve caught up with him and reached out to snatch the pouch, the Archbishop would disappear and reappear fifty metres up the road, still walking and unaware of Steve's presence. So Steve set off after him again. And again, and again…

Christina dreamt that Makarios was making love to her. He was still fully-clothed in his usual flowing ebony robes, but in place of a penis he was pushing a large and glittering diamond into her…

Their minds were that far removed from reality that they would not have heard the third person's arrival even if he had made a sound - which he did not. Three weeks at the KGB Academy Number 311 at Novosibirsk had seen to that.

Ilich Ramirov was always on his guard, his sixth sense permanently primed for the slightest thing untoward. Even at home here in the villa in Cyprus. He had parked his old Volkswagen Beetle car as far away from the villa as he could, around the side near his garage. Before getting out, he had removed the gun he always kept in the hidden compartment in the steering column, and he had then traversed the final fifty metres to his front door in total silence and complete darkness.

He knew as soon as he put his key in the lock that something was not right. As soon as he opened the door, the presence was obvious. The place, which was in darkness, should have smelt musty after four months of disuse. Instead it smelt of people, of use.

He closed the door behind him and stayed utterly still. The smell of cooking still lingered in the air and there was the faintest trace of a cheap scent. So, a female? And most probably accompanied by one or more males. Locals at play while the businessman was away?

He placed his suitcase down on the tiled floor and stood stock still. It took less than a minute for his ears to pick up the sound of breathing from upstairs. A man's breathing. With the even flow of sleep.

Whoever he was he had certainly made himself at home. And

that told Ramirov that there was no immediate danger to his person. Professionals lying in wait would not have domesticated themselves.

He knew exactly which part of each stair to tread on without it creaking. In no time at all he was outside his own bedroom door, gun at the ready. He listened. The male breathing was still regular and heavy. He could hear no other, but then just as he reached out for the door handle the voice of a woman moaned once and then was quiet. The male breathing went on undisturbed.

Slowly the Russian's hand turned the handle…

Christina had to admit she was excited. The old, bearded, hated priest was on top of her, his breath reeking of *houmous*. He was pushing his diamond-hard organ into her. She had climaxed twice already and, although something in her mind told her not to for this was the man she despised above all living things, she found herself moaning, moaning for more and for him to stop, both at the same time.

Suddenly the sun came out and Makarios disappeared like a phantom of the night. The hardness was not pressing between her legs anymore but into her left eye. She awoke, just a fraction before Steve, as her hair was grabbed and the top half of her body was yanked a full metre off the bed. The gun was pressed so hard into her eye that she could not open it.

"Do not move, my friend," the voice spoke in Greek and was addressed to Steve. "Not even the tiniest muscle."

Steve was on his elbows, glaring in bewilderment at the unscheduled interruption of his sleep. It was a few seconds before reality came back. Then he saw a Latin-looking man in tinted specs sitting on the far edge of the bed. He had Christina's head in his left hand, her naked body across him, the gun pressed hurtfully into her eye.

"What the fuck!"

"I said do not move!" The voice was sharp and dangerous, and it had changed to English on hearing the American's oath. He pulled tighter on the girl's hair until she yelped. "Wake up! Wake up both of you."

"Oh, Jesus shit!" Steve was awake and he looked up at the ceiling in resignation. Then he looked across at the girl. "Please, please don't do that. You're hurting her. She's no threat to you."

"*I* will decided that." The gun remained where it was, and Christina grimaced in pain.

"But she is in pain. You could damage her eye!"

"So? If you want me to release your friend, talk to me. Give me a good reason why I should not kill you both right here and now."

Steve's eyes wandered around the room, up the walls, over the ceiling. "Look, you were away. We wanted somewhere safe, somewhere to stay. The place was lying empty... What can I say?"

Ramirov said nothing, he just stared at the American, his head inclined.

"Okay, okay," said Steve in what he hoped was a reasonable voice, trying to quell the anger that was brewing inside, anger at himself. He *knew* they shouldn't have stayed so long. Why hadn't he done something about it? It was against all his training. "We were looking for a safe hideout, see? The TRF are after us. We... we are members of EOKA."

The Russian snorted. "An American and a girl? Members of EOKA?"

"I am Cypriot by birth. My God, can't you see that?"

"Just because you *look* like a Greek..." The sentence was left in mid-air, but Ramirov pushed the girl back down onto the bed, glancing at the full bouncing breasts as she landed.

Her eye was bleeding. She sniffed once and was silent, her hand covering her eye, the good one glaring venom at Ramirov. "Bastard!" she spat the word like a true vixen. "So what do you do now? Kill uss in cold blood? *Mafioso* pig."

"*Mafioso?*" He laughed. "Is that what they say? The *Mafiosi* are mere children." The gun was lowered but remained in his hand. "I see that you are no threat to me." He looked about the room. "You have weapons?"

"Yes," said Steve. "There is a pistol underneath each of these pillows - " Ramirov raised the gun again. "There are no others."

"Please give them to me."

Steve passed his over and then fumbled under the girl's pillow. "Christy?"

She said nothing. She moved her left hand down and underneath the mattress. She pulled out her gun and threw it on the bed.

Ramirov emptied both the pistols with his left hand, letting them fall to the floor. He placed the bullets in his pants pocket.

"You are a sensible man, sir. The thought that is in your mind is correct. I will not have one moment's hesitation in killing both of you at any time I like. You will do well to remember that. Now, there are no other weapons. Are you telling me the truth?" The cold, black eyes bored into Steve's.

"Yes, I'm telling you the truth."

Ramirov continued to stare for another twenty seconds. Then he said, "Yes, you are." He stood up off the bed. "My friends, we have a lot of talking to do." He stood with his back against the door. "Both of you get dressed, and you see to her eye. Then we shall go downstairs - I take it you have stores in? Good. And you have got my generator working, I see. I would like some coffee and something to eat. You, my dear lady, will get it for me."

He looked at her as she raised her head and tried to look defiant. "My dear *Christina*. Christy, of course. Well, well, so it is you. I have heard you sing many times in *L'Eclair* in Nicosia. I have watched you from afar." He seemed to amuse himself. "Before we are through you may be singing for me again. Now, get a move on both of you. I am thirsty."

Ramirov partook of his coffee and left-over *meze*, his gun remaining within millimetres of his right hand. The couple sat on the couch opposite, empty coffee cups next to them. The American was unshaven and rugged. The girl, eyelid distended and with a wicked-looking scab, glared.

Refreshed, Ramirov politely suggested "Talk to me."

Christina was reluctant. "You seem to know everything already."

Steve asked, "What do you want to know?"

Ramirov smiled disarmingly. "Why, everything, my dear sir. Everything. I do not even know your name. Let us start from there."

"My name is Stelios Grivas." Ramirov's eyebrows appeared over the top of his spectacles. "Yes, General George Grivas was my father. My mother was Amy Silver, an American journalist. She lived in Athens and she was the Greek correspondent of a national daily, in the late nineteen-forties. Do you really want to hear it all?"

"Of course."

"Okay. Well, to cut a long story short, she interviewed Grivas in his position as commander of the Greek forces in Cyprus. They hit it off. She became pregnant by him, the usual. I was the result. My mother told no one who the father was, not even the father. We lived on our own. Grivas did not find out about me until I was about four or five and my mother was sent back here to Cyprus to cover the worsening situation. Apparently he went into a rage when he found out - not because of my existence but because he had not been told.

"Anyway, after the rage he went into raptures. A son he never knew about! It was never revealed publicly that I was who I was, and Mom and I stayed here for two years, living on our own somewhere in the south in a place provided and kept by my father. He and Mom met up quite frequently, but the battle for *Enosis* took up most of his time.

"Things went on smoothly like this until the real outbreak of violence in 1955. My mother was on an assignment when one of EOKA's own bombs blew up the car she was travelling in. She lost both her legs."

Steve paused. There was absolute silence in the room.

He continued. "With her mobility gone, she was no use as a correspondent. Her agency - probably out of kindness than anything - offered her a staff job at their offices in Philadelphia. It was either accept that or stay here with the prospect of civil war looming." He sighed and shrugged his shoulders. "Of course she had no choice. And anyway she wanted out. Never, up until her death three years ago, did she completely forgive Grivas for the loss of her legs - although God knows it was not his fault. *He* was not responsible for the detonation of the bomb.

"He let us go, of course. It could not have been easy for him, but having never publicly acknowledged the existence of his bastard son things were not too bad. He would have no loss of face. He and my mother entered into some agreement. I do not know the finer details of it, but it seems that I was to lose my paternity. Grivas would never contact us again, and my mother would never reveal to anyone who my real father was. The agreement was kept.

"I never thought much about my father as I grew up, not until my mother's death. Then I decided to contact him. I felt he had a right to know about her passing. I had some contacts in the Press and, after months of enquiry, I came up with a *poste restante* address for the General down in Limassol. Apparently I was not to put his name on the envelope, just address it to some woman. I wrote him a short note telling him of Mom's death. I heard nothing until six months later when an envelope arrived. Inside was a scrap of paper with a hand-written message: *Thank you, G.* And that was all.

"I heard nothing else. He was obviously determined to keep his side of the agreement even though one partner to it was dead.

"Then in January this year I received another envelope. Inside was a plane ticket and a note that Grivas wanted to see me. So I came here, just three days before his death. He was almost gone when I reached him, but he made one last request, asking me to do something for him. He wanted me to get The Eye of Makarios. That was the last thing he ever said." He paused at the memory. He was aware that Christina and the man were looking at him intently.

"The Eye of Makarios?" prompted Ramirov.

"Quite. What the hell was it? He died before he could tell us. Since January we've been continually on the run. The TRF suspect that we exist, but they are not sure. So there's been no direct pressure, not until recently. That's when we took refuge here."

"On the assumption that they would not think of looking right under their own noses. Most sensible." He looked the girl. "And what part does Christina play in all of this?"

She bridled, tossed her hair back and spoke, reluctantly but with pride. "I was close to Grivas during the last months. When Syros and Demetrakis were taken last autumn he turned to me more than anybody else."

"So! That *is* something I did not know. But pray go on, you have more to tell me?"

Steve continued. "Just over a month ago we intercepted Bishop Rigakis on his way into Nicosia. He was persuaded to tell us what The Eye of Makarios was. And where it was."

"So it was you! No wonder the heat was on and you looked for refuge!"

"The Eye of Makarios," explained Steve, "is, we think, Makarios' personal investment, his pension. Although it could have been a gift. Whatever. It is a diamond. Must be pretty big.

He carries it about his waist at all times."

That shocked even Ramirov. Was it *possible?* That fate should be so beneficent? That all the work and effort had been done for him? By this man and this girl? It appeared so.

He shook his head and then chuckled, a happy, throaty sound. "Magnificent. Magnificent!"

"You do nott belief uss!" snarled Christina.

"Oh yes, yes my dear. I believe you." His eyes filled with a few tears of mirth. "Please forgive me. It is an incredible story, but I believe it."

"And now what?" asked Steve. "Do you turn us in? Or kill us... or let us go?"

The laughing stopped abruptly and there was an ominous silence. Steve honestly thought the man was going to exercise the second option. He thought of throwing himself at the stranger, at least Christina might get clear.

But then to their great surprise Ramirov put the gun in his pocket and inclined his head. "My friends, I am certainly not going to turn you in or kill you. You may go if you want to. But I have a proposition for you. Stay here. Stay with me. I happen to know that there will be an opportunity coming up soon for you to get this diamond."

"How? We haf thought off everything."

"How does not matter. It is sufficient for you to know that there *will* be an opportunity. And I will help you. I will help you get this Eye of Makarios!"

Christina and Steve were stupefied. They looked at each other incredulously.

"Until the opportunity to take the diamond arises you may, if you wish, stay here - as my guests. It is very secure here."

"Well... that... hmm!... but why are you doing this? I don't understand," said Steve.

"Such matters need not concern you. It is sufficient for your purpose that I am. Consider me an old supporter of EOKA."

"Wh-who are you?"

"My name is Martinez. That is all you need to know. Further questions will be a waste of your breath. There will probably be some danger later on. You can handle a gun? We will have time, I will teach you how to use one properly. Both of you. You will be my pupils, I your master. Now," he stretched, his arms above his head. "How about some more coffee, my dear?"

Christina was still in a state of bewilderment. As she got up, she asked, "You - you don't happen to haf a cigar, do you?"

Ramirov would not sleep that night. Grivas and Christina could if they wanted to, but Ramirov had enquiries to make and people to see later that day and he did not want the inconvenience of sleep to dull his senses.

At 03:00 all was quiet and all was dark. Outside a half moon gave soft illumination and cast stark shadows. Earlier Ramirov had moved his car into the garage a few metres away from the villa. Now he walked soundlesly back across the gravel track. The garage door swung open with just a little resistance and no noise. Leaving it open to get the benefit of the moonlight, he stepped to the front of the car which, in a Volkswagen Beetle, was the trunk. The hood opened with a click, and he reached inside and removed a holdall. The contents clinked lightly.

He lowered the hood but did not slam it shut. Back outside, the door resisted again but then closed without a sound. Ramirov remained facing the door as he slipped the wooden bolt back over. He said quietly, "You could be as good as me. Except," he turned. "I knew you were there."

The person was in shadow, a little to the right. "If you say so."

Ramirov nodded back at the villa. "The son of Grivas, eh?"

"Apparently."

"We can hide behind that. Make them think it is all EOKA."

"Have they given the go-ahead?"

"No. It will happen. But not yet. Weeks, maybe."

"Should I report that?"

"That is for you to decide. We will not get the diamond until it happens. I just have to wait for instructions from Athens. Until the diamond is with the supplier, the materiel will not be available. So you have breathing space. That should keep Tel Aviv happy."

"Time for them to get people in place."

Ramirov inclined his head. "As you say." Saying no more, he set off back towards the villa.

Agent Digenis slipped back into the shadows of the night.

Ψ

Tuesday June 11 1974

"Three bombs exploded at the Strensall army training camp near York this afternoon. No one was seriously injured."

London, England

The two men sat in front of Colonel Egginton's desk in his comfortable office in Stuart House. They were representatives from the United Kingdom Atomic Energy Authority's Windscale Works in Cumbria in the far north, although their voices were strictly home counties stockbroker belt.

The Colonel had just sat down after greeting them on entry. "Well gentlemen, I am so glad you had a comfortable journey. I know what the ride from Windscale can be like. Has the transport problem improved?"

It was generally agreed that it had.

"That's nice to hear. Now, you know the reason I invited you here. Needless to say the matter is Top Secret and goes no further than ourselves. The Minister has asked me to undertake a little review of security matters at your establishment. While no disrespect to your current arrangements is intended, he feels that for the whole system to be looked at by an outsider not unknowledgeable in such matters would do it no harm at this present time. I must say I agree with him.

"He has asked me to look at one part of the set-up in particular: the security of the plutonium and uranium." Egginton dragged mightily on his *Dunhill* cigarette and swallowed all of the smoke. "I'll be honest with you. Strictly between ourselves, he hinted to me that the Defence Intelligence boys had got the wind up about a possible attack on one of our plants and the swiping of amounts of the stuff. Until they make the radiation level of plutonium lethal, how easy that could be given a concerted effort by a terrorist army. And we all know what could happen if that stuff got into their hands! It is feasible that the Arabs or the Japanese want some to convert into bombs for use in the Mediterranean somewhere. *[Egginton never knew how close his sheer fabrication had come to the truth.]* But that should really be no concern of ours. Official Secrets and all that, what!

"I'd like to discuss your security arrangements with you today, quite informally and without prejudice, of course. Then perhaps next week I can come up and visit you and have a look at the layout first hand. I've written down a few points here. Firstly, can you really account for every pound of plutonium at any given time…?"

Nicosia, Cyprus

That same day a telegram was collected from the main post office in Nicosia, sent from Vienna a few hours earlier. It read:

TO MARTINEZ POSTE RESTANTE NICOSIA STOP DESPITE EXHAUSTIVE CHECKS NO TRACE CAN BE FOUND OF THE TITLE MENTIONED STOP SUGGEST THAT AND YOUR OBJECT ARE THE SAME STOP PROCEED ACCORDINGLY STOP KATHERINE

Ψ

Friday June 14 1974

"With the results of the Australian general election now all in, the Labour government has failed to gain a majority in the senate.

Whitehall, London

Every non-elected civil servant in the United Kingdom is reported on annually. The report, at that time in the form of a standard ten page questionnaire, is completed by the reportee's immediate superior officer. It is then passed to the next person in the chain of command who is known as the 'Countersigning Officer'. The Countersigning Officer adds his or her own comments and then passes the report ever-upwards for eventual inclusion in personnel records.

Before he gets rid of the report, the Countersigning Officer may also interview the reportee in what is known in the service as a 'JAR' (Job Appraisal Review), a marvellous invention in which the discussion is supposed to be a no holds barred affair concerning the reportee's career prospects, job satisfaction, relations with colleagues, private life, right down to the clothes he wears and any unfortunate personal habits (like halitosis or the way he picks his nose).

Egginton's JAR that afternoon was of the friendly variety, his Countersigning Officer being the Permanent Under Secretary for the Ministry of Defence (Sales Executive) Sir Lovelock Armstrong. The interview lasted just fifteen minutes and was of the "Hello Stan - Hello Lovelock - How's the wife?" variety (for on more than one occasion the Eggintons had dined at the Armstrongs' in Denham, Bucks).

The interview ended with both men agreeing what a bloody waste of time these JARs were, and we must get together again sometime, my love to Margery.

Sir Lovelock Armstrong inked over his pencilled marking of 'Fitted' in the promotion column, signed his name on the bottom of the form, placed it in an orange *Confidential* envelope, and threw it in his Out Tray. His PA would see that it continued on its journey.

He picked up another piece of paper, the small *JAR Completed* form, and put a stroke through the *Comments/Suggestions Made* column and signed at the bottom. According to a recent DCI *[Defence Council Instruction]*, all *JAR Completed* forms on Assistant Directors and above had to be routed via Security for a standard check. Bloody waste of time in this case, thought Armstrong, Stan was straight as a die, a damn good Director. But instructions were instructions, even for a Permanent Under Secretary.

Another orange envelope, addressed to the Director of Security, and that was that over for another year.

The Director of Security received the form via the internal mail shortly before he left for home at 16:30 that afternoon. He gave the contents of the orange envelope just a cursory glance, wrote the name of the Security Officer for Stuart House on the front in pencil, tossed the envelope into his Out Tray, picked up his case and walked out.

Ronald Spencer Arthur, Security Officer for the Ministry of Defence in Stuart House, received the form at 10:15 the following Monday.

Ψ

Thursday June 20 1974

"Israeli planes have again attacked Palestinian refugee camps in southern Lebanon. Reports say that at least sixteen people have been killed."

Reference DO/364/03

CONFIDENTIAL

Director of Security
Room 201
Main Building

DCI 36/74: SECURITY APPRAISAL ON COLONEL S W EGGINTON

Colonel Egginton was last positively vetted in November 1973 (see DI4's minute of 11 November at enclosure 42). Due to the nature of his work, he will continue to be positively vetted every 2 years. No interim vetting is recommended.

Ron Arthur

R S Arthur
SO Stuart House
20 June 1974

Whitehall, London

Ron Arthur was due at the regular fortnightly Heads of Security meeting in the MOD Main Building at 10:00 that morning. The Director of Security would chair the meeting, as always, and it would probably be stretched to lunchtime.

Arthur had decided to bring the minute on Egginton over himself, rather than waste the two envelopes needed to transmit confidential documents outside their parent building. He did not really want to meet The Old Man before the meeting, so it was with a modicum of circumspection that he walked along the corridor at 09:45 and nipped smartly in to the Director's PA's office.

"'Morning Eunice."

Eunice Tate was a thin woman in her menopausal late forties. She had been PA-DOS for the last two years (ever since the current DOS had been promoted from Assistant Director) and was disgustingly efficient at her job. She had the haughty, brisk manner one would expect from a professional spinster in such a position, but she was not a bad sort once she got to know you.

"Mr Arthur! Good morning. Off to the meeting?"

"Just thought I'd pop this in beforehand," Arthur handed over the unmarked, unsealed envelope. He looked furtively at the door leading to the next room. "Is he...?"

Eunice nodded, and as if on cue the door opened and the DOS strolled out.

"Signed 'em, Eunice," he dumped a bundle of letters down onto the desk. "Hello Ron. Business or pleasure?"

Eunice sniffed and pretended not to hear the remark.

Arthur smiled dutifully. "Just thought I'd pop up with Colonel Egginton's report, sir."

"Ah good, good. Coming to the meeting?"

"Of course, sir."

"Good, let's go then. Back this afternoon, Eunice."

As they were walking down the corridor, the Director asked "Anything, Ron?"

"On Colonel Egginton? No, sir," Arthur chuckled at the idea.

"Good."

They reached the lift lobby.

Arthur looked at the DOS. "There is one thing, sir... about the Colonel."

The DOS was about to ask what when a pretty young thing from the typing pool waddled along and pressed the UP button. She smiled coyly at the two men, who were now silent. They smiled inanely back.

The lifts came simultaneously. Arthur and the DOS were the only travellers down, and before the doors had closed fully the DOS asked sharply, "What is this about Egginton?"

Arthur felt uncomfortable and he began to wish he hadn't opened his mouth. Really it was only something to say. "Nothing much, sir. Not worth reporting officially. But he seems to have been drinking a lot recently."

"Stan's always been partial to his wallop."

"Aren't we all, sir? But this has been more than usual, even for the Colonel. Just about every day now he doesn't come back from lunch until three and - well, you know the Colonel sir, he can hold it more than most of us. He never seems actually drunk, but... well, it *is* every day now sir... and considering his position..."

"Of course, of course, yes, you were right to tell me, Ron. And right not to make it official."

The lift reached the basement and they stepped out and turned right. Behind them another lift touched down and ejaculated three other building security officers. In between their mutual greetings, the DOS said as an aside "Let me sleep on it, Ron. Let me sleep on it."

Ψ

The Director of Security must have slept during the meeting, for it was when he returned to his office that afternoon, after a double-whisky lunch, that he asked Eunice to get him a certain unlisted number over in Queen Anne's Gate.

Jamhour, Lebanon

The new Catholic church of Notre-Dame de Jamhour, above Beirut to the east, was only six years old. It was built in the round style of modern churches, long pews set in a decreasing semi-circle narrowing in to the wide, accessible altar. Beige wide-bricked walls held modern uplights at five metre intervals, discreet lighting which added to the calmness of the interior.

The church was quiet and empty as Nathanson stepped into the confessional.

"Bless me Father, for I have sinned. It has been... many years since my last confession."

Only the faintest of diffused backlighting entered through the grill that kept identities hidden, the sinner known only to God. The priest was just a dark shadow.

"And what have you to confess, my friend?" His voice was soft and low.

"My search for justice has made me many enemies."

"Vengeance is mine; I will repay, saith the Lord."

"I have managed to get close," said Nathanson. "To the financier. I am – how should I put it? – in his employ."

"Good. And you are not suspected?"

"No."

"Digenis has been involved also. We now know what the Arabs are up to. It is not good." The priest spelled out the Arabs' plan. Then he said, "But they need to get the diamond first."

"Should we finish them off?" asked Nathanson. "Do you

want me to retreat?"

"No, not yet. Stay in place. You will be useful on the inside. We will do nothing yet. We must let them proceed. The world will not believe us unless we expose them red-handed with the evidence."

"I understand."

"Confess regularly."

"Of course."

"*In nomine patre, filis et spiritus sancti.*"

"Amen."

Five minutes after Nathanson had left the confessional, Monsignor Chaim Cohen stepped out of the priest's side and closed the door behind him. He nodded paternally to two ladies (Madame Renée Ibrahim and her daughter Violette) who had started decorating the altar dias for a forthcoming wedding on Saturday, and, without pausing for them to wonder who he was, walked out of the main door and into the warm darkness of a Lebanese evening.

Ψ

Saturday June 22 1974

"Tension is still high in the Middle East after the Israeli air attack on Palestinian refugee camps in southern Lebanon two days ago. Sixteen people were killed and more than forty injured in the attack. A Palestinian spokesman has threatened dire revenge for what Palestinian sources call 'This cowardly attack by Zionist warmongers on innocent women and children'.*"*

Istanbul, Turkey

Ramirov, dressed in a white cotton shirt and grey slacks, stood in the hot midday sun without perspiring. He was waiting on the quayside on the European bank of the Golden Horn, looking out over the water and watching the ferry approach from Asia. His head was cocked slightly to one side.

Behind him, people of every nationality milled about noisily, a hum of excitement rising as the ferry came nearer. Istanbul, the New York of the east, smelt of spices, sun and body odour.

He looked at the gold Rolex Oyster Perpetual on his right wrist. It showed five minutes after noon. His appointment was late, but never mind. He half closed his eyes and enjoyed the sun.

Two minutes later a voice said, "I apologise for my lateness." 'Akay' Al Khalifa, the financial controller of Black September, appeared beside him from thin air. Any person other than Ramirov would not have been aware of his approach.

Ramirov waited.

"Did you enjoy your recent visit to Cana?" asked the Arab.

"Very pleasant but the Jordan is vast and mysterious."

"Who knows where a river ends?"

They spoke in French and made customary greetings, but they did not shake hands or make any form of physical contact. They both faced the water and gave the impression of speaking casually, as if exchanging pleasantries about the view.

The Russian said, "It has taken time, but I have now discovered the location of the item."

Al Khalifa sniffed with the beginnings of a summer cold. "My colleagues will be pleased with your news. You are able to obtain the... item?"

"Yes." He pointed out over the water as if indicating a point of discussion. "There will be a certain amount of difficulty but nothing that cannot be handled."

"Good. It will take long?"

"Hard to say. Not too long. One week, five weeks. It all depends on various circumstances."

There was a moment of silence, and then Ramirov asked "And what about your supplier? Is he ready? I would advise you not to have the item on hand for too long once I get it for you. But that is, of course, your business."

"Indeed, but we are always glad of your counsel."

"I will contact you to make the arrangements just before or just after the item is secured."

"Please do."

Without further ado, both men turned and disappeared into the crowds.

Ψ

Friday June 28 1974

"Reports are coming in of a coup in Ethiopia in north-east Africa. Members of the Ethiopian army have taken over control of two radio stations in the capital Addis Ababa. The fate of Emperor Hailé Selassié is not yet known."

Houston, Texas, USA

"You've been lucky, young lady. Very lucky. Drive more carefully in future." With a shake of the hand, Dr Louis Thomas of the *Texas Medical Center* turned and walked back into the main area of the hospital.

Sally-Anne Bowker walked slowly and carefully down the two steps and across to the waiting cab. She gave her home address to the driver who, once he realised that his attempts at joviality or conversation of any sort were being met with silence, remained quiet for the length of the journey.

As Dr Thomas had said, she had been lucky. Lucky to have survived at all. Most people would have been killed. More than anything, it was the old broken seatbelt that had caused the damage, nearly pulping her left breast and helping to fracture four ribs on the left side and one on the right. Her chest was scarred for life with deep stitching lines where the breast had been sewn back into some semblance of a tit, and various evil-looking lacerations stretched from shoulder to shoulder. As well as that, her skull had been fractured in three places, albeit the breaks were only 'hairline'. Her head had been shaved and now, some six weeks later, her hair had regrown into a short cropped style, masculine and some two years ahead of its time fashion-wise.

Her huge, school-marm glasses had shattered in the crash and she had been told that she had been very fortunate that the glass had missed her eyes and only caused deep cuts and painful bruises in the cheeks and forehead. Thankfully these had healed completely after a month. Now she had broken in a pair of pure plastic contact lenses.

Yes, the general opinion of everybody in the hospital was that luck had been with her on that fateful May 20th.

Well, fuck that. If she had been so lucky the accident would not have happened in the first place.

One can measure the amount of physical damage inflicted by a car crash but, without very careful examination and knowledge of the patient's previous condition, it is hard to determine the amount of mental damage sustained. Sally had been visited by two psychiatrists who had both pronounced her a mentally normal, if somewhat bitter, young woman. The bitterness would pass, they had decreed, it was caused by latent shock.

So to all intents and purposes Sally-Anne Bowker was a healed human being both physically and mentally when she signed off from the hospital that fine June day.

But she had changed. Physically the change was obvious: hair shorn, no more the huge glasses, sixteen pounds in weight lost, and a predilection for wearing denims to hide her scarred legs. Mentally, it was not so obvious. Determination had set in. Where once there was tolerance and concern for others (under other circumstances she would have returned the cab driver's banter) there was now impatience and concern only for herself.

Apart from the bastard and dead out of town farmer who had been driving the other vehicle, there was one person and one person alone who was responsible for her being in that hospital: Mister Steven Graves - or Stelios Grivas or whatever he called himself and whoever he was. If it had not been for him, her mind would have been more on her driving six weeks ago. If it had not been for her concern for his safety, she might have avoided the other vehicle. If his whereabouts had not been bothering her, she would not have ended up cut to pieces in a hospital bed. If she had not been so damn much in love with him…

At least there was one consolation - she would not now have to lie about the death of her grandmother to have time off. She had the perfect excuse for absence from school! She was not to return to work until at least September, by order. So she had the best part of three months. It would take all her savings and probably more so, but, goddammit, she had decided she would find Steve Graves wherever he was.

Even if it killed her.

The cab deposited her outside the apartment block and, after telling the driver to go fuck himself after he had made some sarcastic remark about her cheerfulness, she walked very slowly into the building.

Ψ

Monday July 1 1974

"From Ethiopia it is reported that most of Emperor Hailé Salassié's advisers have been arrested, but the new controlling army have renewed pledges to the Emperor himself."

Over the Atlantic Ocean

The *Air France 747* lifted into the clear azure sky above Houston, banked sharply to starboard and set course for its direct run to Paris. In the final seat on the left in the first class compartment, Sally-Anne Bowker relaxed the tense muscles of her neck and breathed a sigh of relief. She did not mind flying, it was the take-off and landing that she could not, literally, stomach.

"There now honey, that wasn't too bad, was it?" smiled the woman next to her.

"Guess not, but I'm always glad when we're up." Sally tried to sound amiable but, as usual nowadays, she just did not feel like it.

The woman next to her was a butch-looking character who had introduced herself as Charlotte Rapley, "Call me Charlie." Dressed in a tweed three-piece suit, hair short but fluffier than Sally's crop, face framed by large agony-aunt spectacles, she had been one of the last to arrive in First Class, making an ostentatious display of breathlessness as she entered. The seat next to Sally had been empty and she had just *known* that this loud lesbian would be heading for it. She had been right.

Charlie had tried to strike up a conversation straight away, but Sally had been even less responsive than usual. However, bowing to the continual verbal pressure, she had eventually had to say *something*.

Charlie was unputoffable and, to be fair, Sally knew what the obvious attraction of herself was: short hair, rather hard face, bra-less tee shirted chest (on doctor's advice) and denim jeans. Charlie was trying her out to see if she was one of her own kind. Sally knew that she was not but, after twenty minutes, she had to admit that she did not dislike the chatty, blowsy, personable female.

Charlie was a sculptor and artist, in that order. She came from New York and had been in Houston for the past month conducting an exhibition of her works. Perhaps Sally-Anne had heard of it? ("Well, actually, no.") She was now on her way to Paris to organise a similar showing.

By take-off she had all but told Sally the story of her life, and Sally had reluctantly reciprocated with a few forced details of her own. Charlie had been most concerned when she had heard about the accident.

Now they sat high in the air over Texas, ready for the long flight ahead of them. Charlie smoked on a *Peter Stuyvesant*.

"Gonna watch the movie, Sal?"

"Guess so, not much else to do. Wonder what it is?"

"Dunno, hope it's something good. Something with a bit of spice, know what I mean? Ever seen any of those movies?"

"No."

"Dunno what you're missing, babe. You must come and see me when we hit gay Paree, I'll show you some celluloid to open your eyes - and your legs." She guffawed. "Hey, wanna drink?"

"I don't think so."

"Shit, of course you do. Hey miss!" A stewardess, with a catchy wiggle which did not go unnoticed by Ms Rapley, appeared from somewhere. "Two double scotches on the rocks please honey - no, nothing with it."

Sally looked out of the window and inwardly sighed. It was going to be a long flight.

"*Chinatown*. Shit, what kind of movie was that?"

"A very good one, what was wrong with it? You don't like Polanski?"

"Argh Sally, you're too nice, y' know that? Certainly wasn't my kinda movie."

"So you keep telling me. Never mind, you'll be able to see plenty of those when you hit Paris - as you keep telling me."

"Right. How long - God, two more hours yet! Want another drink?"

"Really no, not this time Charlie. Four is enough."

"Well, p'raps you're right."

They travelled on above the clouds of a rainy Atlantic.

"So, when you get to Paris, what you gonna do?" Charlie broke open her second packet of duty-free *Peter Stuyvesant*. "How you gonna find this guy of yours? If you ask me, you're putting yourself to a lot of trouble over nothing. No man is worth it."

Sally sighed. "Quite honestly, Charlie, I'm not too sure what I'm going to do. Try the airline desks and check their flights to the Balearics for January 23rd last, I reckon. See if they have Steve down."

"Or this crazy 'Stelios Grivas'. One heck of a name that - don't sound unfamiliar though. You got somewhere to stay?"

"Nope, I didn't reckon I'd need anywhere. I'll check the airlines and I'll either be on my way forward or back home again."

"Heck, you're one hell of a devoted gal. But what do you do for sleep, hm? Or hadn't you thought about that?"

"I've slept on the plane."

"Shit, you don't call that *sleep!* Just a doze. Everyone knows that sleep on a plane's not restful. It's not *sleep,* just a way of passing the journey." She drew on her cigarette.

Sally looked out at the milling clouds. For the first time she had a feeling of doubt about what she was doing. *Screw* this woman! Or, she thought cynically, is that exactly what she wanted?

"First time in Paris?" the smoke rolled back out of Charlie's mouth as she spoke.

"Yep."

"And you're just gonna land, touch the wall and fly off again? Shit girl, do you know what you're missing? This is Paree, honey. The City of Light."

"*Gay* Paree?"

"It simply won't let you ignore it. Everything you've read about it is true, and more so." Charlie frowned. Her sales pitch did not seem to be making any impression. She grabbed hold of a soft hand. "Listen, if you don't have anywhere to stay, you can come with me to my friend's place for the night."

The offer was not unexpected. "Oh no, really, I couldn't." Sally moved her hand away.

"Sure you could! Louise won't mind. You've been through a lot recently, you need your rest. This plane ride's enough for one day. You can stay the night at Louise's and then tomorrow we'll maybe help you make those enquiries about this precious Steve of yours. How's that?"

"But, Charlie - "

"Great, that's settled. We'll be glad of your company." She patted Sally gently on the right knee, and Sally wondered what she had now let herself in for.

Paris, France

Much to Sally's surprise, Louise was a small, slim, dark-haired Parisienne of around twenty-five. Quiet and elegant, her features were gamin and Gallic and would appeal to both sexes. She lived alone in a plush apartment at 46 Boulevard Exelmans in the 16th arrondisement, and was a fashion designer by trade. She welcomed Sally as if they were old friends.

The three women enjoyed *omelettes à la poulard* cooked to perfection by Louise, and they then finished off two bottles of *Sancerre* while a Pink Floyd cassette played on the expensive stereo.

"Don't let Claude hear that or he'll be down like a shot," joked Charlie. "Don't s'pose you know Claude, Sal. He's a singer. Lives on the top two floors of this building. Good friend of Looey's. *Clo-Clo* they call him. You'll have to meet him. Hell of a nice guy. For a man."

La Française was deeply interested in Sally's story of her missing lover, which she retold with prompting, interruptions and embellishments from Charlie. Louise offered whatever assistance she could during tomorrow's enquiries at Orly.

Although only early evening, Sally and Charlie were obviously weary after their journey, and so the three women retired early. Each, surprisingly, sleeping in a separate bedroom.

Ψ

Tuesday July 2 1974

"A state of national mourning has been declared in Argentina following the death yesterday of General Juan Perón. General Perón relinquished his third presidency to his wife, Señora Maria Martinez de Perón, just three days ago because of his failing health."

Orly, Paris, France

Orly Airport was invaded early that morning. Sally and Charlie assailed the *Iberia* desk while Louise tackled *Air France*. They then rejoined to assault any other airlines flying south from Paris.

The airline clerks were, on the whole, helpful. But helpfulness is not necessarily synonymous with success, and it was three disappointed ladies who drove away from the airport at midday. They had tried every airline flying to the Balearic Islands and the Spanish mainland, all to no avail.

They travelled back in silence, Louise driving her new green Opel with the motoring ferocity which comes naturally to the French.

As they turned off the A6 autoroute onto the Boulevard Périphérique, south of the city, Charlie broke the sullen silence with a forceful "Shit!"

"Shit is right," agreed Sally, looking out of the front passenger window and the fast moving motley of vehicles heading west.

"*Et maintenant?*" asked Louise in between *merdes* aimed at the unprepossessing form of a Fiat in front.

"Well, I guess that's it. Home to the good old US of A and goodbye Steve. Damn." Sally stared unseeingly at the graceful metal giraffe, *La Tour Eiffel*, thrusting its way heavenwards between the 15th arrondisement office blocks in the distance.

Louise exchanged glances with Charlie via the rear-view mirror.

"Perhaps it's just my imagination," Sally continued, "but my scars seem to be aching more now. Probably outta disappointment." Oh damn you Steve, damn you, damn you, damn you.

"Well you just tell them to quit," ordered Charlie, herself just a trifle more subdued than usual.

"But he couldn't have disappeared into thin air, surely?" reasoned Sally, clutching at straws.

"Seems he has done just that, honey. *If* Stelios Grivas was Steve Graves in the first place."

"Mm."

"As I said yesterday on the plane, no man is worth losing sweat over. Tell you what! Heck, you don't have to go home straight away. Why not stay here with us for a while?"

"I couldn't."

"Zat is ze good idea!" exclaimed Louise. "You will be no problem. *Bâtard!*" They overtook the Fiat.

"You can help me set up the exhibition if you like," suggested Charlie. "But nothing too strenuous, mind. You'll meet some interesting people."

"All our friends would love to meet you. Per'aps even find you a man to take your mind off Steve, hah?" The French girl smiled.

"What say we do the town tonight? Say Looey, how about if we asked Claude - he's not on tour, is he?"

"*Non.*"

"Good! And maybe he could bring along Michel too."

"Michel will be off preparing for his programme tomorrow."

"Shit, yes. Well how about that guy at Isabelle's party?"

"Oo? Guillaume?"

"Guy, yeh. Claude and Guy, wee, they could accompany us an' I'm sure Claude'll have a friend for Sally. We can all make up a sixem - or a sexem as you French would say, heh, heh."

"But I thought you two..." Sally smiled and frowned at the same time.

"Listen, honey," explained Charlie, leaning forward from the back seat, her hands on Sally's shoulder. "Why just sample the rosebuds when there's beefsteak to be had as well? Huh? I'm not purely queer, y' know. Now whadya say? Will you stay on for a while? Are you game for a good time?"

They drove over the Pont du Garigliano and paused at the traffic lights at Rue Chardon Lagache.

Sally looked from one to the other of them: Louise's pretty French face intent on the lights and Charlie's face alive and swashbuckling.

The lights changed and they pulled away, made a quick right into Rue Boileau and parked. Further up the street an armed policeman stood guard outside the Vietnamese embassy.

Both the women looked at Sally. She made up her mind. She smiled broadly, something she had not done for a long, long time.

"Hell, yes, dammit. I'll stay. I'd love to!"

Claude's friend was called Marcel, and in the early hours of the following morning, after a fantastic time at *Don Camilo*, he followed Sally into her room by invitation and, using great care because of her recent injuries, he made sublime love to her.

Ψ

Friday July 5 1974

"The Queen has been at the Edinburgh Academy today to mark its 150th foundation anniversary."

Queen Anne's Gate, Westminster, London

Queen Anne's Gate is a smallish thoroughfare, a tangent from the Westminster Abbey end of Victoria Street. It runs for only half a kilometre to St James's Park underground station and then loses its identity to the narrower, curiously-named Petty France. In 1974 a vast portion of Queen Anne's Gate was in the process of being demolished.

At the western end of the street, opposite the underground station, the modern monstrosity that is Number 50 was nearing completion. Part of this monolith was destined to house the security section of the police Special Branch, but until it was ready for occupancy the security section was dotted about various parts of Westminster.

Special Branch Security (Operations) Division 1 was based on the top floor of the ancient, but very secure, Queen Anne's Mansions, just across the road.

The Special Branch of the British police is a curious organisation, a cross between the American FBI, CIA and National Guard but without the overt thuggery. In addition to its well-known roles of Diplomatic Protection and Diplomatic Investigation, it also handles certain internal security matters and many other concerns subversive. And it does it without treading on the toes of MI5, MI6, DI6 and the SIS. *Almost.* For the Special Branch are a strange mob.

And there were none stranger than the unfortunately titled S(O)D 1. For a start, it was rumoured that they harvested their personnel from spent SAS men, the most elite soldiers in the world. For another thing, they never referred to each other by their police rank. They always used 'mister'.

Thus it was that at 10:30 that Friday, Mr Ramm and Mr Woods (in fact Detective Inspector and Detective Chief Inspector respectively) were summoned into the inner sanctum of the S(O)D 1 suite at the behest of Mr Metcalf (in fact a Detective Chief Superintendent).

"Come in, lads, come in." The bald-headed Metcalf was a good boss, but he had one embarrassing habit: when he addressed you he would always unconsciously touch his genitals.

The two men approached the desk and sat down, exchanging 'Good mornings'. They looked nothing like coppers, which of course was the whole idea. The bespectacled Mr Ramm looked like a rather shabby pin-striped civil servant from the lower echelons of Whitehall. Mr Woods would not have looked out of place on a building site.

"How's Janet?" asked Metcalf solicitously.

"A week overdue now," nodded Ramm. "And still no sign. I think she's got a bloody elephant up there."

"Told you you shouldn't have gone to Kenya last year," quipped Woods. "Never know what those witch doctors get up to. Mind you, you could always sell its tusks. Worth a bob or two."

"And we could certainly do with that. Can't go on fiddling expenses forever, can we Mr Metcalf?"

"Quite," Metcalf brought his hands up from his lap and opened a buff file in front of him. "How's the workload?"

"As ever," reported Woods. "No further forward on the Sieff

shooting. Coupla reports on IRA activity in Kilburn - I think they're building up for Christmas. A certain Central African diplomat fucked four suburban housewives in one night last week, paying their husbands five ton each for the privilege."

"God, I wish he'd come to me," grumbled Ramm. "I could just see five hundred off nicely. And Janet wouldn't feel a thing in her condition."

"Apart from that, the usual irons in the fire."

"Hmm," Metcalf nodded, one hand disappearing again beneath the table. "I've got another little job for you. Long-term effort. Surveillance job probably."

"Phone tap?" Woods.

"Not at this stage."

"Who's our client?" Ramm.

"Chap at the MOD. Probably nothing. Straight as a bat for years. Still is. Just something that came up during a routine security check. Been imbibing to excess. We've been asked to have a little look. Over the OBN *[Old Boy Network]*. Leave Five out of it."

"A big boy?"

"Big as they come," Metcalf threw the file across the desk with his one available hand. "One of the defence sales directors. Colonel Stanley William Egginton..."

Ψ

Saturday July 6 1974

"There is growing concern in America over the role of President Nixon in the Watergate scandal. Pressure is mounting in Washington for his impeachment. On Monday, the Supreme Court will hear arguments concerning the President's claim that he had a right to withhold sixty-four White House tape recordings."

Paris, France

That night Sally and Charlie and Louise slept together, forming a bond of friendship in a very special way.

Ψ

Friday July 12 1974

"In America, President Nixon is still retaining the controversial sixty-four White House tape recordings, which were the subject of a Supreme Court hearing during the week. He awaits the final report of the Senate Watergate Committee which is due to be published tomorrow."

Paris, France

It had been a wonderful week. Helping Charlie set up the exhibition at the gallery in the Avenue Matignon had been fun. Sally, the new alive Sally, had no intention of leaving her friends and the wonderful city for a long while yet. And there was no pressure on her to do so. Her lovers, both male and female, had asked her to stay, if not forever then at least until the passion on both sides had abated. And that could take a long, long time.

But fate was to move its prophetic hand that Friday evening.

Sally had stayed home in the apartment that afternoon, it being her turn to prepare the evening meal (*boeuf en daube*). Louise arrived home at her appointed time of 16:30, and she and Sally supped *Dubonet* and talked about the events of the day to a stereo background of their neighbour Claude François. Charlie had promised to be home "at least by five" but, knowing Charlie, Sally had scheduled dinner for 18:30.

As it was, Charlie burst upon the scene at 17:15.

The door slammed open with such force that it rebounded off

the stop and stood trembling on its hinges. "Sally! Sally! It suddenly came over me on the way home!"

Sally looked up, startled. "What? Who did?"

"Whadyamean *who*? You sex mad or sumpn? No," Charlie threw herself down into an armchair. "Remember I said I thought his other name was familiar? Y' know, the *Grivas* one?"

"Yes, I do."

"Well, I've been so dumb! I've known all along but it didn't occur to me till just now, as I was parking. Grivas. He was that guy in Cyprus, y' know that terrorist leader. Died not so long ago. January I think it was."

"January! But that was when Steve - !" Sally sat bolt upright. "Do you really think - ?"

"Holy shit, it seems logical! Why it should be, I don't know. Why the hell he should travel under that name in the first place, d' you know?"

"No, but that doesn't matter right now."

"We must find out." Louise picked up the excitement. "Flights on *vingt-troisieme Janvier* to Cyprus or that area."

"Let's do it *now!*" Charlie jumped up, loose change rattling in the pockets of her tweeds.

"But what about the *boeuf en daube?*" Louise was forever practical.

"Shit the berf on dowb, Looey," Charlie reached down, snatched Sally's glass and swilled down the remaining *Dubonnet* in one. "This is love we're talking about. C'mon, let's get moving!"

Their joy, however, was short-lived. Again a descent on Orly, again all the airlines most helpful, again nothing. No Graves or Grivas on any flight to Nicosia, Istanbul, Athens, Beirut or any other likely place on January 23rd or in the week following. They noticed a Mr Golkadas and a Miss Casceri on the early morning flight to Nicosia on January 24th, but it meant nothing to any of them.

It does not need recording that the most prevalent word in the volcabulary of Ms Charlotte Rapley on the morose journey back to the apartment that evening was one consisting of just four letters and associated with the movements of the bowels.

That night Sally asked Charlie to sleep with her, out of need for comfort and to quell her feelings of loneliness and abandon, rather than out of any need for sexual gratification. Charlie understood this and, although she touched the intimate parts as they held each other in their arms, nothing more happened between them.

They must have lain awake for two hours, talking spasmodically in between long periods of silence. This time the older woman had nothing to offer, no hope, no optimism. They both knew they had tried everything. The final inspiration had failed.

Outside, the late evening chatter of a summer Paris gave way to the stillness of night.

It was nearing 01:00 when Sally said, "I'm going anyway."

"Mm?" Charlie had been dozing off, and her bedmate's voice startled her back to consciousness. "What, honey?"

"I'm going anyway, Charlie. To Cyprus. I just *know* that's where Steve is."

With an effort, Charlie sat up in the bed, her full baggy breasts wobbling as she turned to switch on the dim bedside light. "Shit kid, is that wise? Whadya gonna do when you get there?"

Sally also sat up, and the woman in Charlie winced as the raw scars on the girl's chest came into view.

"I don't know, I just know I have to go. I have ample money, I'll find a hotel or something. I don't even know how I'm going to set about finding Steve, but he's there, Charlie, he's there. And I'll find him."

For a moment Charlie was silent. Then she smiled a big, warm, friendly-bear smile. "Y' know, I think you're right. It's probably the best thing you can do. It'll either kill or cure you." She looked again at Sally's scars and thought that perhaps that was not the right expression to use. "I mean of this love you have for this guy. I only hope he'll appreciate what you're doing."

A rueful look crossed Sally's face as she said wistfully, "So do I, Charlie. So do I."

Ψ

Sunday July 14 1974

"The new Prime Minister of Portugal is Colonel Vasco Goncalves. He was named yesterday following the resignation of Professor Adelino Palma Carlos last week."

Nicosia, Cyprus

At 21:30 that evening, Ramirov met someone in a secluded corner of the noisy *Picnic* nightclub in northern Nicosia. Few words were exchanged and Ramirov left the club just twenty minutes after he had entered it.

Yeri, Nicosia District, Cyprus

Steve and Christina were in the bath together when Ramirov returned to the villa. Without even the courtesy of a warning knock, the bathroom door crashed open. They made no attempt to cover themselves, but Steve frowned angrily at the sudden intrusion. "What the hell, Martinez!"

"My partners," Ramirov knelt by the side of the bath, addressing the couple like old and trusted friends. "The time has come. It is to be tomorrow. Tomorrow Grivas, you will have The Eye of Makarios!"

"At last! What exactly is going to happen? What do I do?"

"Later. Tonight we have a lot of work to do and a lot of planning. Come, we must not waste time." He had hold of

The Eye of Makarios

Steve's arm and he was literally lifting him from the water.

The American fought him off with a series of splashing slaps. "Hey buddy, do you mind!" He had never seen the other man like this before. Was he high? "At least give me the chance to finish my bath!"

Ramirov's eyebrows narrowed and then rose. "My goodness! I am sorry! Of course. But downstairs as fast as you can, Grivas. We have a long night ahead of us!"

He went out, bubbling with excitement. The bathroom door slammed behind him.

Steve paused to get his breath back. "Jees, I don't even think he knew we were naked. So our cold, hard teacher *can* get excited. I wonder what's coming down?"

Christina shrugged. "Excitement is not necessarily a good thing, Stelios. If a man gets too excited he can make foolish mistakes."

"And a woman?"

"What?"

"A woman can get too excited and make foolish mistakes too, you know."

"Ah, but for a woman it is different."

"Cascianis?"

"Yes?"

"Think, will you?"

"Of what, Stelios?"

"Just think of this afternoon."

"This afternoon...?"

"About a woman getting excited...?"

A cat-with-the-cream smile oozed across the olive face.

"Now," continued Steve. "You're thinking, right?"

"Oh yes Stelios, I am thinking." She closed her eyes dreamily.

He picked up the soap and lathered his hands. "Well now, gorgeous Christy, don't you give me any of your Cypriot bullshit about women not getting excited, huh? I can still feel your nails in my back."

"Just the claws of a pussycat, my Stelios."

He reached forward and lathered both her breasts simultaneously, the soft-yet-solid mounds quivering beneath his palms. "A pussycat or a tiger?"

She kept her eyes closed. "Maybe both."

Very gently, with the softest of caresses, he rinsed the soap off. "But tigers can bite."

"So can pussies."

He bent down and took her hardened left nipple between his teeth. He sucked at it and then bit it sharply.

She squealed and pushed his head down her body. The water lapped at her pubic line.

"I didn't think pussies liked water," he said as she forced his head down and between her legs.

It was the first saturation diving he had done since January.

And the excited Martinez/Ramirov had to wait quite some time for them to come down.

"And what do *I* do?" asked Christina with a pout. They had been talking and planning for two hours now. Ramirov had informed them that tomorrow a great turmoil would be unleashed on the island as history took its ineluctable course, but he would not be drawn on specifics. "The diamond is your only concern. You and I, Grivas, are going to attack Makarios."

Christina had tried to bully, coax and seduce further information from him, but he was not to be drawn. That had started off her sulks and she had moodily puffed her way through three pungent panatelas which looked and smelled as if they had been made out of the eviscera of a rotting goat corpse.

Now the man they knew as Martinez was giving Stelios his instructions. They were to raid Mouskos' palace. And this had prompted her question of her involvement.

Ramirov looked towards her, his mouth smiling but the black

eyes behind the tinted glasses remaining cold. He inclined his head. "You, my dear, do nothing. You remain here and prepare for our return. Be ready to move if things do not go according to plan. If things go all right, there should be no necessity for us to move. But we must be prepared just in case. Every circumstance must always be catered for."

"But that ees not right!" Her accent became more pronounced with her increased emotion. "I must comma weeth you. You *cannot* leaf me here!"

The look Ramirov gave her would have turned anybody to stone. She stared back at him, but then her resolution began to waiver and her eyes faltered from the stare, came back again, then away again. She rammed the butt of the panatela back between her teeth.

"Best do as he says, babe," counselled Steve. "He's the master, don't forget. Our *sempi*. And besides, we do need you here as he says. You never know what might happen."

"So, the two off you are going to raid the Presidential Palace, take a priceless diamond and comm back and liff happily effer after, hah? You will need help, you know. You cannot do itt on your own effen if you are supermen like Meester Martinez here seemse to think he iss. You must get help from somewhere." She scowled at Ramirov. "Why will you nott tell uss exactly what iss going on?"

"Baby, I think - "

"Shut up, Stelios! You will be risking your life tomorrow in somsing that seemse bigger than oll off uss, and *he* will not tell you what you are getting involved in." The eyes glared again. "Just who are you anyway, to come with your threats and then leaf uss again for a month and come back and order uss about with the promise of geeting The Eye of Makarios? I think Meester Martinez that you are using uss. How can we be sure that we will effer see thees diamond - ?"

It happened so suddenly that Steve did not have time to

move.

All Christina was aware of was a black blanket descending over her eyes. Ramirov had been sitting with his hands clasped together on his lap, head tilted to one side, taking in the woman's vitriol. Suddenly his right arm shot outwards, hand and fingers rigid, slicing sharply through the air. It met Christina's right temple with a sickening thud. She dropped back on the chair immediately, totally limp, the panatela rolling onto the floor.

For a second Steve was speechless, then he leapt over to her, grabbing her wrist to feel for a pulse.

"For Christ's sake man!"

"She is alive," Ramirov announced with an air of total disinterest. He walked over, picked up the panatela and killed it in a rush of effervescence in her half-empty glass of local champagne. "If I had wanted to kill her I would have aimed thirty millimetres lower."

Steve let her wrist drop and turned to look at the other man. "You callous bastard."

Ramirov spoke as if scolding an errant schoolboy. "I said when I first met you that there would be no questions, that you would do as I say. I could have killed you both that night, please remember that. Do you *want* this diamond? Or is this little piece of Cypriot ass worth more to you? In five hours time we will get The Eye of Makarios. May I suggest you also get some sleep? Shortly we will both be very busy."

"What kind of animal are you?"

"The kind that is helping you fulfil your father's last request. She will awake with a headache, nothing more. I will take my rest in the outhouse. I have things to do. Five hours, my dear Mr Grivas, that is all. Five hours."

Outside, two hours later.

"Do you want this?" Digenis held up the syringe. "For the

woman?"

Ramirov shook his head. "I can use the cyanide gas."

"No. We're not into death - "

"I am."

"Maybe so. We are not. This will keep her out for a few hours. Use it, please."

In the darkness, Ramirov actually looked disappointed. He took the syringe.

"It will keep her out long enough for you to be on your way," Digenis continued. "Get the diamond and she will never see you again. And she does not know your real identity."

"Nobody does," said Ramirov.

Except you, he thought.

For a summary of the events leading up to the attempted coup in Cyprus on July 15 1974, please see Appendix 3.

Ψ

Monday July 15 1974

"Reports are coming in of a rebellion in Cyprus. No details are available as yet, but it is known that members of the EOKA terrorist organisation have taken over Nicosia radio. Unconfirmed reports say that President Makarios has been killed."

Cyprus

The Presidential Palace is on the south-western perimeter of Nicosia, just over two kilometres from the southern walls of the old city. To reach it direct from Yeri village it is not necessary to enter the city itself, passage can be made via Strovolos and round the back of Engomi.

But Ramirov had one last piece of business to attend to that morning, and in the early hours his battered grey Volkswagen Beetle was seen thundering through Athalassa and heading straight on for Eylenja.

"Hey, it's that way!" shouted Steve above the roar of the supercharged engine as they swept over the intersection. He shifted in his seat, uncomfortable with the weight of the sub-machine gun on his lap.

"Not yet my friend, just one last thing. How do you think we are going to reach the Presidential Palace in an old Volkswagen and looking like two stupid tourists who just happen to be carrying a whole arsenal of weapons?"

Steve said nothing but looked grimly out of the window. It was hot inside the car, but even hotter outside, even at this early hour, and the window remained closed against the heat and the dust.

He thought of his life. Of his *lives*. The one people knew about, the one they didn't. He thought of the madness of the last months. He thought of his father.

He said a silent prayer for the soul of George Grivas.

Eylenja was reached in no time, and the Volkswagen pulled up outside a ramshackle old dwelling on the eastern side of the town.

"Wait here." Ramirov climbed out and ran into the house without bothering to knock.

Inside it was dark, and it took just a second for Ramirov's eyes to adjust from the glare of the early morning sun before he could make out the old peasant waiting patiently in a wooden rocking chair by the bare wooden table.

The old man looked up as the door burst open.

"Martinez," snapped the visitor. "You have something for me." He spoke in Greek.

"I have," said the old man calmly, and he reached down the side of his chair and handed over a brown package tied up with string, like a bundle of laundry.

"My thanks, old man," Ramirov leant forward as if to kiss him on the cheek.

The old man was surprised by the action. He was even more surprised as he felt the knife slide into his body just below the breastbone and push upwards into his heart. He died immediately.

After two jerks up and down to ensure death, Ramirov removed the knife, wiped it on the old man's dirty trousers, and replaced it in its sheath.

Back in the car, Ramirov slit open the parcel, yanking off the brown paper and string. Two uniforms were revealed.

Steve sniffed in irony. "Well, well, the Tactical Reserve Force.

I'd recognise *that* uniform anywhere."

"Not quite the TRF, but they were the best official uniforms they could get hold of."

"Who are 'they'?"

Ramirov did not answer. Roughly he rewrapped the uniforms and tossed them onto the back seat. He gunned the car into action and took a quick left at the end of the road, heading into the capital.

"Martinez, who are 'they'?" Steve repeated.

"EOKA, of course," Ramirov answered smoothly. "More precisely, EOKA B."

"But I thought they were finished?"

Ramirov was searching the road on the right with his eyes, and they had slowed down to a reasonable speed. "You are a fool if you believe that and such thoughts are not worthy of the son of Grivas."

"But we were told - "

"You were told nothing. You refused their offer of leadership, therefore you were excluded. You were not required - you and that meddlesome female. You are Grivas' son in name only. The two of you had your own little mission and they were content to let you get on with it. EOKA has grown stronger since the death of Grivas. People revere his memory. And today is their day, today is *the* day of *Enosis!*"

Steve remained quiet. Two minutes later, Ramirov cried "Ah, here we are!" and he turned the car sharply to the left between two rows of old and not very well kept houses.

About a hundred metres along, three men waited anxiously beside an old jeep. They were wearing the uniform of the Cypriot National Guard. They tensed, hands on their holsters, as the Volkswagen approached. Then, at a word from one who must have been the senior officer, they relaxed as the Beetle came to a halt and Ramirov could clearly be seen.

"Our way into the Palace," explained Ramirov. He reached

into the back seat. "Get out and change into one of these uniforms and sit with me in the back of the jeep. Talking will be superfluous. They are genuine members of the National Guard and under orders. They know who you are and not so long ago would have shot you on sight. Today you will be quite safe. Prepare your gun and pistol for action. From now on it is kill or be killed. Come, Grivas, let us go."

Stelios Grivas stepped from the vehicle and did as he was told.

As the jeep with the five men on board drove swiftly through the streets of Nicosia, Grivas noticed how quiet everything seemed. It was not that there was a lack of activity - for the majority of the people who were not in on the coup would not know what had happened until it was all over - but there just seemed *something*, something almost tactile in the air, as if the Gods from high up on Olympus knew exactly what was going on and disapproved.

And it was hot. So, so hot. Grivas' shirt was saturated and it stuck to his back uncomfortably. The back of his curly hair was matted and gritty. And, he had to admit, he stank. Yet Martinez next to him did not seem to be sweating at all.

They took the main Dhiyeni Akrita, hooting the tourists out of their way.

And then he saw her.

Or at least he thought he saw her.

Or it was someone who looked like her.

But it could not be her, of course.

They had flashed past her in a moment, and Grivas was too cramped between Ramirov and one of the others to turn around. He laughed to himself. His mind was playing tricks on him! That tourist they had just hooted out of their way looked like Sally, the girl he had left behind in Houston. Wasn't her, of course. This one had cropped hair, was decidedly skinnier than

Sally, and the glasses were missing. Also she looked wan, as if she was not well or was just recovering from some illness. No, it was not her. But just for one moment, one crazy moment, he thought he had seen someone from another, forgotten world…

They travelled on.

Michael Mouskos, His Beatitude Makarios III, Archbishop of the Autocephalous Church of Cyprus and President of the Cypriot Republic, had not slept well that night. And he had good reason. For he knew of the probability of the attempted coup that morning and, worse, of his proposed assassination.

Makarios was a man of vast intellect and personal charisma. He prided himself on the intricate intelligence network he and his intimate counsellors had built up over the years. It was only natural that he had known of what would be attempted that day nearly two weeks in advance.

After spending many nights alone in the Archbishop's Palace considering the avenues open to him, Makarios had come to an important conclusion. During the four previous assassination attempts he had been able to meet threat with force, either prior to or shortly after the event. This time it would be different. This time, if his intelligence was correct, it would be himself against the army. Odds much too numerous. This time he would not be able to meet force with force. This time, in all probability, he would not even be able to defend himself.

Needless to say, he had been particularly circumspect that morning during his daily four kilometre journey from the Archbishop's Palace within the old city wall of Nicosia to the Presidential Palace on the south-western outskirts.

Some ten days previously, as soon as Makarios had evaluated all the possibilities of this rumoured new attack and had decided on his action, he had summoned someone from Kykko Monastery, his own home monastery in the district of Marathasa, Paphos. That someone was a priest Makarios had used before.

Makarios was a commanding figure. Over six feet in height, he looked even more imposing than his size already allowed due to the combination of the tall hat, the flowing black robes and the Greek Orthodox bishop's long staff. His eyes were sharp and penetrating, and he wore the thick greying black beard. He was, therefore, very hard to impersonate with any conviction. Hard, but not impossible. And that was his little secret.

Makarios had stumbled across the priest many years before on one of his return to visits to the monastery that he loved. The priest was younger than Makarios, but he was of the same height and identical build. His facial features were roughly similar, at least to withstand perfunctory examination, and his black beard was the same shape. Dressed in identical robes to the Archbishop, beard greyed with powder, Andreas Papadopoulos could have been a twin brother.

He had been used successfully in the past when it had been necessary for Makarios to be in two places at once: once during an assassination bid (when a forlorn EOKA attempt on the President's life had missed even his stand-in by metres) and, more notably, on the famous occasion eighteen years previously in 1956 when Makarios had supposedly been taken from the island into exile in the Seychelles, escorted ashore by the Chief of Police Trevor Williams. *[Makarios was, in fact, stripped of his robes, shaved and immured by the British for over twelve months in Limassol, unbeknown to the rest of the world. Whether he underwent deliberate physical intimidation or just the discomfort of gaol is not known.]*

Andreas Papadopoulos had not been used for a while, but today The Red Priest would need his services like never before...

In the cramped, bumpy rear seat of the jeep, Ramirov raised a suntanned arm and looked at the Rolex on his wrist.

"One minute," he said. The head inclined itself a few degrees to the left.

In front of him, a member of the National Guard blocked his right nostril with his finger and snotted over the side of the vehicle.

Archbishop Makarios looked up from his desk and responded quietly to the knock on the door. "Come in."

The priest entered diffidently.

Makarios smiled. "Ah, Father Andreas, come in, come in. I believe we do not have much time…"

The tanks of the National Guard had just started firing into the Presidential Palace as the jeep turned the last corner of the main drive and screeched to a halt. There were people everywhere, those in uniform heading towards the palace, the rest fleeing for their lives.

The five occupants of the jeep leapt out. Ramirov and Grivas headed as planned directly for the huge main door, which had already been blown apart from a blast from one of the tanks.

There was noise everywhere.

And it was hot.

And it was dusty.

And it was hell.

When the tanks started firing, Makarios and Papadopoulos were together in the palace on the broad landing looking down onto the wide main lobby below. Anybody seeing them at that time would have thought they had suddenly been inflicted with double vision. Here was Makarios in duplicate. Both men were fully robed and standing erect, holding themselves with the Mouskos calm, the Mouskos self-assurance. The only difference was the eyes. One held the charm, the cunning, the slyness, the greatness, that was the embodiment of the genuine Makarios.

The other held almost nothing.

The second tank blast shattered the main door, and Makarios sprang into action. While his double watched, the Archbishop flung down his staff and pulled off his headgear, revealing his bald pate. The black robes were whipped off carelessly and left in a bundle on the floor. Underneath, Makarios wore a pair of old brown cord pants and a dirty white shirt with beige stripes. The transformation had taken only four seconds, yet no one would now have recognised the world-famous priest.

"All right," Makarios busily tucked his shirt into the pants. "Give me half a minute's start and then flee yourself, dear Andreas. I fear this time we may indeed be in serious danger." He paused for the briefest moment. "And may God be with us both."

Papadopoulos grabbed the Archbishop's hand and kissed the ring of office in genuine devotion.

"Goodness, yes." Makarios tugged the ring off his finger and grabbed Papadopoulos's hand. The ring slipped onto his finger, a macabre marriage of souls.

Papadopoulos's eyes held tears. "He will protect you, your Beatitude."

The eyes of Makarios watered also. A swift blessing, a smile, and then Makarios was gone, down the wide staircase and out of sight somewhere into the back of the palace.

Dust began to fly in all directions as more tank shells thudded into the walls and through the shattering windows.

Papadopoulos stayed his ground and silently prayed as he allowed thirty seconds to pass. On the thirtieth second, amid the noise of the tanks and the chatter of machine guns, a shard of the ceiling directly above fell away and exploded on top of his head. It shook him but he did not collapse. His head hurt but he was alive. Now he must escape, and quickly...

The masonry had stunned him, and instead of running deeper into the palace as would have been expected, Papadopoulos went full pelt down the stairs, head on into the firing. Halfway down his foot caught in the hem of his robes and he fell, his knees thudding on the stairs, his face ripping against a piece of rubble as he came to rest at the bottom, knees oozing warm liquid.

His face was cut just below the left eye and was bleeding savagely, but the smash on the head had dulled his sense of pain. He staggered to his feet, bent down, picked up the fallen headgear and jammed it back into place. Then he turned to head for the back of the palace.

Just as he did so, two men charged over the shattered main door, their guns blazing. One was swarthy and had a chubby face, the other tall and with a black moustache and - *my God!* Didn't he look like the young Grivas! No, it couldn't possibly be!

Papadopoulos turned away to run, but he knew it was hopeless. His feet slipped across the heavily polished tiled floor and he tried to reach a door.

"MOUSKOS!" shouted an accented voice from behind.

But he kept on running.

One of the machine guns fired and for a moment it seemed to the priest that the bullets had missed. But then all life went from the right side of his body and his right leg was whipped away from under him. He span around, robes swirling, in a wild, macabre pirouette. He saw the tall man's mouth move and flames shoot from his gun.

Papadopoulos never heard the fire of the gun, and at his moment of death - as pieces of his chest flew away at all angles and the floor came up to meet him - he heard the man shout "FOR GRIVAS!".

Then all was tranquility.

Ψ

Ramirov and Grivas dashed over to the body. Ramirov was mumbling to himself. Above the din, Grivas heard "You did it. My God, you did it!"

Ramirov's hands scrabbled frantically at the clothing, ripping the bloodsoaked cloth away.

"Where the hell is it?" shouted Grivas. "It's not here. For fuck's sake, it's not here!"

"Wait." Ramirov's hand withdrew something from near the body's genitals. It was a small leather pouch connected to a leather cord still around the waist. Ramirov's knife appeared and the cord was instantly cut. Quickly, he opened the pouch.

The Star of Sierra Leone slipped out into his hand, a huge but ungainly rough diamond.

"The Eye of Makarios!" said Grivas. "Holy God!"

Without a word Ramirov replaced the diamond in the pouch and went to put it in a top pocket. Grivas grabbed his arm, the barrel of his gun pointing between Ramirov's eyes.

"Mine I think."

Their eyes locked. Then Ramirov let the diamond and the pouch be removed from his hands.

Then he said, "Come on, quickly!" and the American rose and followed him through the back of the palace.

Two civilians appeared from an office, and Ramirov shot their faces away without thought.

They reached a side door, already gaping open like a corpse's jaw, and ran out of the palace and into the grounds. They did not know that just two minutes before the real, live Michael Mouskos, Archbishop Makarios III, had fled this very same way.

The firing into the palace did not last for long. The first genuine members of the National Guard to enter the building found the body of the fake Makarios, hence the radio reports later that day that Makarios had been killed. It was not until the body was moved some hours later that the headgear fell off to reveal Papadopoulos's full head of jet black hair, the main feature that had distinguished him and Michael Mouskos in mufti. And by that time Makarios had hitchhiked into the mountains and would soon be picked up by the British troops. Two days later he was in London.

Christina Cascianis surfaced slowly from the man-made oblivion. She had the worst headache of her life. It began at the cranium and travelled upwards over the top of her skull to erupt above the eyes in a whirlpool of ache, pain and nausea. The side of her head hurt like hell. She touched the spot gingerly as she moved herself gently into a sitting position. And what was the bruise on her arm?

How long had she been out? Where was Stelios and that bastard Martinez? What had happened? The last thing she remembered was berating Martinez over something, and then... nothing.

What time was it? She had no watch. Carefully she straightened her stiff neck and moved her head to look around the room. She had been in the villa long enough to know that there were no clocks about the place, but one of the men might have left a watch somewhere.

There were no watches, but there was something else. A person.

Standing just inside the half-open front door was a man. A tall, broad man with dark brown hair and a sallow, gaunt face which was distinctly out of place above the broad and obviously muscular body. He was dressed in a lightweight brown suit of old-fashioned design, and ancient brown brogues. A small-collared once-white shirt and thin knitted brown tie completed the ensemble.

"Who - who are you?" she stammered in Greek.

The main raised an eyebrow and looked quizzically at her. The eyes held no trace of comprehension.

She tried again in English. "Who are yoo?" She could almost hear his brain computing the language.

After a moment he said, "Ah! In-gleesh. Mine not good. Turk?"

Christina spat unladylike on the floor. The man paused again, computing the gesture. Then his cheeks twitched upwards, once, and then down again, and he walked over towards her.

"In-gleesh not good. I... friend of Ramirov. He here not yet no?"

A sharp stab of pain pierced the back of her skull and came out through her right eye. The stranger was standing three metres away. "Who iss Ramirov? I do nott know heem."

"This howse hiss," the gentleman gestured.

"Martinez. His name iss Martinez."

Information computed once again, then the gaunt face turned even paler as he realised his error. "Oh... I wait. You... well?" He came nearer.

He was just a metre from Christina when she snarled. Without warning, her right hand shot out and grabbed him mercilessly in the groin. She could feel the balls beneath the cheap cloth of the pants. She squeezed with all her might.

The man screamed with the sudden agony. His hands fumbled ineffectively at her wrist, trying to pull her off, but she was not going to let go. He tried to kick her but found it impossible to move his legs up. He screamed again and again, spittle flying from his mouth, until the red haze overcame him. His legs gave way.

Christina maintained her emasculating grip as he fell, and she twisted the balls wickedly for good measure. The screams had died off into a whimpering gurgle, and the spittle has changed to drool oozing from the corners of his mouth.

Christina released the organs, stood up, swung her right foot back and brought it down heavily into the man's crotch. He grunted and rolled over onto his stomach, his knees raising themselves in protection.

She wasted no time. Disregarding her complaining head, she ran over to the door and out into the hot, dazzling sunlight. As she went through the doorway, a gun cracked from behind and the lintel splintered above. But she did not pause, she just kept on running, running…

On the floor of the villa, the gun slipped out of the Russian's hand, all strength gone, and, crying in sheer agony, he rolled his face to the left and spewed all over an expensive rug.

The old Volkswagen pulled up outside the villa two hours later. Ramirov and Grivas, both now back in their own clothes, climbed out. The sub-machine guns were in the front in the trunk of the vehicle; Ramirov carried a simple pistol tucked into the waistband of his pants. The American was unarmed, the diamond buttoned safely in his shirt pocket.

The mood of both men was euphoric.

"Did you see the way that son-of-bitch's back exploded?" asked Grivas as they walked towards the house. "Do you *see* it, Martinez? Jees, I only hope my father did. Revenge is so, so sweet."

"It was remarkable, all of it," nodded Ramirov. "Not a hitch. And Makarios just where I thought he would be. Stunned and stupefied and running like a frightened animal. Well, he will run no longer."

He turned the handle of the front door and they entered the villa. Ramirov was not at all surprised to see the gaunter than usual visitor sitting uncomfortably in one of the armchairs, and he greeted him with "Sergei!".

Grivas stopped in his tracks just inside the front door. "Who the hell…?"

Ramirov totally ignored him as he walked towards the other man. "All is ready?" he asked eagerly.

Sergei nodded and said something in Russian.

"Hey Martinez, who *is* this guy?" Grivas continued on into the room. Again he was ignored.

"What happened here?" asked Ramirov in Russian, indicating the big damp patch on the rug.

"There was some bastard woman here."

"Oh yes, a minor hindrance which I had to put to sleep."

"Not permanently enough."

"I told him that."

"She was just waking when I arrived. She attacked me. In the bollocks." A weak gesture towards the rug explained everything else.

Ramirov could not resist a guffaw. "I think a spell at Novosibirsk would do you good, Comrade! But I am sorry about the female. As you say, I should have made it permanent."

The foreign tongue was aggravating Grivas. "Do you two mind? Who *is* this, Martinez?"

Sergei sniffed. "And what about him? This is the famous Son of Grivas, huh? When will you deal with him?"

"Martinez, will you *answer* me?"

Ramirov turned and looked at the American, his head inclined to one side. He said in English. "Now is as good a time as any."

"As good a time as any for *what?*"

Ramirov drew the gun from his waistband and shot Stelios Grivas through the heart from a distance of only two metres.

PART FOUR

Ψ

OBJECTIVE DELIVERED

Christina kept running. Running and running. Wildly at first, the pain in her head increasing with each stride until she thought she would pass out. The wide ethnic skirt entangled itself around her legs as she moved.

After half an hour her legs began to tire and she slowed to a walking pace, her breath coming uneasily. In a further fifteen minutes she had reached the village of Laxia. People seemed to be going about their business as normal, but there was an eerie quietness about the place. She accosted a villager and asked what had happened that morning, but the old woman just gave her a stony stare and hobbled on.

Christina came to the main Nicosia-Limassol road. The traffic seemed unusually thin, and what little of it there was was heading for Limassol, away from the capital. She had a nasty feeling that she knew exactly what was going on in Nicosia. Stelios had probably got embroiled in an attempt to overthrow Mouskos. She only hoped that he and Martinez had been successful, because such was the nature of their mission - to steal a diamond from the very person of Makarios - that they must either succeed or lose their lives.

Resting under a tree by the side of the road, she realised that her best bet lay back at the villa. Stelios would need her help - *if* he came back. *If it was ever Martinez' intention to have him come back.*

She accepted her thoughts with resignation. She had been near death too many times for the thought of it to horrify her any more, even the death of General George Grivas's son, her lover. But she must not run away. She must return to the villa to see what she could do.

As she arose a jeep thundered past her on the road, heading towards Nicosia. In the back she thought she saw one of the old EOKA members of the good old days, but the jeep had gone in a second in a cloud of dust, and she could not be certain. Not until days later did she realise that she had seen Nicos Sampson on his way to take up his short-lived Presidency.

She returned to the villa by the route she had come, half walking, half trotting.

Arriving back an hour later, the first thing she noticed was that the door of the place was ominously open, and there was not a sound from within...

It was evening by the time the Volkswagen arrived at its destination, Sergei driving, Ramirov asleep in the front passenger seat. They had gone south from Yeri to Athienou where they had turned east, heading through Arsos, Lysi and Kondea. They had followed the road for Famagusta, turning south about two kilometres out and then picking up the main road through Dherinia and Paralimni. They were now stopped to the south of the village of Ayia Napa in a secluded spot to the east of the Nissi Beach Hotel.

The evening was warm and still, a calmness which belied the events of the day.

Ramirov awoke immediately the car's engine was switched off. "We have arrived?"

"Just beyond the trees," confirmed Sergei.

"And now we wait." Ramirov touched the inside pocket of his cord waister jacket to confirm the safety of The Star of Sierra Leone. "Till dark?"

"Immediately it gets dark we descend to the beach. A motor boat will pick us up. It is arranged."

"And you are sure we will not be seen from the hotel?"

"There is a small headland on the way, it will give us sufficient cover. And anyway, the tourists are evacuating, they will be much too preoccupied to notice us."

"That is true. If only we had a radio to know how things were going. If it has gone according to their plan, things will be over by now. Makarios is dead, that I know."

"You can get all the news you want on board the yacht." Sergei opened the door.

Abruptly, Ramirov reached across and grabbed him by the forearm. "Where are you going?"

"Piss."

"We do not want to risk attracting any attention now. Can't it wait?"

"I have just driven over seventy kilometres non-stop, Comrade. No, it cannot wait." He pulled his arm free.

He was back in a couple of minutes. "There was blood in it and the balls are a deep purple."

"We must get you to a doctor. There will be one on board the yacht?"

"Yes. He was thought necessary in case anything happened to *you*."

Ramirov chuckled. "Such are the vagaries of life, Comrade. It is causing you much pain?"

"Discomfort, the pain has subsided. You should have killed that bitch, you know."

"Quite, but I was talked out of it. I did not expect you to arrive so early. I had planned to deal with her and the American at the same time. Still, wherever she went she will be of no trouble now. I have what I want and her beloved EOKA now has power. Why, she should thank me and the late Mr Grivas for our part in it!"

Ramirov's good humour lasted for the half hour until darkness had settled. Then the two men simply left the vehicle where it was, for all intents and purposes abandoned by fleeing tourists.

There was little moon and it was almost pitch black on the beach, sparse and intermittent illumination being provided by a pencil torch carried by Sergei. The sibilant waves slid along the sand towards them and then crept away again diffidently.

They did not have to wait long before they heard the sound

of an outboard motor approaching from their right. Sergei raised the pencil torch and gave three flashes of five seconds duration and one of two seconds. It was answered by three flashes of two seconds duration and one of five.

The small motor boat contained two men in crew uniform. With simple acknowledgements, Ramirov and Sergei waded out twenty metres through the undertow and climbed in. They hardly had a chance to sit down before the boat had been pushed around and they were off, raking into the night.

They travelled in an easterly direction for ten minutes, Cyprus lost in the darkness behind them. Then all of a sudden the yacht loomed up from nowhere. Only a few lights were on but Ramirov could tell that it was huge, much bigger than the normal rich man's vessel. *[The vessel belonged, and still does belong, to K – a very influential Arab.]*

On board they were met by 'Akay' Al Khalifa, smart in dark suit and white polo-necked sweater. This time he shook Ramirov's hand. "My friend, congratulations! Mr Hernandez, welcome once again." He spoke in French. "Did you enjoy your recent visit to Cana?"

"Very pleasant, but the Jordan is vast and mysterious."

"Who knows where a river ends?" Al Khalifa smiled. "Please excuse the lack of illumination, for obvious reasons. And this night air out here leaves something to be desired in warmth. Come, I will show you to your cabin." The three men passed through a doorway and down some steps. "You know, of course, that Sampson is now President?"

"I guessed as much, that was their plan. Everything appeared to go extremely well, entirely as arranged. What happens now is up to them."

They were walking on thickly-piled carpet, and the walls were tastefully finished off in well-polished wood. Through another doorway and down some more stairs. Al Khalifa opened the second door along, and Ramirov followed him inside.

"Your cabin," said the Arab. "Mr Hernandez is situated just next door."

"I must see the doctor," said Sergei from the doorway. "He is awake?"

Al Khalifa looked concerned. "No, but I can wake him. You are hurt, unwell?"

"Both," sniffed the Russian. "Some accursed female attacked me."

Al Khalifa raised an eyebrow but pursued the matter no further. "I will see that he comes to your cabin immediately."

Sergei walked away, and the door to the next cabin could be heard opening and closing.

The Arab turned back to Ramirov. "The item is safe, I trust?"

"Of course, and it will remain in my care for the time being."

"*Mais naturellement.* We can talk further in the morning. I will have some hot food brought in to you and something to drink. There is also a bar," he indicated a cupboard set into the wall next to the wide and extremely opulent bed. "Is there anything else you wish at this time?"

"Just to relax, that is all. What time do we arrive in Beirut?"

"We are scheduled to dock at noon tomorrow."

"Good."

"Relax well, my friend." Al Khalifa left the cabin, closing the door noiselessly.

A few minutes later the muted hum of the vessel's engines increased as it picked up speed, and by this time Ramirov was lying on the bed, naked except for a black jock strap, and gazing up at his reflection in the mirrored ceiling, willing himself into a state of relaxation.

Another few minutes passed. There came a gentle tap on the door. "*Venez!*" called the Russian.

The door was pushed open and a trolley was wheeled in by an attractive red head. She was dressed in a green knee-length kaftan, nothing adorning her legs. She smiled, natural gaiety in her green eyes. "Good evening," she said in English, her voice deep, lilting.

Ramirov raised himself up on one elbow. "Good evening. You are English?"

"That's right. Akay - Mister Al Khalifa - has sent this food along for you."

"You are the waitress?"

She chuckled. "No, I was coming this way anyway. I believe you wish to relax? I am a qualified masseuse." She left the trolley behind the closed door and walked over to him, red hair bouncing, green kaftan rustling. "May I help you relax?"

Ramirov smiled and removed the tinted glasses. "But certainly."

"My name is Melanie."

"And I am - "

"You are… to relax." She undid the kaftan and let it fall from her body. Underneath she wore just the smallest pair of red G-string pants. Her breasts were firm and stood out from her body without support; they wobbled gently as she knelt down on the edge of the bed.

She put her hand firmly on the front of his jock. "You have far too many clothes on. May I remove them?"

Tel Aviv, Israel

At the same time that Ilich Ramirov was surrendering himself to the ministrations of the delectable Melanie, a very special meeting was taking place in a room on the top floor of an office block in northern Tel Aviv.

Usually the Controllers of the five branches of *Mossad Aliyah Beth* (Israeli intelligence) met informally in this room once a week on a Wednesday morning. This week, however, an extra-special meeting was being held on Monday night.

They sat at a round table, each man in his shirtsleeves and no tie. All were in the forty to sixty age group, each one a tanned, anonymous-looking Jew. Outside of government circles few people, if any, would have guessed their occupation.

Up above the table the blades of an old and only partly effective fan moved around noisily and reluctantly, a token effort against the heavy summer heat.

The mugginess of the evening did not aid the men's collective testiness at having to meet extra-ordinarily. They did not want to be here, but they had to be. It would be a short meeting, that was for certain.

They had started by expressing regrets over certain events in Cyprus.

Then the Controller of *Sherut Bitachon Klali,* or *Shabak,* the Israeli internal security service, gave a short discourse on the effects of an attack the previous week by Arab terrorists on an apartment block in Nahariya, a town near the Lebanese border. Now the other four men digested the information about the dead and mutilated.

"Are we certain it is the work of Black September?" asked the Controller of the external security services branch (also known under the title of *Mossad*), who was the overall Controller of the other four men.

The Controller of *Aman,* the military intelligence unit, cleared his throat. "I have reports that Hassan had a private meeting with Qadhafi only two days before. You can bet your mother's life that baby Colonel is behind it, either directly or indirectly."

"I see. Any other proof?"

"We do not need proof!" hissed the *Shabak* man stiffly. "Let us hit them as we did last year."

"But not too much," said the sixth man in the room, Chaim Cohen the Deputy Controller of the external security services. "They are planning something big. We have people in place. We need to catch them in the act."

"But their actions cannot go unpunished," argued the *Shabak* man.

"Of course not. But let us not over react."

The overall Controller blew his nose on a large white handkerchief. Then he asked, "Can we agree then on a limited but effective response?"

The *Shabak* man reluctantly nodded, as did the other three.

"Right. I will arrange it. I should have something to report on Wednesday. Thank you, gentlemen. I am sorry to have kept you."

Ψ

Tuesday July 16 1974

"Archbishop Makarios is alive. Following yesterday's rebellion by Greek-backed members of the Cypriot National Guard, it was reported that the Archbishop had been killed in a dawn raid on his palace. In fact he escaped and was taken by RAF helicopter to the British base at Akrotiri on the southern-most tip of the island. Today he was taken by RAF plane to safety in Malta."

Beirut, Lebanon

The yacht docked at Beirut at 12:30. Ramirov and Al Khalifa were on deck to observe the intricate manoeuvring.

It was a hot, musty day in Beirut, not even the slightest breeze from the Mediterranean to take the edge off the heat. The smells of Lebanon rose off the dock to greet the vessel.

Ramirov was dressed in the same clothes as the night before. Al Khalifa was smart, as usual, in a crisp white short-sleeved shirt and cream slacks.

"You are sure you're not known?" asked the Arab as the vessel moved sideways to position itself correctly.

"No, it is all right," said Ramirov. "I have been here on two occasions in the past, both times as a guest of the Palestinian exiles. Why should anyone be worried at my coming?"

"Look at those faces down there. Any one of them could be Israeli."

"And what of it? I have done nothing to interest the *Mossad*. Yet. Worry when worry is due, *amigo*, not before. This is your home territory. I am safe."

"Of course," nodded Al Khalifa, but he wished tonight would come and he would have this foreigner off his hands. He was an organiser and accountant, not a minder.

"Go over it just once more," instructed Ramirov. "The meeting is at nine tonight?"

"Correct. Until then you and Mr Hernandez are requested to remain in the Hotel Phoenicia where separate suites have been reserved for you. I am to stay with you and this evening I will take you to the place."

"In other words, you are to watch me like a hawk."

"That is not in my instructions. You are trusted, surely that is not in doubt? Once the item was in your possession you could have gone anywhere, but you chose to complete the mission. Of that we are grateful and eternally in your debt."

"You are not in my debt. You are indebted to the cause of peace and justice."

"Of course."

"Just one thing…"

"Yes?"

"The English girl, the masseuse. She comes to the hotel with us."

Al Khalifa knew argument would be pointless. "I see."

"You can stay in Mr Hernandez' suite. I am in need of more relaxation."

Moscow, USSR

It was sunny that day in Moscow, but the warm rays hardly penetrated into the courtyard of the Arsenal. It was a chilled Ekaterina Furtseva who pulled up in the black, chauffeur-driven limousine.

At that time the Arsenal was the one-third of the Kremlin

that was totally forbidden to both tourists and most Russians alike. Only the upper echelons of the Soviet hierarchy, their workers and their guards were permitted to enter the area. It consisted of a rectangle of office blocks surrounding a central courtyard. On the third floor of the six-storey eastern building was the room which housed the most powerful caucus in the world at that time: the *Politburo* of the Central Committee of the Soviet Union. Every Thursday the *Politburo* met in the room, and only a very select few (including three transcript secretaries) knew exactly what went on around the huge T-shaped table.

That Tuesday afternoon the room was empty save for one man. He stood at the window, gazing down onto the courtyard below as the limousine pulled up.

Alexei Nikolayevich Kosygin had been Prime Minister of the Soviet Union for ten years. Born in 1904 in St Petersburg, the son of a turner, he had fought with the Red Army in the revolutionary war, but it was not until 1927 that he became a party member. From then it had taken him just eleven years to rise to mayor of his home city, by then called Leningrad. In 1940, aged only 36, he was made Deputy Premier in Stalin's wartime government. Just after the end of the war, further elevation saw Kosygin into the *Politburo* where he shone with his expertise on economics. His career remained dormant during the reign of the peasant Nikita Kruschev, with whom he never saw eye to eye. With the ousting of Kruschev, Kosygin became Premier. His economic brilliance did much to remould the structure of Russia's ailing industry, but he was destined to become the quiet, stern half of the partnership with the showman Brezhnev.

In 1974, the craggy, severe Premier was still a force to be reckoned with, and an unexpected summons from him could make even a hard-faced bitch like Furtseva tremble in her Y-fronts.

Kosygin turned from the window as Furtseva was shown into the room, her shoes - which looked as though they were made of cast-iron - echoing on the floor.

"Comrade Prime Minister," nodded the woman bravely, holding the edge of concern from her voice.

Kosygin nodded. "What are you up to in Cyprus, Comrade Ekaterina?"

"Prime Minister?"

It was not Kosygin's habit to repeat himself, and he did not do so now. He just looked at her.

"The coup was known about," she explained. "We spoke about it. It was not the direct responsibility of my division."

"Of course, of course," he said gruffly. "But there's something else going on, isn't there Comrade? Something you have not told me about." He walked forward to stand on the opposite side of the baize-topped table. He did not ask her to sit down.

"My division has certain... interests in the area, Comrade Prime Minister."

"And you did not see fit to tell me, your Controller? What are they?"

She stared at the iron jowls. "One of my agents is assisting certain middle eastern factions."

"The Palestinians?"

"Among others, Comrade. They are formulating certain plans which necessitated their obtaining a diamond which was in the possession of Makarios. My agent has an assisting brief, and I authorised that he use the coup as the opportunity to obtain it."

Kosygin scowled. "The orders from the *Politburo*, from this office, were that Makarios was to die."

"And according to the reports - "

"The reports are wrong! It has now been confirmed that Makarios is alive and well and with the British." He raised his right fist and brought it crashing down onto the table. "And I have been told by impeccable sources that a certain gentlemen, *unknown to me*, led the attack on him. And yet Makarios is not dead. The instructions from the *Politburo* must never be interfered with, do you understand that *Comrade?*"

"Yes, I - "

"As it is, your man's meddling could have wreaked untold damage. We wanted Makarios out of the way forever. Now he is still around our necks." He turned sharply back towards the window, biting off whatever else he was going to say.

Furtseva remained still and said nothing.

When Kosygin spoke again, his voice had subsided to normal, the hysteria vanquished.

"It is... unfortunate." He turned to face her again, motioning to a chair. "Sit, sit, Comrade, please."

They sat facing each other on opposite sides of the table. The Premier's hands were clenched together, resting on the baize top. Furtseva's hands were in her lap.

"Tell me about this 'secret' agent of yours. What exactly is he doing? What is his brief?"

Furtseva opened her mouth and then closed it again. There was so much she could say to the man. How Ramirov had been her idea, not even known by the head of the KGB. How she had been briefed about the planned activities in Cyprus and had considered it within her discretion to authorise her own man to become involved to his own particular ends without the authority of her Controller. How she had stressed that killing Makarios would be a bonus but the diamond must come first, despite Kosygin's ruling to 'other parties' that Makarios was to die at all costs. How she accepted the kudos for her division's many successes. How she must now accept the responsibility for its interference. How she was getting old...

Instead she told Kosygin in detail what she had outlined in private to certain members of the *Praesidium*, about the Arabs' plan to explode a nuclear device in Britain, and also (garrulous now, hoping to save face) about her future plans for Ilich Ramirov. How it was her intention that he should become a discrete entity in the co-ordination of world terror, with only a tenuous umbilical connecting him to the KGB. How her plan was succeeding and how Ramirov was within a year of permanently adopting the South American cover. How it was hoped that he would have untold successes in, say, the next decade.

At the end of it all, Kosygin was quiet. After a while he nodded. "I see," he did not expand on the comment. Then, rising, he said "All right, Comrade. Thank you. But in the future you are to inform me of all your little escapades in advance. No more discretion. The only initiative in the Soviet Union is taken in this room."

"Yes, Comrade Prime Minister." Furtseva leapt to her feet, snapped to attention and turned away.

"Oh, Comrade Ekaterina?"

"Yes, Comrade Prime Minister?" She turned back, puzzled.

"I wish you continued luck with your Ramirov. *But keep me informed. Always.*"

She almost smiled. "Thank you, Comrade Prime Minister." She turned and left the room.

Kosygin returned to the window. The basic premise was good, he had to give her that. Ekaterina had a brilliant brain for subversion, that was why he had agreed to giving her her own division in the first place. An itinerant agent with an open ticket... And it would be easy enough for him to persuade the *Politburo* that the failed assassination of Makarios was just another example of the extraordinary fortune that surrounded the magical priest.

But Ekaterina Furtseva - was she really now the right person to run such an agent? Should it not be put in the hands of someone younger. Or perhaps, because of its international delicacy, in the hands of only Shelepin himself? Was Furtseva getting too old?

He watched from the window as, three floors below, the woman left the building and climbed back into the limousine.

Was it time she was retired?

Beirut, Lebanon

The same members of Black September met in the safe house near Sidani Street that night as had met there the previous January, when Michael Mahoney's request for the diamond had been revealed to them by Al Khalifa: Ali Hassan Salameh, controller of the intelligence and action arm; Abu Ayad, the IRA liaison man; the man from the Fateh intelligence agency, Jihaz-al-Razd; and Hassan's quiet personal assistant, Faisal Ibn Musaed.

They met at 20:30, for they had other matters to discuss before the arrival of Martinez and the diamond at 21:00.

As it happened, Al Khalifa, Ramirov and Sergei were to be late that evening. That afternoon, after two hours of sex and massage in the sumptuous suite in the Hotel Phoenicia with the delectable, wanton and genuinely red-haired Melanie, Ramirov had foolishly (for he was usually so careful about everything) ordered oysters from Room Service. A dozen prime, and incredibly expensive, specimens had been promptly delivered, and Ramirov had swallowed his way through seven of them.

About thirty minutes later the stomach cramps had begun, and he had spent the rest of the time in self-incarceration in the bathroom, defecating. It was a final ten minute shit that had delayed the three men leaving the hotel that evening. Had it not been for the oysters, Ramirov would have delivered the diamond and been away before the major events of that night took place. But fate, God, chance, call it what you will, had decreed differently.

It was 21:15 before the three men arrived at the house, by which time the nervous Abu Ayad was extremely worried. He still harboured the feeling that to return to Beirut after the massacre of his brothers last year was folly of the highest order. However Hassan, as overall leader on these matters, had overruled him.

The five members of Black September were waiting patiently when Al Khalifa entered, accompanied by Martinez and followed by Sergei Hernandez. They all rose in welcome to much scraping of chairs.

"My friend, my dear, dear friend! My brother!" effused Hassan, swallowing a candy and gripping Ramirov in a tight embrace. "Welcome, it is good to see you again. And congratulations! I hear the coup in Cyprus has been one hundred per cent successful." He nodded greeting at Sergei, who remained by the door. "The island is rid of the devil priest at last. But there are rumours, you know, that he is not dead. Sit down, please, sit down. Faisal!"

Musaed pulled out a chair next to Hassan and on the opposite side of the table to where he himself was sitting.

"But still," continued Hassan, "that is not our concern, is it?" He took another sweet from the candy bowl on the table.

"He is dead," assured Ramirov. "I saw his back explode with my own eyes. And," he removed what looked like a chunk of glass from the breast pocket of his shirt, "I took this from his corpse." The diamond was placed on the table in front of Hassan.

The Arabs looked at it in awe. The room was still, no man daring to move or speak, as if paralysed by some force emitting from the rock.

Then Abu Ayad picked it up. "It does not look much," he sniffed. "Can this really be worth two million pounds?"

Ramirov inclined his head and gave a false smile of respect.

He kept the intolerance from his voice. "That is The Star of Sierra Leone, otherwise known as The Eye of Makarios. It is an uncut rough diamond, that is why it does not sparkle. That," he nodded at the stone, "is a piece if natural magnificence."

Abu Ayad replaced the piece of natural magnificence on the table.

From the corner of his eye, Ramirov noted that Faisal Ibn Musaed was staring at the stone in a curious, trance-like manner. Still, the peccadilloes of the Arabs were no longer his business. His task was completed.

"Well gentlemen," he said chirpily, "my task is complete." He made movements to rise. "I would advise you not to hang on to the diamond for too long. But, as always, that is your business. Your plan is progressing?"

"We have not heard from the supplier for a time," commented Al Khalifa. "But then, neither has he heard from us. I must chase him."

"Just take care of the stone," Ramirov flashed another insincere smile, "there is no other like it. Now, I must leave." He rose and Sergei came over to join him.

"Both so soon?" frowned Hassan amicably. "You will not join us in celebration? We know a place where there is good food... and good women..."

"You are kind," again the inclination of the head. "But I must refuse." His bowels twitched ominously and he had a silent breaking of wind. "I have an urgent engagement."

"Whatever you say, my brother," Hassan rose and clapped him on the shoulders. "How can we ever thank you? The Palestinian people will be forever in your debt."

"Just win, my brother," said Ramirov and meant it. "Just win your fight."

"Oh, we will, we will. It may take some time, but the Zionist war machine - "

It was at that moment that the attack started.

Ψ

The first blast of gunfire echoed from downstairs and, although the men in the room did not know it, the first two of their six bodyguards were already dead. The guard on duty immediately outside the door began firing as he screamed hysterically *"Israelis, Israelis!"*

They all jumped to their feet. "Bastards!" screeched Abu Ayad.

Ramirov and Sergei had guns in their hands.

"The window, quickly!" instructed Hassan.

It opened out onto the back of the building, and there was a drop of four metres to the roof of the extended ground floor, then a further drop of an equal distance to the ground.

"Hurry, hurry!" snapped Hassan. "Quickly!"

Ramirov grabbed the stone and replaced it in his pocket, knocking the candy bowl over. "I have the diamond!" *Damn* this intrusion!

The roar of gunfire from the stairway was deafening. From a building nearby, a woman screamed.

Musaed was the first through the window, quickly followed by Abu Ayad, the intelligence man, Abu Jihad and Al Khalifa. All landed safely on the roof and scrambled down to the ground. Swiftly they dispersed into varying, pre-planned directions.

Up in the room, Hassan stood by the window ushering Ramirov and Sergei through. The firing was louder, and a torrent of Arabic and Hebrew obscenities could be heard through the din. The stench of cordite swept its way into the already stinking room.

As the two foreigners jumped, Hassan pulled a set of keys from his pocket and leapt over to a small, triple-locked cupboard set into the wall. He swore as he dropped the keys, picked them up, and then opened the door. His hand darted inside and emerged with a cold, pineapple-shaped object. He slipped back to the window, swung one leg over the sill and waited.

The door of the room started to splinter as the final guard outside lost his battle.

Hassan pulled the pin from the grenade with his teeth, and threw it as the door slammed inwards. He jumped into the darkness as the room exploded behind him. *[One member of the four-man Israeli hit team died in the explosion and another died of his injuries back in Israel two days later.]*

As he slid over the ground floor roof and down onto the ground, Hassan saw the foreigner in the shadows bending over the wriggling figure of his gaunt companion. The man's left leg was twisted at an hideous angle. Hassan bent over and rasped into the foreigner's ear "Rome. We will contact." And then he was up and away.

The room upstairs was now burning, but that did not prevent a shot being fired into the shadows near where Ramirov crouched. His left hand was pushed tightly over Sergei's mouth, and he looked straight into his comrade's agonised eyes. Both of them knew what had to be done.

Ramirov positioned his gun pointing upwards behind the left ear. He fired once, the sound muted by the hair and skull. With a final twitch, Sergei was still, the agonised eyes still starting at Ramirov, all life extinguished.

Ramirov did not dally. Quickly feeling to ensure that the diamond was safe, he moved away, blended with the shadows, and was gone.

Ψ

Friday July 19 1974

"General Franco has stood down as Spain's head of state. The health of the general, who is eighty-one, has recently been deteriorating. The heir to the vacant Spanish throne, Prince Juan Carlos, who is thirty-six, is taking over as provisional head of state."

London, England

Pandemonium. Or possibly mayhem. Or turmoil. Whatever it was, it was happening in the S(O)D 1 suite in Queen Anne's Mansions that morning. When Detective Inspector 'Mr' Ramm entered through the main door at 10:00, it was a fact that not one member of the staff was sitting down or even in a stationary position. Papers rustled as if a window had been left open, telephones rang, the drawers of filing cabinets banged incessantly, and bodies flitted in all directions.

"Bloody hell!" murmured Ramm to himself. He intercepted a passing WDC. "What's up, Roz?"

"A biggun." She hurried on.

He didn't know whether it was a comment on the state of affairs or a dream of her boyfriend.

"Boss in?" he shouted into the air.

"Yeh," came an unidentified voice from beneath a mountain of paper.

Ramm passed through the two general offices, knocked on Metcalf's door and entered. At least the Boss was sitting down, but he was talking excitedly to someone on the telephone. His free hand came up from beneath his desk, where it had been comforting his willie, and motioned Ramm to sit down.

"Yes... yes, sir. Right away. Any staff? Right." Metcalf replaced the receiver. "By crikey!" he blew out imaginary steam.

"Something up, Mr Metcalf?"

"Makarios. Sir Robert's ordered additional protection. Apparently there've been threats to get him while he's here. An iron curtain has been ordered around him. He's not even gonna be allowed to pick his nose without us looking up there first. And because of shortage of men, I'm to co-ordinate it."

"You, sir?" It was not meant to be rude and it was not taken as such.

"Right. So I'm just having a swift run-through of our current workload before I nip across to the Yard. I'll be working from there."

"Who - ?"

"Mr Woods will take over here. Where is he, by the way? Shouldn't take more than a few days until all the fuss dies down. Sooner we get Makarios out of Britain the better. Still, we've got our obligations, I suppose." He fiddled with some papers.

"Mr Woods is out on reccy. Actually, that's why I came - "

"I'll call him. What's the state of play on your jobs?" A sandwich appeared from a drawer and was crammed into Metcalf's mouth. His left hand reached for the mug of steaming tea on his desk.

Ramm briefed him on this three current assignments: a certain embassy using the diplomatic bag to import nasties, a junior government minister's unusual sexual proclivities, and Egginton.

"It's Egginton I've come to see you about, sir."

Metcalf grunted through a piece of fruit cake.

"We've come up with nothing. Certainly he's been taking the booze, lunchtimes and evenings. But he's able to handle it. No question of a security risk. He's been working on some hush-hush job for the Minister. Been up north a lot at the nuclear place. We can't make out what's causing the drinking. The only thing is that his wife has a chronic heart condition, and his daughter's got a wedding coming up. Maybe he's just anxious."

Ramm thought he translated Metcalf's words as "Want to call it off?" but they got caught in a mouthful of apple.

"There seems to be nothing," said Ramm. "However, I want to be safe than sorry. I want your permission to tap his phones. You said it probably wasn't worthwhile before."

A young member of the civilian clerical support staff entered, handed a buff file to Metcalf, nodded to Ramm and withdrew. Metcalf studied the front of the file, frowned, and then looked back at Ramm, distinctly preoccupied.

"Er… you think a tap'll reveal something?"

"No, sir. No, not at all. But we want to be sure."

"Hmm… " Metcalf was thinking more about the file than the Inspector's request. Then he said, "Yes, yes okay."

"Thank you, sir." Ramm rose to leave.

"Oh, Matthew?"

"Sir?"

The applecore sailed through the air, bounced off the edge of the wastebin with a dong and flew off across the room.

"Don't forget, this is all over the OBN. Unofficial. Five or Six not to be involved. Why cast doubts on the poor sod when it looks like there's nothing there? Home phone only."

Bugger it, thought Ramm. Out loud he said, "Yes, sir."

But Metcalf already had his nose deep in the intrusive file.

Ψ

Wednesday July 31 1974

"Watergate. President Nixon's former chief adviser, Mr John Ehrlichmann, has been sentenced to twenty months to five years imprisonment for his part in the break-in at the office of Mr Daniel Ellsberg's psychiatrist. In France, the prison riots continue and the death toll has now reached seven."

London, England

Colonel Egginton was depressed that morning. In fact, he had been descending into such a state for the past month. In his guise of working on a hush-hush review for the Minister (a guise which no one had thought to check), he had visited Windscale Works twice for informal meetings and checks on security, and had also had three meetings here in his office in Soho Square.

Security was first class at the place. There was no way, simply no way, that any fork from the canteen could go missing, let alone any plutonium. Not one hardly-radioactive ounce of it, let alone twelve pounds. Short of hiring a battalion of mercenaries to raid the place, there was no way he could get in.

And Windscale was his only hope. He was not sufficiently known at any of the other British nuclear establishments to start even the most initial of enquiries without attracting unwanted attention to himself.

He could have gotten Mahoney any armoury he wanted. Absolutely anything. He had done so in the past. But plutonium was out of the question. Mahoney was asking the impossible.

So what could he do? If he could not come up with the stuff, Mahoney would send the incriminating photographs to Margery (and he would, of that Egginton was sure). And that would kill her.

He was at a loss. Mahoney had given him three months on May 16th. That meant that in just fifteen days time the evil Irishman would be in contact again. And it seemed to Egginton that he was helpless. All he could do was sit and wait. Thursday August 15 1974 was to be his day of reckoning.

Egginton took his pipe out of his mouth and gently laid it against the ashtray. Then he pressed a button on the intercom and instructed his secretary that he would be engaged to callers until lunchtime.

He leant back in his chair, arms lifelessly dangling towards the floor, and stared at the opposite wall. His eyes became vacant and his mouth opened just a fraction. His mind switched off.

Slowly, a dribble of snot ran from his nose and settled on his upper lip...

Ψ

Monday August 5 1974

"No one has yet claimed responsibility for the bomb which killed twelve people and injured forty-eight others aboard the Rome-Munich Express yesterday. It exploded as the train passed through a tunnel in the Apennines, thirty miles south of Bologna."

Paris, France

Charlotte Rapley and Louise were in bed together and sleeping when the doorbell rang at 04:00. Neither woman heard it the first time, but Louise began to surface after the second ring, suddenly snapping into consciousness when her brain realised that the ringing had become continuous.

With great difficulty she awoke Charlie who, swearing, dragged herself from the bed and pulled on a robe. They fumbled in the dark, reaching the front door before putting any light on.

"Okay, okay, who the shit is it?" shouted Charlie. "Key est eel? Take yer finger off the goddamn bell!"

"Charlie?" The voice from outside was weak and distant. "Please let me in."

"*Sally?*"

Bolts withdrawn and dead-locks undone, the door was hurriedly opened. Charlie stood staring at her fellow-American, not believing what she saw. "Oh shit."

"*Sacré Maria!*" gasped Louise. "*Ma chère Sally, entrez, entrez!*"

Sally-Anne Bowker was dressed in torn denims and a filthy

white T-shirt made of the thinnest material. Her nipples showed through the shirt without any concealment. Her hair was untidy, and there was dirt on her face mingled with what could possibly be blood.

"I - I'm sorry for wakening you, the *concièrge* let me in," she said emptily.

"For shit sake, don't worry about that," said Charlie. "C'mon inside, honey, c'mon."

Sally was ushered into the lounge. Sitting down on the couch, she at once began to cry, heavily and uncontrollably.

The two other women let it come, not saying anything, not even touching her in consolation for whatever grief had caused the tears. Look at the state of her, poor kid, she looked… as if she had been through a war.

It took five minutes for Sally to take control of herself, and she readily accepted a large brandy offered by Charlie. Louise had gone into the kitchen to prepare a pot of strong, sweet black coffee.

Sally dabbed her eyes with a tissue donated by the older woman. "Oh, I'm sorry. Whatever must you think of me? I'm sorry to get you up like this, but…" Her face creased and she almost started again, but instead she leant forward and put her head in her hands. Charlie's face was creased with anxiety but she said nothing.

They stayed like that until Louise reappeared with the coffee. "*Ici ma petite*, drink zis, it will do you good."

Sally accepted the hot mug and cringed as the liquid burnt her lips. Charlie came over and sat next to her. "It's all right now, baby, you're with friends." She put her arm around her, but it was roughly shrugged off.

Immediately Sally regretted her brusqueness. "Oh, I'm sorry Charlie, I'm sorry, really I am. Whatever must you think? It's just… I… I can't be touched. Not at the moment."

"I understand honey." Then: "You want to talk about it? Or

do you want to get some sleep? We can talk in the morning if you like."

"No! No, I'd rather talk now. You deserve an explanation, of course. I - I don't know where to begin..."

"Don't rush it, hon. In your own time."

"Try some *café*," suggested the French girl. "You would like *crème*, per'aps?"

"No, no this is fine," she made an attempt at a smile.

A minute later she took a deep breath and said, "I didn't find him."

Charlie gave a resigned nod, as if she had known it all along. She tried consolation. "Aw, gee, that's nothing to get yourself so upset about, sweetheart. At least you got back. We were worried when we heard of the trouble out there."

"It - it's not that. I didn't find Steve, but there really wasn't much chance that I would - oh God, you just don't know... When the fighting began, I - I was in the capital, Nicosia. My first morning. I saw the army vehicles speeding through the streets, even thought I saw Steve in one of them, wasn't that crazy? I wondered what was happening... " She sipped the coffee. "There was panic. I tried to find somewhere to go, in case shooting started in the streets... I don't know, somehow I managed to get back to my hotel. They advised me to pack up and leave immediately, all the rest of the tourists were going and some of the residents. There was a coach leaving for Limassol, where the British are. I went up to get my bag, which I hadn't even unpacked, but by the time I got back downstairs the coach was gone. There wouldn't be another one. They said it was everyone for themselves. I didn't know what to do... so I just stayed there." She stopped, the fact of remembering painful. So, so painful. Steve, where are you?

"The next day things seemed to be getting back to normal. I heard rumours that President Makarios had been killed. There were a few other tourists left in the hotel the same as me. We got together and began to help out in the kitchen. Only some of the staff were left, the others had fled. There was a sort of... camaraderie, all helping together, you know? Well, there was nothing we could do, all transport was at a standstill. It was reported that the British were coming, but they never did. I heard they had reached southern Nicosia, but I was in the north.

"And then... a few days later, we heard that the *Turkish* army was coming... That same night a group of men raided the hotel – I don't know who they were or what they wanted – they just seemed to want trouble... to hurt, to steal... One old man, I think he was Dutch, was hit across the head with a pan full of hot oil. They... they killed him with it, just hitting and hitting him...

"And then... three of them... they grabbed hold of me... there, right there on the kitchen floor, and they... they fucked me. They just pulled my denims off and... did it... one after the other... Then some others came and... while one was doing it, another ripped off my shirt, and when they saw my scars, they... they started to laugh and spit at me and call me names, said I was a freak... and then they started to punch me and kick me... and then something wet started to splash on my tummy and I opened my eyes and one of them was... was pissing on me... oh God... " The tears came again, and they fell without interruption. Louise was crying openly too, and Charlie fought a losing battle with her twitching lips.

A while later, with half the mug of coffee inside her, Sally continued her story. "I - I passed out, at least I think I did. I can't recollect anything happening. I remember walking... buildings either side of me... then no buildings... and then I was in a truck with some other people, mostly Greeks I think, and then a soldier and a guy in a white coat were helping me out... I don't know...

"Anyway, I found out later that I had been picked up by the British in southern Nicosia. They said I was lucky as I was in the last truck out before the Turkish army arrived. We were all taken to the British base at Akrotiri. They guessed what had happened to me - I don't think I was able to speak right then - and I was hospitalised and given a good clean-out inside. I think I stayed there for two or three days. But they said they were evacuating and there was a place reserved for me on one of their air force planes. They told me after that I was in shock and couldn't walk at this time.

"Well, they took me to Malta, and I was in hospital there until last week. Then they offered me a flight to some air force base in England, and I accepted.

"They'd washed my denims and T-shirt for me and, so they said, found a hundred dollars folded inside a back pocket - really I think they were just being kind. They gave me some sort of identity card, said they weren't supposed to as I wasn't British, but they thought it would stop any problems on arrival. Anyway, we landed in a base in... Wiltshire, I think it was called? No problems. And they fed me and gave me a warrant to get a train to London and precise directions on how to get to our embassy.

"I went to London, but didn't go to the embassy. I used the hundred dollars to come here. There was some blockade on at Calais, a strike or something, and we were delayed for five hours, that's why I'm here only now. The train arrived an hour ago. It's too late for the metro, so I walked from the *Gare du Nord*." She sighed and downed the rest of her coffee.

Really there was nothing Charlie or Louise could say. Words or sympathetic clucking would have been superfluous. Charlie lit her third *Peter Stuyvesant* and stared into the exhaled smoke. Louise dabbed a moist eye.

It was Sally who broke the silence after five minutes. "So here I am." A little laugh, totally devoid of mirth, jumped from her lips. She was aware of the French girl frowning at her.

"But your clothes, your face, the condition," said Louise.

"Somsing must 'ave 'appened after they were washed."

Sally looked down at the torn jeans and filthy T-shirt. She laughed again, pathetically. "This? *This?* I was looking up at your window and I fell up the kerb outside here. Can you believe it?"

Again silence.

Then Charlie rasped "SHIT!" forcefully.

Ψ

Wednesday August 14 1974

"As a reaction against further Turkish military incursions into Cyprus, the new Greek Prime Minister, Mr Constantine Karamanlis, today announced the withdrawal of all Greek armed forces from NATO, and he has threatened to take suitable measures against what he calls 'The Turkish menace to world peace'."

Crowthorne, Berkshire, England

Stanley William Egginton stayed up until all hours that night in a state of total anxiety. He had kissed Madge goodnight at 22:30 and had then retired to his study in a final vain attempt to think something out. By midnight he was quite despondent.

To beg, borrow, steal, hijack or even buy twelve pounds of plutonium in Britain was just impossible. Security in this country was watertight. Two days ago he had made yet another visit to Windscale, and he had even made a half-hearted attempt to offer a couple of employees a bribe (which, when refused, had been passed off as a security test). Then, to top everything, when he arrived back at his office yesterday morning, he had been telephoned by the Head of Accounts over in Shell Mex House. His frequent trips to Windscale had been noticed and he was asked for an explanation. Being in charge of defence sales security, he had managed to fob the fellow off with some extemporaneous story which he had even by now forgotten.

So, it was not on.

And tomorrow the Irishman would call.

And it would be the end. The photographs would be sent to Madge, and it would kill her. Or if not, it would at least mean the end of their thirty-year marriage. How could thirty years be shattered just like that by some stinking, blackmailing, conniving Paddy bastard?

By the time the clock dragged round to 01:00, Egginton's mood had changed. As usual with over-stress and over-anxiety, his mood had swung from one of concern through deep depression to sublime insouciance. He had realised, quite suddenly, that there was nothing he *could* do. The Irishman would just have to do his worst. To hell with him.

Even this realisation gave the Colonel great relief, and he decided that it was now time to go to bed. At least he could catch six hours sleep before the moment of reckoning.

With the Irishman still in his mind and another "To hell with him" on his lips, Egginton turned out the study light and left the room, closing the door softly behind him. Then he froze in his tracks. My God, *why hadn't he thought of it before?*

Quickly going back into the study and closing the door, Egginton switched the light back on and nipped over to his antique mahogany bureau which held all his paraphernalia. *It had completely slipped his mind!* He unlocked one of the four drawers and pulled it out nearly to its limit. With his right hand, he rummaged in the back. Ah! There it was.

He pulled out a plastic bag wrapped tightly around something and secured with sticky tape. Mumbling to himself, he ripped the plastic off the greasy old *Colt .455* automatic, a keepsake (unlicensed) from his field activities in the fifties.

He examined the gun and decided that it was in good working order, the grease and the plastic had preserved it well. Now, somewhere in the back of this drawer was an old box of ammo… yes, there it was.

Egginton wiped off the surplus grease with a tissue and

slipped the safety catch off the gun. He practised firing at a picture of his old regiment on the wall. The gun clicked ominously as the pin fell on the empty barrel.

Satisfied, he loaded the maximum seven rounds into the magazine, replaced the box of ammunition and closed the drawer. Always tidy, he picked up the torn plastic and screwed-up tissue and put them into his waste bin. The daily would see to it in the morning.

Placing the gun in his jacket pocket, Stanley William Egginton, a much happier man, left the study once again and went up to bed.

For some incongruous reason, his mind took that moment to remind him to ring the Post Office in the morning. There was something wrong with his phone. For about a month now there had been a click on the line every time he picked it up. And when he spoke down it he could hear a strange hollow echo...

Ψ

Thursday August 15 1974

"Today is Princess Anne's twenty-fourth birthday, and it has been announced from Buckingham Palace that the Princess has been made a Dame Grand Cross of the Royal Victorian Order for her 'calm and brave behaviour' during the attempt to kidnap her in March. Her husband, Captain Phillips, has also been admitted to the same order for his 'excellent conduct' during the same incident."

London, England

Michael Mahoney telephoned Colonel Egginton at his office promptly at 10:00 that morning. Perhaps the jauntiness, the actual eagerness in Egginton's voice should have warned him, but Mahoney thought it was because the stuff was available as required. An appointment for 12:30 was arranged, and Egginton turned up five minutes ahead of time, tapping on the side window of the brown Cortina parked at a meter in Greek Street.

Mahoney let him in and he could sense at once that the Colonel was different. "You seem happy today Colonel, good news is it?"

"Get driving," ordered the older man peremptorily. Mahoney raised an eyebrow but made no comment.

"Where to?"

"How about… let me see… Hyde Park. Yes, that will be an ideal place. Nice day for a trip to the park, don't you think?"

"Okay, here he comes." Mr Ramm nodded towards Stuart

House, just a little to the south of where they were parked in Soho Square.

"Wonder what pub it'll be today?" mused Mr Woods dryly as he threw his half-finished cigarette out of the open side window.

Ramm sniggered. "Last day, guv. Might as well make the most of it. I've been doing this on my jack for the last four weeks while you were made up." He gunned the white, unmarked Rover 2000 into life. "You on foot? You've got a nice day for it."

"Bloody well suppose so." Woods climbed out. "Keep in sight."

He sauntered past the front of Stuart House and fell into a deceptively casual stroll some twenty metres behind Egginton. What with being in charge of S(O)D 1 these past weeks in Metcalf's absence, this was the first chance Woods had had to 'meet' the Colonel in the flesh. Egginton was more jauntier than Woods imagined he would be, and the heavy drinking had not taken one iota of toll. Looked like S(O)D 1 was on a fool's errand, just as they had expected all along.

Egginton disappeared round the sharp corner into Greek Street. No rush, thought Woods; all his drinking emporia were within five minutes of the office.

By the time Woods reached the corner, Egginton was just climbing into a brown Cortina a little way down the road. There was somebody at the wheel, but Woods could not clarify any descriptive features. It looked like a man.

Bloody hell! He turned back and signalled frantically to Ramm. The white Rover had only just pulled away from the kerb , but when Ramm saw his partner turn back he shot out into the traffic, thundered down the road, and pulled up sharply by the corner.

"He's bloody got into a car!" Woods jumped in.

"He's *what*? Which?"

"Brown Cortina."

Ramm frowned, focussed on the vehicle now at the far end of the street, and sped off after it.

"Anybody in it?"

"Someone. Couldn't see. Male."

They saw the Cortina turn right, heading south on Shaftesbury Avenue.

"Get the number?"

"No." Woods could feel the unspoken criticism. "For Christ's sake, it was all too sudden. *You* didn't expect him to get into a car, did you?"

"No, sir."

"Thought he was going to the pub as always, didn't we?"

"Yes, sir."

They arrived at the junction with Shaftesbury Avenue. The traffic was heavy and there seemed to be an inordinate number of taxis about. Ramm nudged the Rover out and to the right, to the background of a complaining cacophony of horns.

"Don't make yourself too conspicuous. Where is the bugger? Ah, there." Woods pointed unnecessarily ahead. The Cortina was just passing the Queen's Theatre, heading towards Piccadilly Circus. There was a group of four taxis between hunter and hunted.

"This is a turn-up for the books," continued Woods. "I wonder where he's going. And who *is* that driving?"

"Could be just an MOD driver," suggested Ramm. "If we had the number…"

"If those buggering taxis would get out of the way we could see the bloody number!"

The Cortina made the then compulsory left turn into the Piccadilly one-way system in front of the Eros statue, heading down the Haymarket.

The four taxis turned, followed by the white Rover.

"C'mon, c'mon," mumbled Woods impatiently.

Then, outside the London Pavilion cinema, the taxis stopped. Right there in the street, two abreast, completely halting the flow of traffic.

"What the hell - ?" Ramm slammed on the brakes. No sooner had he done so than another black machine pulled up to their left.

"Christ!" shouted Woods. "I don't believe it!"

Both policemen turned around in their seats. More taxis and a couple of other vehicles had stopped behind them, completely pinning them against the railings of the Eros island.

Ramm banged on the horn irascibly. The vehicles in front did not move even though the road was clear ahead of them. People were beginning to look.

Woods had his head out of the window. "Move you bastards, move!"

A friendly, lived-in face rolled down the window of the cab next to them. "They can't, mate."

"What?"

"They can't. This is a cabbie stoppage - in protest over Wilson's refusal to raise our rates."

"It's *what?*"

"You won't get out of here until three o'clock," chuckled the cabbie.

"What?"

"Might as well sit back and relax, mate."

"But we're police officers!"

"Good! Per'aps you can put in a good word for us with the PM."

"I demand - !"

"Our Association advised the Yard this morning. Didn't they tell yer?" He stretched out his right arm. "Wanna Polo mint?"

Woods looked at him aghast and then turned back to Ramm. The Detective Inspector was staring resignedly ahead. He did not look at Woods as he spoke. "He's clean anyway. It might have been an official trip - you know he's been travelling all about the country recently. Or it could have been just a friend. We'll pick him up back at the office this afternoon... after three o'clock."

"Sure," fumed Woods. "Sure."

"If only they'd've let us tap his work phone..." mused Ramm.

A moment later, Woods leaned back out of the window and shouted at the top of his voice, "Fuck your bloody Polo mint!"

Mahoney became more and more bemused by the Englishman as they drove west through sunny Piccadilly, unaware of the stoppage behind them. Around Hyde Park Corner and into the park. Egginton matched the Irishman's usual patter, but he was not to be drawn on the subject of the plutonium.

It was not until they were on the main road by the Serpentine that the Colonel suggested they pull over. Mahoney did so with alacrity.

Mahoney shifted into neutral and turned off the engine. "Now, me ole Colonel, yer hoigh spirits must mean yer have good news."

Egginton shifted so that he was facing Mahoney, his back against the door. He beamed.

"Oh, I have good news all right, but not for you, you stinking Irish bastard."

Mahoney frowned. There was something not right about the Colonel's eyes, something that told him this time it was no joke. "What?"

"The news is splendid, you blackmailing lump of crap. Shall I tell you what it is?" Egginton's left hand went into his jacket pocket. "The news is that I don't have your plutonium. Not one single fucking ounce of it. And I am so, so pleased."

Mahoney's face was stone and he was tensed in caution, his eyes riveted on the other man. He spoke softly and with deep menace. "Well, you know what this means Colonel."

"The pictures you mean?" grinned Egginton. "You know what you can do with them. I don't give a damn. To hell with the pictures. And," he said calmly, "to hell with you." His hand came out of the pocket with the pistol. It was pointing straight at the Irishman.

Mahoney shrank back in his seat, his hand reaching for the door handle. "You fool. I should have guessed something like this. You mad English prick." Beads of perspiration broke out on his brow. "You'll never get away with it, you know. Yer might kill me, but you'll have a lot of talkin' to do. D' yer think oi haven't left a letter in case I die under mysterious circumstances? It'll all come out and you'll be finished."

"Oh shut up - *and take your hand away from that door!* Mahoney, I am sick, sick, sick of hearing your haunting bloody voice. I have had enough of it, do you hear? Enough!"

Mahoney said nothing.

"Now, where are the rest of the pictures?"

The Irishman swallowed, freely perspiring now. "I - I don't have them on me."

"No, no you wouldn't, you little runt. Well, never mind. I just wanted to see what they were like, that was all. It doesn't matter."

"Perhaps we could still do a deal, Colonel? The photos *and* you keep the two thousand you already have."

"Shut up! The time has come, runt. You will never blackmail me again." His finger tightened on the trigger.

"Now Colonel, wait, please..."

"There's no more to say."

"Stan - !"

"Irish bastard!"

"Colonel - !"

Egginton raised the gun, by-passed Mahoney and, turning his wrist, pointed the gun into his own mouth. He fired once, up into his brain, and slumped…

Mahoney sat there staring, mouth open, lips quivering. He tried to move or say something to the corpse, but only animal grunts came out of his mouth. His bowels moved violently and the immediately rising smell told him he had shit himself.

"B… b… but… "

Tiny rivulets of blood trickled from Egginton's nose, and with a thud the gun slid from the dead fingers onto the floor. The head slipped a few centimetres, and Mahoney could see brain, light and pink, smeared on the window.

But…

Then there was a scream. A loud, piercing scream which shocked Mahoney back to his senses. Outside, a woman with a pram was staring into Egginton's side of the car and pointing.

"Oh Jesus, Mary and Joseph!" Mahoney was out of the vehicle in a flash and running. A voice from somewhere shouted "Hey, you, stop!" but stop was the last thing he was going to do. He ran and ran and ran…

Back by the car, the woman with the pram had been joined by other people, mostly office workers out sunning themselves in the lunch-hour. More than one lunch was brought up by the side of the road before the police arrived to clear the area. One lunch, regrettably, even ended up spewed into the baby's pram. The child, who was happily playing with teddy, could not have cared less, and it splashed merrily amongst the diced carrots and tomato skins…

The irony of it all was that Mahoney had no other negatives or photographs. His collection of eight had been accidentally destroyed back home about a year before. Only one photograph and its matching negative had survived, and that was the one he had already given to Egginton with the two thousand pounds.

Ψ

Wednesday September 11 1974

"In trouble-torn Ethiopia, Princess Tenagne-Work, only surviving daughter of the now virtually powerless Emperor Hailé Selassié, has been arrested. Today is the country's New Year's Day."

Somewhere in the Irish Republic

With Egginton's suicide, the worry, concern and anxiety shifted like an evil spirit from the body of the Colonel into the soul of Michael Mahoney. The Colonel's death had been widely reported in the newspapers on the first day, with wild speculations about the identity of the man seen running away. Then it had died the death of most newspaper stories. An inquest had been opened and adjourned indefinitely.

After fleeing from the car, Mahoney had travelled immediately to Heathrow Airport by the most inconspicuous route: underground from Hyde Park Corner to Hounslow West and then express bus *[The Underground link to Heathrow was not yet open in 1974. The* Heathrow Express *overground rail link was nearly a quarter of a century away]*. Just three hours after the incident in the park and before the body had even been moved by the police, he was landing at Dublin Airport. His Mini-Cooper awaited him in the long-term car park, and by early evening he was back home in his mansion, somewhere in the south.

His worries had started on the plane after the anaesthesia of the initial shock had worn off. He could not be connected to

Egginton's death, of course, he was too careful for that. The car had been hired under the name of Christopher Whelan, and his travelling alias for this trip had been Thomas Doherty. His fingerprints were not on any police file, so he was clear there.

No, the source of his worry was the Arabs. They would very soon want him to produce the goods, the infernal twelve pounds of plutonium, and there was no way he was going to be able to do so. He had been so sure Egginton would supply him. And, although the Arabs understood that sometimes there had to be failure (not like some of his other customers), they would not forgive him on this one, they had too much at stake - especially as they were probably going to a lot of trouble to get that diamond for him. Mind you, he had not heard from them for nine months: was it too much to hope that their plan had been abandoned?

Black September had not forgotten. That Wednesday morning the telegram arrived for him. Al Khalifa would be arriving at Dublin the following Saturday; transport would, of course, be waiting for him?

Throughout that Wednesday afternoon Mahoney tried to lose himself in the soft, delectable body of Lizzie O'Toole, who had now moved into his mansion permanently. But he just couldn't get business out of his mind, and he knew that he did not perform well (although the girl did not complain).

Then, at 18:00 that evening, whilst swilling poteen in his office, it came to him like a bolt from heaven.

Glory t' Jaysus, Moichal, he thought, *yer nothin' if not Oirish!* Why hadn't he thought of it before? It was really the only course open to him, if he did not want to be immediately exterminated. *He would bluff it out.* Take it all the way and see what happened. If it came off, it would be the biggest ever con trick played on the Arabs. And if it didn't...

He had nothing to lose but his life.

Ψ

Friday September 13 1974

"A bomb exploded in a restaurant in Madrid earlier today, killing at least twelve people and wounding forty more. No one has yet claimed responsibility."

Frascati, Italy

It had been nearly two months since the affair in Beirut, but Ilich Ramirov had not been idle. The diamond had been deposited in a sealed package in a bank on Rome's Via del Corso, and from his house in Frascati, fifteen kilometres south of the city, Ramirov had spent his time organising certain other matters. That very morning he had had to leave Madrid in something of a hurry.

It was waiting for him when he arrived back at his house. Posted in London six days before, the envelope contained a small piece of sepia paper with just three typewritten words:

MILANO. GCONTINENTAL. 2MARDI.

The meeting was to take place at the Grand Continental Hotel in Milan on the Tuesday of this month whose date fell in the twenties. Ramirov consulted a small pocket book. That would make it 24th, eleven days hence.

Right, he had a few other things to settle and then he had to pay a visit to his bank manager to reclaim a very special package. Then he would drive to Milan to enjoy a few relaxing days seeing the sights (hopefully there would be a race meeting on), with perhaps one or more of Milan's prostitutes for carnal company, before getting down to business again on Tuesday 24th...

Ψ

Saturday September 14 1974

"The three members of the Japanese Red Army terrorist organisation who yesterday took Count Jacques Senard, the French Ambassador to Holland, and ten others prisoner in an attack on the Ambassador's office in The Hague, have now made their demands known. They are asking for the release of a member of their group who is held in a Paris jail."

Somewhere in the Irish Republic

"Akay, my dear, dear friend!" Michael Mahoney rushed from the front door of his mansion as the Arab stepped out of the chauffeur-driven Rolls-Royce. "How are yer? Goodness, yer lookin' well!"

All the charm was there, and the empressement sickened Al Khalifa, but he smiled pleasantly. "Michael, how are you? It gives me pleasure to see you again."

"Indeed it should," winked the Irishman, "indeed it should. Come insoide, come insoide. Fitzgerald'll take yer bag. Did yer have a pleasant flight? Weather's still very warm for mid-September, isn't it? What's it like in your country?" These and other banalities poured from Mahoney's lips as he led the way to his office.

Mahoney plonked himself behind his large mahogany desk and produced the ubiquitous half-drunk bottle of poteen. He also switched on the hidden tape recorder.

Al Khalifa sat down in the gigantic maroon leather armchair

in front of the desk.

A shot of the whiskey inside him, Mahoney wiped his mouth on the back of his right hand and spoke, the exuberant culchie gone. "You have the diamond?"

"You have the plutonium?"

Mahoney stared into the Arab's black eyes and then said, "I think we can take the answer to both questions as being positive."

"That is good. Then we are in business."

"Right. When and where do you want the stuff? It can be delivered anywhere in mainland UK."

"We will notify you. It will not be where you think. The fact that the plutonium is available is sufficient for now. I take it that there is no immediate urgency to remove it from wherever it is?"

The Irishman thrust the bottle at the Arab. "A drink? Oh no, of course, I forgot, you gentlemen don't, do you?" Swig. "No urgency whatsoever, my friend. In fact it is being looked after by none other than my very good friends the British government." He saw Al Khalifa's look of consternation. "Over the past nine months, twelve pounds of the stuff has been spirited away, bit by bit - *on their books*. In fact, it has remained exactly where it is, so they now have twelve pounds more plutonium than they can account for. And, because my men are very clever, it does not show up on any audit or security inspection. How about that for brilliance?" It was brilliant, he thought. If only it was for real.

Al Khalifa was frowning. "If the plutonium has not in fact been moved then you are sure you will have no problems in transportation?"

"None whatsoever." Total confidence. "My contacts are good, you just name the place and date you want it and... Seamus is your uncle!"

"That is good Michael, and very clever too, as you say. I will advise you of the collection and delivery details. A date early in seventy-five has been suggested for the operation. Therefore we will have to take delivery - when? Late November or early December? That is what I am told, it is not really my department."

"Then late November or so it will be, Akay. Now, about my little gift...?"

"The diamond can be delivered as soon as you like. You will wish it brought here, naturally."

"Not on your bloody life, boyo! Here is the last place oi want a two million pound diamond. I already have the *Garda*, the income tax boys *and* the VAT gestapo on my tail. If they ever got a whiff that oi had such a magnificent and expensive jewel - glory be! They would have it off me before you could say 'distraint'."

"Then where?"

Mahoney pondered for another mouthful of gut-rot. "I'm due in Amsterdam soon, deliver it to me there."

"That can be done."

"My meeting is on, let me think... the fifth of November. Then I'll be stayin' for a few days after. Make it on the eighth, a Friday I believe?"

Al Khalifa was writing in his small pocket book. "A Friday is indeed correct. When and where?"

"I always stay in the Park Hotel, Stadhouderskade. Have someone contact me there, say eight o'clock that evening. I'll be in the bar."

"Good. That shall be done." Al Khalifa finished writing and put the pocket book away.

Mahoney exhaled deeply. The thick accent returned. "And now Akay, me ole friend, come wit' me."

He led the way from the room, talking as they walked.

"To celebrate the successful conclusion of our business oi have a little surprise for yer. D' yer remember those two friends of mine who were here last time, Lizzie and her sister Philomena? Well, they're here again, and positively oozing at the chance to entertain yer after dinner. Philomena's been working out and my God you should see the superb arse she's got on 'er now..."

Ψ

Tuesday September 24 1974

"Australia and New Zealand have both devalued their currencies, Australia by twelve per cent and New Zealand by nine per cent. In Honduras, the number of people killed during the recent Hurricane Fifi has now been estimated at between seven and eight thousand. Six hundred thousand people have been made homeless."

Milan, Italy

"Water."

"Signore?"

"Water."

"Certainly, *signore*." A glass was produced and filled.

"No ice."

"As you wish, *signore*." The barman sidled off to serve some other customers.

Ilich Ramirov turned on his stool and gave the impression of casually looking around the adjacent tables. In fact he was scrutinising very closely every one of the twenty or so persons in the plushly decorated bar of Milan's Grand Continental Hotel.

He sipped his water slowly and inclined his head to one side as he surveyed the legs of an Italian girl seated at one of the tables. Whores, even high class ones, were not usually allowed in hotels But hotel managers did not know every girl who plied her trade in the city. Perhaps she was new on the job?

His answer came two minutes later when a man who was

undoubtedly her husband approached, and she arose and walked out with him. Ramirov gave a mental shrug. He could not be right all the time. Anyway, to him all women were whores. He pushed the tinted glasses up on his nose and waited...

Just before 21:00 Faisal Ibn Musaed, Hassan's aide and the silent member of the Black September caucus, walked in. He stopped, picked out Ramirov and walked over. He spoke in French without preamble.

"Did you enjoy your recent visit to Cana?" His voice was soft and low, and Ramirov realised that it was the first time he had heard him speak.

"Very pleasant but the Jordan is vast and mysterious."

"Who knows where a river ends?"

Musaed, tall, olive-skinned and with long tight curly hair, stood looking down at Ramirov on the stool. "Abu Hassan sent me and bids you greetings. He asks if you would come with me."

Ramirov did not move. "Where to?"

Musaed's voice became even softer. "There is a house. To the south of the city. It is safe."

Ramirov said nothing but he slid off the stool. The Arab led the way out into the street and to a white Lancia parked nearby.

It was an acceptably warm Italian evening and the stars in the heavens had turned out in full force, a scintillating celestial panorama.

The journey took twenty minutes and during that time the two men uttered not one word. Ramirov stared out of the passenger window, smelling the countryside, remembering every detail of the route, and secure in the knowledge that his favourite blade was strapped on the inside of his right forearm. Occasionally he moved his left arm to check on the security of the diamond in an inside pocket of his leather jacket.

Musaed concentrated on his driving, now and again casting cautious glances at the man to his right. He well knew this man's reputation. He was the man behind a great many of the operations of the world's freedom fighters, and he was, first and foremost, a lethal killer.

The 'house' was a low, rambling, two-storey villa set at the end of its own drive at least two hundred metres from the road. It had been built in Roman style and was brilliantly illuminated by two floodlights which stood to either side of the turn of the drive. Ramirov was surprised and not a little vexed by the glowing advertisement of their presence.

"If you will come this way?" asked Musaed politely as they stepped from the Lancia.

They entered the villa by the main double doors. Two huge, smelly eastern types with ominous bulges under the left armpits of their jackets patrolled inside the main hallway. At a nod from Musaed, they allowed them to pass without hindrance. Musaed knocked gently on another double door to the right, and they entered.

Three people were sitting with their backs to the door watching television, hoots of canned laughter coming from the box. Musaed coughed and the occupant of the chair on the left turned quickly and then stood up smiling.

"My brother, again we meet!" Hassan came over and embraced Ramirov. "This time in a more friendly climate, I hope. I do apologise for that little incident on the last occasion. As you will appreciate, it was beyond my control. At least we escaped with our lives, for that we must give thanks."

"Indeed." Ramirov smiled politely and tried not to show his distaste for the embrace.

"Come, sit down," ushered Hassan. "You know Akay Al Khalifa of course."

The occupant of the furthest chair nodded in greeting.

"And he has brought along a mutual friend of yours."

Ramirov came level with the centre chair and looked down at the smiling freckled face of Melanie, the English girl from the yacht. He smiled back in genuine pleasure and bent and gallantly kissed her proffered hand.

"Melanie, it is a renewed pleasure."

"Hello again." The green eyes sparkled with that wicked promise.

Musaed had pulled over two more high-backed chairs and Ramirov sat down between Hassan and the girl, Musaed placing himself on the other side of Hassan.

Al Khalifa switched off the television.

"You will drink?" asked Hassan.

"Just water, please. No ice."

"Good man. Faisal."

Musaed rose and walked over to a large refrigerator against the far wall. He began to pour liquid.

"This place is new to me," commented Ramirov. "I thought I would have known about it."

"You like it, eh?" Hassan with a new toy.

"The little I have seen of it."

"A new *Fateh* purchase, just finalised last week. As far as the Italians are concerned it belongs to a Saudi banker."

"I see." Ramirov accepted the cool tumbler from Musaed. He declined a toffee from the bowl offered by Hassan. The big Arab could not resist temptation so easily.

"My dear," he chewed and smiled at the same time. "I wonder if you would be kind enough to leave us while we discuss our boring business? I will not keep our brother here long."

"Certainly." Melanie stood up, looking totally desirable in her green baggy fisherman's jumper and incredibly tight blue denims. Her hand brushed Ramirov's shoulder as she passed him.

They waited until the door had closed, then Hassan asked

"You of course have the diamond?"

"Safe and sound." Ramirov produced the small leather pouch and pushed the diamond out into Hassan's big, hairy right hand.

The Arab felt it awkwardly, like a giant caressing a new-born babe. "Magnificent!" he grinned.

PART FIVE

Ψ

OBJECTIVE RELINQUISHED

"Magnificent. Not its looks but the fact that this one stone could be worth so much."

"Indeed." Ramirov did not really care about that side of things.

"Cut, it will be worth even more," explained Al Khalifa. "Our supplier has chosen his reward well."

Ramirov took a mouthful of water and then said, "That, I think, concludes our current business. You know how to contact me for future assistance. I would not be prepared to involve myself in the exploding of the bomb in Britain, but if you have anything else more in my line you have only to let me know." He moved to rise.

"Actually, there is something," Hassan sounded just a shade sheepish. "Still to do with this diamond. We have to hand it over to our supplier in Amsterdam on November 8th." He looked embarrassed. "Normally it is a task we would undertake ourselves. However just a week ago, as you probably know, two of our brothers were arrested by the Dutch police. They were in Holland quite innocently, as it happens, but we fear that our network in that country is split open. Except for Faisal here, my face and those of my brothers are too well-known in northern Europe since the Olympics *[the Olympic Games in Munich in 1972 during which Black September murdered most of the Israeli competitors]* for us to attempt it." He smiled ingratiatingly. "We wondered if you would undertake to deliver the diamond for us?"

Ramirov was irked. This diamond was beginning to weigh heavily around his neck. He was getting tired of it. But he had offered his services so, after reflection, he agreed. "November 8th is some five or six weeks away. Yes, if you would feel happier, I will deliver it for you. You will need to keep the diamond safe, I suggest you put it in a safe deposit box in a bank."

"So public?" queried Musaed softly. The three other men were surprised to hear him say something, and for the briefest of moments they stopped dead in their verbal tracks.

Then Ramirov explained. "Yes, indeed. The chances of the bank being raided are remote - even in Italy. Thousands to one against. Admittedly, the chance of your safe here being robbed is remote also but the odds are not quite as good. The diamond has to go somewhere for five weeks and I suggest a bank. It is only my counsel, of course. Really it is up to you what you do with it."

"Oh I agree with you," nodded Hassan, looking reprovingly at Musaed. "Who is to say that the *Mossad* will not find out about this place and raid it? We hope not, of course. Then what would happen?"

"I agree," said Al Khalifa. "Our brother's suggestion is sound."

Musaed frowned sulkily.

"Now gentlemen," Ramirov looked at each of them. "If you have no further use for me this evening...?"

"We know somebody who has!" laughed Hassan. "Enjoy yourself, my friend. Come, I will show you to your room." The diamond was still in his hand. "I will put this in our safe tonight, then in the morning you may care to accompany Faisal and myself into the city?"

"Of course - but I hope you will not be up too early!"

Both men roared with laughter as they left the room.

After the door had closed, Musaed looked at Al Khalifa. "You trust him?"

"The foreigner? Of course, he has never let us down or cheated on us. There is no reason why he should now."

"I am unhappy. Not just because of the bank. Why must it be *he* who takes the diamond to Amsterdam? He is becoming too involved in *Fateh*'s personal affairs. I do not like it."

"Then why do you not have a word with Hassan?" suggested

Al Khalifa with just a trace of scorn.

Musaed looked back towards the closed door.

"Maybe I will. Yes, maybe. Things have progressed too far to be ruined at this stage."

Al Khalifa sniffed and leaned forward and turned on the television. Musaed stayed staring at the door, frowning.

Ψ

Thursday October 24 1974

"In Greece, the four army officers who seized power in 1969, among them former President Papadopoulos, who were arrested yesterday, have been banished to the island of Kea in the Aegean Sea."

Moscow, USSR

Ekaterina Furtseva died that night. The official version is that she died in her sleep of a heart attack, having resigned earlier that day. How much credence is given to this should be measured against the fact that the official version of her career, as previously stated, was that she was Minister of Culture and had been so for fourteen years.

Precise facts about her death cannot be ascertained. It is known that Kosygin was displeased over her meddling in Cyprus. It is known that for the past thirty years the Russians had employed, on numerous occasions, the untraceable cyanide gas which induces heart failure. It is rumoured that the only way out of the KGB was death.

Exactly what happened concerning Ekaterina Furtseva must be a matter for conjecture.

Ψ

Wednesday October 30 1974

"Finally, sport. Muhammad Ali has regained the world heavyweight boxing title. His bout with George Foreman in Kinshasa has just ended with a knockout for Ali in the eighth round. These have been the headlines from Independent Radio News. The time is three minutes past nine."

Milan, Italy

"My brother, greetings again!" Hassan's huge face smiled welcome as his hand pumped Ramirov's. They were in the wide hallway of the villa, the two hear-nothing see-all guards by the front door. Hassan motioned the Russian into the room on the right and then bade greeting to Faisal Ibn Musaed as he came in, having parked the Lancia. The young Arab closed the door and followed them into the room.

"I hear your other activities have been meeting with success," conversed Hassan. "Long may it remain so. Drink?"

"Just water. No ice. Indeed, I have been successful with certain matters in Syria." Ramirov's voice sounded clipped. The matter of the delivery of the diamond was now an irritating inconvenience.

He was more concerned about the death of Ekaterina Furtseva five days before. He could not have cared less about the woman, it was the future of his own position he had to look out for. And she had died of a heart attack. So sudden. And rumour had it she had *retired*. If so, why had she not informed him beforehand? It was suspicious, but he knew better than to fan embers. He had yet to contact his new Controller - whoever that might be.

"Now tell me," Hassan handed over the water. "When will you be leaving for Amsterdam? Contact has to be made with this Irishman in the bar of the Park Hotel, Stadhouderskade, at twenty hundred next Friday, the eighth."

"I will leave tomorrow and I shall travel by car, so avoiding any airport security checks."

Hassan's brow creased. "But what about the borders?"

"Customs do not worry me, they are no threat. I will stay overnight in Frankfurt, arriving in Amsterdam late Friday. That will give me a full week to reconnoitre, to get the *feel* of the city. It is a long time since I have been there."

"Just as you wish, we place the matter entirely in your hands. You wish to collect the diamond tomorrow?"

"Today. Preferably right now. It can remain in your safe here overnight."

"Are you sure that is wise?" asked Musaed softly.

Ramirov looked at him, his head inclined to the right. "Yes."

"I am sure our brother does what is best, Faisal," scolded Hassan. "We need no quibbling at this stage."

The young Arab said no more.

Ramirov removed the glass of water from his lips. "You will accompany me, Hassan? Now, to the bank? Or I can do it on my own. It does not need both our signatures, either will do, though I would prefer it if you were there."

Hassan looked a little put out. "Actually, my brother, I had not planned on going into the city today. I did not expect you to want to collect the diamond so soon. I have made other arrangements for this afternoon."

"So be it. Faisal can drive me."

Musaed remained silent.

"I have hunger," announced Ramirov. "When we get back,

there will be food ready?"

"Whatever you wish," Hassan spread out his hands.

"And I have another hunger," Ramirov smiled. "Melanie is here?"

Hassan chuckled. "Indeed, my brother, indeed. I believe she is upstairs bathing right at this moment."

"That is good," Ramirov's head was inclined and nodding at the same time. "That is good."

In fact Melanie was not bathing but was waiting patiently in Hassan's bed, for she was his 'other arrangement' for that afternoon. A fact which, in the light of subsequent events, was to cause Ilich Ramirov great anger.

It took three hours for Ramirov and Musaed to travel into Milan, complete the necessarily strict formalities at the bank, and return to the villa. By this time Hassan had completed his gyrations with the English girl and felt much the better for it. Although powerful and bulky of physique, the Arab was a five-star performer when it came to matters carnal, and it must be said that Melanie felt much the better for it also. She had bathed, douched, and was waiting with Hassan when Ramirov entered, Musaed as always on his tail.

There were smiles all round, Ramirov's reserved mainly for the girl. Her hair had been permed into a frizz since he last saw her, and she wore a one-piece full-length black pants suit, unzipped provocatively so that a glance from the side would receive a generous view of her magnificently taut breasts.

"All went well?" asked Hassan, suddenly realising, and for no apparent reason, that he was always the first to speak. The foreigner never opened a conversation.

"Of course," the reply was confident. Ramirov now seemed in good spirits, sullenness ebbing. "Here is the..." He remembered that the girl was not party to these matters and he changed verbal course deftly, placing the pouch back into his pocket. " - item. I shall have a relaxing night and then tomorrow things can get under way." He smiled. "How are you, Melanie?" he asked in English.

She smiled warmly. "Absolutely radiating with health. But I think I feel lonely."

"That is a situation that must certainly be remedied," He reverted to French. "Hassan, there is food?"

"The dining room is ready. We have a woman - dear old Signora Garofalo - who is cooking something delicious for the kind Arab businessmen. Come we must not keep her. I believe she has a husband and seven *bambini* to go home to."

As they walked from the room, Musaed asked. "What about the di- the item? Should it not be put in the safe?"

Hassan thought and then said. "Perhaps you are right, Faisal. We do not wish its security to mar our evening's enjoyment. You are in agreement, my brother?"

"I intended leaving there overnight, so yes, let me be rid of the thing now, at least for tonight," agreed Ramirov.

"The safe is in my office. Faisal will show you. He knows the combination."

The office was to the rear of the villa, behind the stairway. It was a small room containing a filing cabinet, desk, three chairs and two telephones. On the far side a pair of French windows led out onto the back patio and then to the villa's spacious garden.

The safe was a small standard house-safe set into the wall at head height behind the desk.

Ramirov closed the door of the room behind them. Faisal stood in front of the safe, and Ramirov said "Open it please."

Musaed began. Five or six turns to the right to clear the combination and then the first of the turns to the left. He deliberately blocked Ramirov's view so that he could not read the numbers. What he did not realise was that Ramirov had been taught at a very special training school to *hear* the combination of a safe.

It was open in moments and Musaed stood back to let Ramirov pass.

Inside the safe were various sealed envelopes and substantial amounts of different currencies. There was also a solitary key, for what Ramirov did not know. He walked past the young Arab and took the pouch from his pocket.

His back was to Musaed for only three seconds, but that was all it took. Ramirov heard the sound of the phone being lifted, but he turned too late. The instrument came crashing down onto the left side of his head, he heard a mighty bang like a volcano erupting, and then he fell into total darkness...

His rage was white hot, an emotion he had not experienced for years. But as always he kept his feelings under control and he sat at the dining table tight-lipped. His glasses were off and in front of him was a plate of *caponata* which was receiving the bulk of his visual venom. It had been two hours, and Musaed and the diamond were long gone.

Melanie also sat at the table, her meal devoured, but she knew better than to say anything to this unusual and frightening man. She had tried to administer to the cut under his hairline earlier on when Hassan had led him into the dining room dazed, but she had been brushed off with a curse in some language she did not know.

Hassan now entered the room, his face grim. "Well, that is done. All airports and seaports east of Greece are under surveillance. He will be held immediately he sets foot in any of them, the diamond will be retrieved and he will be executed. We cannot cover everywhere, of course. If he decides to go west we will have no immediate pick-up. My men are covering the airports here, as you know, but it is just possible for him to have got out before I found you and signalled the alert."

"How long was it?" The voice was tight.

"Fifteen minutes at the most, no more."

"Fifteen minutes!" Ramirov's hand smashed down onto the table. The *caponata* jumped into the air.

Hassan sat down two seats away, shaking his head. "I just cannot understand it. It is not like him. I have known Faisal since he was a youth. He is dedicated to *Fateh*."

"But he is not Palestinian."

"No, he is Saudi. But he believed deeply in our cause. He has been involved in many of our campaigns. He was the reconnaissance man for our Japanese brothers at Lod Airport, in fact he was still in Tel Aviv when the incident happened. He was fortunate to get out of the country. I - I just don't understand. He was truly Palestinian, even though he was not of our nationality. He believed in world revolution. Why would he do such a thing? Just for money?"

Ramirov replaced his glasses, wincing as they touched the left side of his head. He said nothing.

Melanie looked from one to the other of them. "Excuse me, but may I say something?"

They both looked at her, Hassan realising with horror that he had been speaking in English.

"Well," she shrugged nervously, "it might not mean anything, but, well, Faisal has said on more than one occasion recently that he doesn't trust you." She looked at the visitor.

"Does not trust me? *Me?*" Ramirov's index finger jabbed into his own chest. "That, my dear, is *ironic!*"

She continued. "Well, if he doesn't trust you - sorry, but that is what he said - if he doesn't trust you and he is as dedicated and fanatical as Hassy tells us... could he not have taken the diamond to its destination himself?" She went on quickly, "You just said it was a diamond Hassy, that's how I know."

The two men were silent. Slowly their heads turned towards each other.

"Well?" asked Ramirov.

Hassan was almost speechless. "That... that is amazing! It had not occurred to me. But of course! *That* is totally in line with his character." He gave a sharp half-laugh. "That *must* be what he is up to!"

Ramirov stood up. "In that case I will follow. He is a fool. An Arab face in Amsterdam would be sure to cause suspicion if seen in the wrong quarters, especially at this time. I must get the diamond before he gets picked up." He brushed a scab off the side of his head. "Or no, he is no fool as you say. In fact, looking at matters objectively, one might say that he was brave and intelligent to take such action if he did not trust me. One *might*. I believe he knows all the risks involved. He will not let himself be taken. Yes, the first thing he will be concerned about is the security of the diamond. He will no doubt bank it, just as we have done here, until contact can be made with this Irish supplier, this Mahoney." He was nodding his head in rumination. "He will have gone by road?"

"Most probably, for the same reasons as you." Hassan also rose.

"I will need a car, fast and in good condition."

"I have an Audi sports available, full tank."

"Ideal. I want you to alert the German Fraction. Musaed is not to be intercepted but I want him located and tailed as soon as he enters that country. I will call at the addresses in Stuttgart, Frankfurt and Duisberg. I expect someone to be waiting with news. And I need a good map."

"There is one in the car."

"Right. You have any food I can take with me?"

"There must be something in the kitchen. I will see while you prepare yourself."

Both men left the room, leaving Melanie on her own. She stared at the empty doorway. "Well, thanks a lot boys," she said. "Nice to be appreciated."

Ψ

Ten minutes later Ramirov was in the car at the front of the villa, Hassan leaning in through the open window.

"You are sure you are in a condition to travel?"

"Yes."

"Then I wish you well, my brother. For the sake of us all."

Ramirov nodded and turned the ignition key. The engine purred into life. "I will report back here if anything happens or, if not, on safe delivery of the diamond. There is one thing, of course."

"My brother?"

Ramirov's right arm moved fractionally to touch the gun in his jacket pocket. "Good intentions or not, I will not have my authority undermined. Musaed dies."

With a kick of gravel the Audi shot away, off down the drive, and turned north for Milan, leaving Hassan nodding his head reluctantly in the half-light of evening.

That night, while Hassan snored loudly beside her, Melanie crept out of bed and walked quietly to the office downstairs. She was naked, but there was no one about. At night, the guards were on duty outside the villa.

She dialled a thirteen-digit number on the telephone. It was answered after one ring.

"It's Melanie. How is our friend? Good. Listen, I have some very interesting news..."

At the end of the call, she replaced the receiver softly and went back upstairs.

Melanie Nathanson, one of the many female operatives of Israeli intelligence, climbed back into bed with the leader of Black September. She prayed to God he would not wake up, her sex was raw enough already.

Ψ

FINALE

Ψ

Thursday October 31 1974

Italy/Switzerland/West Germany

Ramirov travelled fast but remained within the speed limits at all times. To be picked up by the police was the last thing he wanted to happen.

He took the E9 from Milan and had reached the Swiss border in just over an hour. His Swiss passport (one of fifteen supplied by his masters) saw him safely across.

He stopped once, just outside Chur, to relieve himself, and he munched cold pizza, bread and crackers as he drove. There was not too much traffic about and he found driving through Switzerland at night quite peaceful, if a little chilly. The heater was off in the car and would remain so. He did not want himself getting drowsy. And his head still throbbed with what was possibly a mild concussion.

He reached Zurich by 03:30 and here he had to slow his speed down from the motorway maximum of 130 to the town limit of 60. He entered the city along Mythen Quai, Lake Zurich lambent in the still moonlight.

Through the city and then out into the suburbs towards Winterthur. As he hit the motorway again he willed the car forward. He wanted to get to Stuttgart quickly and receive a report. Once he knew that this was the way Musaed had come then he could relax and take it easy, let the Arab do all the work.

He reached the E70. Now it would be a straight run, across the German border and up to Stuttgart. Swiss passport again, a cursory couple of questions by a bored Customs Officer, and he was through.

He arrived in Stuttgart at 06:30 and made his way through the awakening city and to the apartment up near Hohen Park. Parking was easy, and he was greeted like an old friend by the woman and two men who met him. They were members of the German Fraction. *[Sometimes known as the Baader-Meinhof Gang, named after two of their leaders – Andreas Baader and Ulrike Meinhof – both of whom were later to be executed whilst in their prison cells.]* He was given the news straight away: Musaed was indeed heading for Amsterdam, the white Lancia had been picked up immediately it crossed the border. He was two hours ahead and was at that moment nearing Mannheim.

Ramirov was pleased. That was all he wanted to know. He could now take his time.

He was given a rough but filling meal consisting mostly of potatoes and some green vegetable, he drank vodka with his colleagues and then he settled down on the couch to sleep solidly for twelve hours.

Ψ

Saturday November 2 1974

Somewhere in the Irish Republic

Oh God, what time is it? Half-eight already?

I knew I shouldn't have taken *mavourneen* Lizzie to me bed last night - Lord, but she's gorgeous though. Look at her, lying there fast asleep, tits on display like two beached jelly fish. Wish she'd close her mouth though...

Well Michael, me ole fella, it's no good lying around here, yer've a plane to catch in Dublin this afternoon. And in just seventy-two hours from now you'll be meeting with Eyskens. Then you'll have three nights to enjoy yerself until Friday.

Friday...

It will be yer day of reckoning, boyo. Take the diamond and run, that's yer best bet. Whatever yer do, it's too late to worry about it now. Yer in lad, up to yer neck. Play it as it comes.

Come on now, yer lazy git. Up outta this bed... that's me boy. God, it's cold this morning. Must have a pee. Funny how a good session always makes yer want ta pee. Let's just have a look at yer face in the mirror here...

My God, but yer a handsome bastard, d' yer know that?

Amsterdam, Holland

Ilich Ramirov arrived in Amsterdam at 16:00 that afternoon. He had received his last report about the Lancia two and a half hours before in Duisberg. Musaed was now over a day ahead of him. He could be anywhere, of course. And it was that fact that had decided the Russian's course of action.

He would do nothing in the way of trying to find the treacherous, misguided Arab, nothing at all. All he would do was check into the Park Hotel, where the meeting was to take place next Friday, and wait. It was simply a waste of time and effort to try to trace Musaed in the city. He would wait, look around the town (he had not been to The Red Light District for years) and then on Thursday night (just in case) and Friday night he would be waiting in the bar of the hotel.

He entered the city on the E9 and turned left into President Kennedy Laan and up Ferdinand Bol Straat.

He turned into Van Baerle Straat, passed the Stedelijk Museum on his right, and then he was there.

At last, the Park Hotel…

Ψ

Tuesday November 5 1974

Amsterdam, Holland

Ramirov left the hotel early that morning to reconnoitre an area up by West Docks. He arrived there around lunchtime. It was good to see the old warehouse was still in use. Ostensibly it was a front for a firm of flower wholesalers; in reality it was a convenience for the KGB. Earlier he had picked up the keys to the place from a travel agency (also with KGB connections) on Kalverstraat in the centre of the city.

The warehouse was still in good condition, and it was the ideal place for what Ramirov had in mind: the death of Faisal Ibn Musaed. There were a few rats in the dingy corners but, he thought unemotionally, they could gnaw on the Arab's bones.

Ramirov caught a tram back into the city. He did not notice the man who got on the tram directly behind him, who walked past him and sat in the back. He was a tall man, slim with a noticeable hunch in his shoulders. His hair was iron-grey and it was beginning to fall out at the front. He wore a full beard which was just a shade darker than his hair.

And his eyes were something else. For he had no whites, none at all. Where the whites should have been was, quite simply, blood. As if all the blood vessels in his eyes had burst simultaneously, through some strain, shock or traumatic experience.

The Man was pleased the Russian had not recognised him.

His Controller in Israel had been right. They had given him his chance and it must be taken. But not here, not now. It was too public.

The Man got off three persons behind Ramirov. He followed him to the Park Hotel and up into the foyer where he saw him ask for his key.

The Man walked over to Reception. "You have a room?" His voice was a raucous croak, devoid of any accent, and with a constant rasp as he breathed.

The hotel was always busy, of course, but *ja* there were a few vacancies at this time of the year *mijnheer*. How long would the gentleman be staying?

"Not long. Maybe three days." It would take no longer than that.

A room was booked and The Man, smiling all over his ashen face, went off to retrieve his luggage from the safe house. The clerk frowned at him as he walked away. The man moved slowly and seemed to have to gasp for breath before every step. A modern Quasimodo.

On his way out of the hotel, The Man passed a jovial Michael Mahoney entering, but as neither knew each other they hardly even noticed their mutual presence, although Mahoney did wonder what the sudden gasping noise was.

The Man was back at The Park within the hour. As he was signing in, he rasped to the clerk casually in English: "I believe you have a friend of mine staying here. A Mr Martinez?"

"Martinez?" The clerk consulted his records and tried not to stare at the ghoul in front of him. "N-no sir, no one by that name. We have a Swiss gentleman, a Mr Martini." He chuckled. "Not the sort of name one forgets."

"Martini! Of course, that's the guy. So he *is* here, that's good."

"Shall I tell him you are enquiring after him, sir? I can have him paged."

"No, no! Whatever you do, don't do that. I want to surprise him when I'm good and ready. What room's he in?"

"Er... on the floor below yourself, sir. Room 203."

"Thanks. You've been a great help." The clerk was rewarded with a magnificent fifty guilden tip.

"Thank *you*, sir !" Perhaps he was not so bad after all, thought the clerk. The poor man could not help the way he looked. But his breath was so rank! It smelled of dried blood and grit...

Ψ

Thursday November 7 1974

London, England

When it came to it, the girl's head shattered easily and she was dead by the time her body hit the floor. It had been an instantaneous but very painful death, shards of skull penetrating deep into the brain. Sandra - the one person whom the police later thought might be able to name her killer for definite - never knew who her murderer was.

Richard John Bingham, 7th Earl of Lucan, looked down at the inert body and shivered. It was dark in the basement of his town house at 46 Lower Belgrave Street, but he could clearly see the dark patch which had once been the back of the nanny's head. Already there was an unpleasant smell.

His breath came fast and deep, and his hands were shaking. Strangely enough he did not feel sick, as he had thought he would. He felt somewhat relieved. Relieved that this part of it at least was over. But the worst, of course, was yet to come.

Thirty-nine year old 'Lucky' Lucan gathered himself together and got down to business. *They* had specifically instructed that everything must go according to plan. Ten minutes delay at any stage and it could all go wrong and land him in an English cell for life. He must get on with it.

Quickly he retrieved the sack from the darkened corner and began to shove the dead body into it...

When the top of the bag was tied and the macabre bundle

propped back into the corner, Lucan left the murder weapon where it could easily be found - as instructed - and rushed up the stairs two at a time. His small bag was already packed with the very few things he was allowed to take with him, and now he just had time for the cosmetics. Then would come the chat with his wife, which the police would make so much of but which the Press would virtually ignore, and his escape in the borrowed car.

Everything went according to plan and soon Richard John Bingham, without the moustache which had been his trade mark around the gaming clubs of London, was driving south out of central London towards the suburb of Croydon. The night of November 7 1974 was crisp but not necessarily cold in London, and his thick Arran jumper was ample coverage against whatever the elements had in store. It was a dry night and rain was not predicted. This time Lucky Lucan hoped that the weather forecasters would be right. He had a long way to go.

His only regret was that he had to miss his dinner date at the *Clermont* with Greville, and without a word of apology or explanation. It was damn caddish of him. A gentleman really did not do such things.

He only hoped that, if the truth were ever known, England would be grateful...

Ψ

Friday November 8 1974

Across England

Everything had gone according to plan and Lucan's nervousness had now abated. He had met with the inconspicuous member of the British SIS as instructed, outside a public house in the suburban town of Crawley, fifty kilometres south of London. The SIS man had said nothing to him, he had simply given Lucan a set of keys, pointed to a red Morris Mini parked on the opposite side of the road, and had then climbed into Lucan's car and driven off. He would get to Newhaven on the south coast in under two hours, and there he would abandon Lucan's car and travel back by another waiting vehicle. The police would find the deserted car and the false trail would be laid.

Lucan, on the other hand, drove the Mini back into London, up through Streatham, across the river into Chelsea, Knightsbridge, Oxford Street, Swiss Cottage, Hampstead, Highgate, and out of the capital once more, heading north-east.

He arrived in Harwich three hours later, right on schedule, and he had only gone wrong once in finding his way to the docks. His instructions were to wait in the car outside another specified public house and he would be contacted.

Five minutes after his arrival, there was a single rap on the passenger window. A man in a grubby mackintosh, cap pulled down to his eyes, looked in. Lucan wound down the window. There were no introductions, and the voice that came from underneath the cap had a Northern Irish accent.

"Leave the car here, it will be taken care of. Get yer things and come with me."

Harwich was quiet at that hour of the morning. As soon as Lucan stepped out of the car, it started to rain. The forecasters had been wrong.

He was led through a maze of backstreets, some so narrow as to be sinister. The rain became heavier, so that by the time he came out on the quayside it was lashing the street with some force.

"Not a very nice night for it, what?" He tried to make conversation as they crossed the deserted road. The street lighting was poor and clouds obscured all traces of the moon. He nodded at the rain. "This wasn't forecast."

"No." The reply did not invite any further exchange.

Lucan shivered as his sopping jumper finally gave up the fight against the rain and the water oozed through to his skin.

They walked to the edge of the quay. The other man climbed down an unsafe iron ladder and stepped into a small boat with an outboard engine, moored below.

Halfway down the ladder Lucan dropped his bag, but he was relieved to hear it thump into the bottom of the boat and not splash into the sea. The craft was unsteady and he sat down quickly, facing the other man.

The mackintoshed figure pulled two oars from underneath their feet. "Here, sit next to me. We'll row out a little before startin' the engine. Don't worry about the rain, I believe it's quite calm out there. For the North Sea, that is."

They were about a kilometre from the shore before he decided that it would be safe to start the engine. Then they were off, carving through the water, the tangy mixture of the now dying rain and the salty spindrift of the North Sea splashing into Lucan's face and completing his drenching.

The North Sea

They met up with HMCC Venturous as planned, five kilometres out.

[The original manuscript of this book contained a detailed description of the vessel and its activities in the guise of a UK Customs cutter, together with details of the short discussion which took place on board, and the truth – finally – about Richard John Bingham. The material has been deleted at the 'request' of the British security services.]

The final briefing completed, Lucan settled down inside and began to dry his hair with a towel. Soon, in Holland, it would be styled and dyed to disguise his appearance even more, and then he would continue on his pre-planned way eastward.

He suddenly felt quite tired and he leant back against the bulkhead and closed his eyes, only to be disturbed by one of the crew offering him a mug of steaming hot tea, which he accepted with his usual urbanity.

He thought of England and of what he was doing for her...

Amsterdam, Holland

Interpol Amsterdam received news of the Lucan murder by telex at 09:00 that morning. By midday, a copy of the telex and a preliminary description of the Earl 'wanted for questioning in connection with' was on the desk of every senior ranked member of the Amsterdam-Amstelland police.

The preliminary description was: 'Tall, about six foot, aged 39, hair black parted on right and pushed back, well built, special feature thick black moustache probably removed." A wire photo would follow, it was promised.

Middle-aged, world-weary Chief Inspector Johann Versleas assimilated this information on his return to his office at 41 Constantijn Huygensstraat at 13:30, hmphed to himself that the description could fit anybody, and put the copy telex to one side.

The Man entered the bar of the Park Hotel at 19:45. His grizzly eyebrows raised as he saw the unmistakable back sitting on the stool at the bar.

He walked over, stood deliberately close, and ordered a *John Collins*. The seated man did not give any sign of recognition.

"Nice evening," said The Man in the flat, dry rasp. "I find Amsterdam in late fall most beautiful, don't you?"

The eyes behind the tinted glasses turned to look at him. The head inclined to the left.

"I - I am zorry," said the familiar but deliberately deeply accented voice. "My Inglish, not good." The eyes turned away without even a glimmer of recognition.

The Man smiled. "Ah, forgive me. I understand."

He paid for his drink and found himself a seat by the wall. He sat staring at the Russian's back and occasionally sipping his sharp drink (too much lemon), pondering.

A sudden, sharp pain shot across his chest, and he held his breath and concentrated on not letting the agony show on his face. The pain subsided and he exhaled, safe again this time. But one day, he knew, the pain would not stop.

At 19:50 Ramirov vacated his stool at the bar in favour of a seat at an empty table near the entrance, his back towards the wall.

Seconds later, Michael Mahoney entered and strolled over to the bar, plonking himself down on the very stool Ramirov had just left. Ramirov heard the thick Irish accent order a whisky and then begin to pass the time of day with the barman, making casual enquiries about a girl who was on her own at the end of the bar.

They waited, The Man watching Ramirov, Ramirov watching the Irishman, who in turn was intent on the generous tits of the young lady who, as anyone but Mahoney could see, was a whore of the highest order. If Mahoney had not had other business that evening, he would be over there now whispering sweet begorrahs into her ear.

By 20:05 a third glass of whisky was being swallowed, the *John Collins* was just a trace in the bottom of the glass, and the water, no ice, had gone completely.

Musaed appeared at 20:06.

He stood in the entrance surveying the occupants of the place, not noticing Ramirov right underneath him. He went over to the bar. Three men and the whore were there, two of the men talking in German and one man on his own.

"Mijnheer?" The barman.

"For me, nothing," said Musaed in French. "But the same again for that gentleman there." He nodded at Mahoney who, as he knew no French, sat in ignorance of the attention given to him - until the drink was placed in front of him and he looked up questioningly.

"From the gentleman," explained the barman in English, with a nod towards Musaed.

Mahoney frowned, and then comprehension dawned. He said, "Ah, yes! My friend. Thank you!" He held the glass up and smiled at the Arab. The contents disappeared in one. "Won't you join me for a drink, sir?"

Musaed came over. "No drink for me, thank you."

"Oh no, of course, I'm always forgettin'. You fellas don't, do yer?"

"But I believe we have some business together?"

"Indeed we do, me ole son."

"You are Mr Mahoney?"

Mahoney put a hand inside his jacket pocket and threw a

green Irish passport down onto the bar. "I sure am meself," he grinned.

Musaed gave the passport a cursory look and handed it back.

"Please excuse me, but this is not my regular area of employ. You know of discreet place where I may make delivery?"

Mahoney sniffed and looked about. "Here's a good a place as any, oi reckon, don't yew?"

"As you wish."

Musaed's hand went to his jacket pocket. He tried to pull it back out with the diamond but something had suddenly gripped his forearm, as if a dog's jaws had tightened around it, and the arm was paralysed. He looked to his right and gasped with shock as the bespectacled face of Ramirov glared angrily at him.

For a moment the three men were silent. Musaed staring in fear, Ramirov glaring in hatred, Mahoney, mouth quivering, wondering what was going on. Was his plan going to fail at the last minute?

Ramirov stared down Musaed and then turned towards the Irishman, his grip not diminishing on the Arab's arm. "You must excuse me, Mr Mahoney," he said in almost unaccented English. "This gentleman and I have a little unfinished business."

The Irishman was alert, alarm bells ringing. "What's going on?" he asked softly. "If this is Arab against Arab I'm out of it, you can keep the sodding stone." He went to get off the stool but Ramirov's other hand restrained him.

"There is no need for alarm, I assure you. The stone is yours. But I do not think it wise that these things are done in public. If you will come with my friend and me, we will give you the diamond."

"Really, I don't - "

"Please." Ramirov's hand had left Mahoney and was now in his right jacket pocket, the unmistakable outline of a gun poking outwards underneath the cloth.

It was done so discreetly that only Musaed and Mahoney knew anything was wrong. Not far away, the barman went about his business, and likewise the whore who was now being propositioned by a small, balding American.

Ramirov stood back to let Mahoney off the stool, pulling Musaed back with him and laughing as if it was the meeting of old friends. With one hand on the gun in his pocket and the other still painfully gripping Musaed's arm, he ushered the party out of the hotel and into Stadhouderskade.

A chill had descended and their breath turned to vapour in the Amsterdam air. They walked southwards.

Musaed's Lancia was parked just along from the hotel.

"Into the back if you would, Mr Mahoney," directed Ramirov. He pulled Musaed to a halt while the Irishman climbed in. "You are unusually quiet tonight, Faisal. Cat got your tongue? No opinions to express? You will drive. Follow my directions."

The gun was produced from his pocket and he pushed the Arab into the driver's seat. Ramirov got into the back, next to Mahoney and directly behind Musaed, all the time the gun pressing hard into the young man's head.

Ramirov gave instructions and they were off, Musaed nervously jerking them out into the traffic towards Constantijn Huygensstraat.

None of them, not even Ramirov, noticed The Man with the grey hair, beard and stoop, come out of the hotel, hail a cab, and climb into it, giving instructions as he did so. The cab pulled out in the wake of the Lancia…

It had been a long day and Chief Inspector Johann Versleas was tired. Ever since his transfer to the Drugs Squad his working day had been getting longer and longer, some days melting into the next without pause. And, of course, this did not please his wife. She was going through the change, so he received little or no physical attention these days, but she was one of those women who objected to her husband being away from home and yet could not tolerate him when he was there; the ball-crushing vicious circle.

Versleas' day had started at 08:00 that morning and now, over twelve hours later, he was on his way home in his old Opel. Home to a couple of hours of nagging while he tried to watch television, and then seven hours merciful oblivion in his single bed. Oh well, roll on Christmas when his children would be home from school. He had lots of trips and visits to the theatre lined up which he hoped they would enjoy - he would, at any rate.

Versleas smoked placidly on his *Ritmeester* cheroot and drove up Biderdijkstraat, pausing at the intersection with de Clerq Straat for a chance to turn right into the busy traffic.

A white Lancia pulled up next to him, the driver - a young Asian-looking type - trying jumpily to edge his way into the flow, but with little success.

More intent on the traffic, Versleas gave a casual glance into the back of the vehicle where two men sat. One, on the far side, thin, long faced, looked very sombre and absentmindedly picked his nose. The other, on this side, looked well-built, from what little Versleas could see of him, and had dark hair, probably black, parted on the right and pushed back. He looked to be in his thirties, and he wore a pair on tinted spectacles, unusual and quite unnecessary in Amsterdam at this time of year and at this time of night. This one was speaking to the driver, possibly giving him directions, and he had his hand on the back of the driver's seat.

Versleas found a gap in the traffic and neatly slipped out into de Clerq Straat. In his rear-view mirror he noticed the white Lancia also take the same opportunity, then the gap in the traffic was closed before a cab could pull out.

Versleas took the cheroot from his lips and held it between the first two fingers of his right hand as he steered. He drove with the traffic along Rozen Gracht and thought of nothing in particular.

It did not hit him until he was waiting at the traffic lights at the next intersection.

My God! The man, the one with the dark glasses in the back of the Lancia. Well-built, in his thirties, black hair parted on the right. It was almost an identical description to the one he had read that afternoon of the missing English Lord! What was his name? Lew... Loo... Loosen? Loo... Lucan, that was it! Otherwise known as Bingham.

Could it be? Could it actually be the fugitive earl in the back of the Lancia? No, absolutely not. Yet it would certainly explain the incongruous dark glasses. The history of police detection was rife with chance incidents like this. Could it be?

Versleas felt a tingling in his stomach.

The lights changed and Versleas drove on, keeping an eager eye on the car behind. The traffic began to thin at Raadhuis Straat, and he pulled over to the side and stopped, forcing the Lancia ahead of him. As it went past he took a good look at the man in the back. This second look did nothing to allay his suspicions. He let a cab go past and then pulled back into the traffic, eyes glued on the Lancia two vehicles ahead.

He noticed that it had begun to rain, and he switched on the Opel's wipers...

The Lancia kept to the main streets and Versleas kept with it, the cab still separating him from his quarry. By the main Post Office the Lancia made a left turn, then left again a few hundred metres on. Curiously enough, the cab did too. Versleas was now deeply interested. This seemed to be a two-man tail. If it was, who was in the cab?

The Lancia turned right and continued on under the railway

bridge into the West Dock area. The smell of the city decreased as the smell of the docks and the sea overcame the gentle odour of the canals.

Soon the Lancia began to slow down. It turned right into a narrow lane and stopped a little way along. The cab did not turn but went past the intersection and then pulled suddenly to a halt. As he drove by, Versleas saw a tall grey man with a beard and marked stoop shuffle out and quickly hand over money. Versleas pulled over a little way along. As he turned to look back, the now passengerless cab shot past him.

The rain was heavy now, coming from the west, and it tappy-tapped on the roof of the vehicle like the fingers of a thousand devils. Versleas peered through the back window into the darkness. The sinister, stooped figure had crossed the road and was just entering the lane which the Lancia had pulled into.

Reminding himself that he was unarmed, Versleas sat and wondered what he should do…

"Right, if you would be so good as to step outside and accompany us, Mr Mahoney, this transaction will not take too long."

"But it's pouring down with bloody rain, oi'll be soaked!"

"As you are about to receive a diamond worth a considerable amount of money, I should think that would be the least of your worries. Please. Faisal - out!"

Swiftly Ramirov climbed out of the Lancia, gun still pointing doggedly at the forlorn Arab. Mahoney clambered out after him, being extra careful not to get in front of the gun as Musaed nervously joined them on the narrow, puddled sidewalk.

"Walk," ordered Ramirov. He looked at the Irishman. "You no doubt wonder what is going on, Mr Mahoney. Unfortunately it is not my province to offer you explanations. This is an internal matter, which I shall resolve shortly. Meantime, I apologise for the inconvenience caused."

"I don't want to be involved in no internal matters, thank you very much."

"Just bear with me."

"Hm."

They walked for one hundred metres, the lane dark and illuminated only by the moon which peeked through the rainclouds at irregular intervals. Mahoney became wet and he did not like it one bit. If he was honest with himself, he had to admit that he was as scared as hell. What *had* he got mixed up in?

Ramirov stopped them outside the entrance to some sort of warehouse and motioned them inside through a wicket-gate. It was dank inside, seemingly through years of unuse, and but for a few old soapboxes and straw on the floor it was empty.

Leaving the wicket-gate ajar, Ramirov went over to the wall on the left and switched on a dim lightbulb which was suspended by a hideously worn wire from the high ceiling. All the time his gun was trained on Musaed, who had turned and was looking at him.

As the light went on, Mahoney could have sworn he saw something with four legs dash for cover into the darkness of a far corner. Then he too turned to face the man with the gun. God, this place stank of cats.

Keeping at least four metres from the other two men, Ramirov came back over and stood with his back to the open doorway. The gun jerked at Musaed.

"The diamond."

Musaed hesitated, fear in his eyes as he again tried to stare down the foreigner and failed. His hand came up to his jacket pocket and he slowly pulled out the familiar leather pouch.

Ramirov inclined his head. "Good." He kept his speech in English for the benefit of the Irishman. "Now please remove the diamond so we can see it." *What was that strange smell?*

The top of the pouch was pulled open and the diamond was

tipped out, filling Musaed's left palm.

Mahoney was staring wide-eyed at the huge stone. "Jesus, Mary and Joseph, look at the size of that!" A wicked, greedy gleam came into his eyes. Sheer avarice. "The Star of Sierra Leone."

"I THINK NOT!"

The satanic rasp came from no more than half a metre behind Ramirov. The Russian went to spin round but he was halted by the unmistakable hardness pressing into the small of his back. Musaed and Mahoney looked up in shock.

For a moment there was silence. Then the man with the beard and stoop said in his flat, grating, lifeless tone, "No sudden moves, eh? Especially you."

The gun jabbed painfully into Ramirov's back, but he showed no reaction whatsoever.

The demonic eyes looked across at Mahoney. "You, put the stone back into the pouch... That's good... Now keep it in your hand where I can see it. Hold it up! Good." Again the jab in Ramirov's back, "You, drop the gun onto the floor at your feet - don't lower your arm, just let it go."

Thud.

"Kick it behind you. Careful now, my finger isn't as steady as it used to be."

Ramirov kicked the gun behind him. Slowly he turned. He frowned as he looked at the man with the lifeless grey hair and beard and the nasty stoop which made him look as if he was permanently raising his head. For the first time in a long time, Ramirov felt a pang of apprehension as he looked at the eyes, black and surrounded with blood.

The Man caught the frisson and grinned. "Scare yer, huh? Well, so it should - *you* did this to me, Martinez."

Ramirov frowned again. He had never seen this man in his life before the casual meeting at the hotel, yet the man knew one of his aliases.

Now a laugh came from The Man's lips. "Don't recognise me, huh? Well, how do you think I came upon you without you sensing me, eh? You told me in Cyprus you knew I was there – well you didn't this time, did you?"

"I do not believe it," Ramirov almost smiled in admiration. "Mr Digenis. I indeed would not have recognised you."

"Why should you?" growled The Man. "Last time you saw me, I was a normal human being. I had a *life*. In Cyprus, remember? And you, you shit, shot me through the fucking heart. Call me by my real name. I AM GRIVAS. STELIOS GRIVAS! You shot me, you double-crossing bastard. You. You did this to me!" The horrible sound as he breathed in. "You shot me through the heart but you forgot to check that I was dead. Now I have a bullet in there and I have to stoop to ease the pain, and it has sent me grey. And they tell me that the bullet only has to move one centimetre to complete its work. One centimetre, Martinez. One fucking centimetre…"

The hand with the gun whipped upwards into the Russian's face. Ramirov staggered back and fell into a sitting position. The tinted glasses had shattered with the impact of the gun, and he brushed them off his face. Glass had entered his right eye and blood began to roll from it.

"That's from Christina Cascianis, bastard! Stand up. Stand up NOW!"

Ramirov did as he was ordered.

"Now come back over to me."

Ramirov walked slowly over and straight into another smack with the gun, three teeth spinning from his mouth as he fell back again onto the straw.

Grivas looked at the other two men. They were stiff with terror. "The diamond," he ordered.

Musaed weakly proffered the pouch.

The inhaling gasp. "It is for my father. Give it to me. The diamond is The Eye of Makarios."

Musaed went to pass it over.

Grivas reached out a hand.

At that moment a wet, unstoppable figure came hurtling through the doorway, bowling Grivas over with a tackle.

Then all hell broke loose.

The gun fired as Grivas fell, the bullet narrowly missing Mahoney's left ear. Ramirov was up in an instant and he kicked the fallen gun out of the reach of the grasping Chief Inspector Versleas.

Versleas pushed himself off the top of Grivas and grabbed Ramirov's right ankle, jerking the bloodied Russian down as he went for the gun. Ramirov's nose hit the floor with an almighty crack, but he turned around and rammed his heel savagely into the face of the policeman.

Mahoney took two steps and planted a foot firmly into the Russian's testicles, then he saw Musaed sneaking around the edge of the warehouse and leapt over after him.

"No yer don't, me boyo." A push, and the pouch was snatched away.

Cringing with pain, nose broken and face completely covered in blood, Ramirov rose, looked once at Mahoney and once at the gun, saw the man beneath him grabbing for his feet again, and decided on the diamond. He leapt over and aimed a blow at the Irishman's head.

Mahoney ducked but not sufficiently. The top of his head was struck and he was knocked of balance, dropping the pouch into a dim corner.

Musaed jumped forward and grabbed hold of both sides of Ramirov's bloody, chubby face, wrenching downwards. This time the pent-up scream burst from the Russian's lips.

Versleas had shaken his cut forehead and was now coming out of his momentary daze. He saw the gun three metres in front of him and he began to crawl towards it.

Ramirov lashed out at Musaed but his fisted chop was

knocked off target as Mahoney rammed his head into his stomach, lifted upwards with all his might and sent the bulky Russian right over the top of him. Mahoney fell back down with the effort, but then he dragged himself to his feet again, chuffed...

Versleas could see two of everything. His two right hands stretched out and made contact with both the guns...

Mahoney had Musaed by the collar when he saw the other man pick up the gun.

"He's got the gun!" He and the Arab almost fell over each other as they dashed from the warehouse and out into the rain. Mahoney tripped over the bottom slat of the wicket-gate, sprawled across the wet, dirty sidewalk, pulled himself back up and was away...

Versleas turned in a seated position with the guns in all four hands...

Ramirov saw the Irishman go and, not realising he had dropped the diamond, he staggered to his feet and headed for the doorway, blood pouring from his eye, nose and mouth, dripping off his chin and staining the old straw red...

Versleas fired.

Ramirov span around and then sank to his knees, right hand clutching his left collar-bone. He got up once more, then fell back again, then got up again, staggering towards the gateway...

Versleas pulled the trigger again.

There was no report.

Ramirov stumbled out into the lane and away...

Versleas threw the jammed gun towards the gateway and shouted "Lucan! LUCAN!"

He tried to get up but nausea overcame him and he fell back down. He heard a car start up outside and skid away, and he knew it was too late...

Ψ

All was now quiet again in the dank, seedy warehouse.

In the middle of the floor, Stelios Grivas lay motionless. As he had fallen, the bullet had been jogged that one feared centimetre, and by the time Versleas had crawled off of him he was dead of a myocardial infarction.

Versleas succeeded in getting to his feet. It did not take him a moment to realise that the stooped, sinister man was dead, although quite why he did not know at that stage. He noticed something on the floor in a far corner and he walked gingerly over to investigate. It seemed to be a pouch or something.

Cautiously he picked it up. Hmm, leather… He pulled open the top and looked at the contents, laying the object in the palm of his hand.

It looked like an opaque, roughly-cut chunk of glass…

Ψ

POSTSCRIPT

There the story fades. A few more facts are known and, under the UK and US Freedom of Information legislation, some of them have now been incorporated into this second edition of the book.

And what of the protagonists?

Michael Mahoney died just three months after the incident in Amsterdam. Working on a tip-off from a very high up grass in the IRA, the Gardai (Irish police) were already two months into an investigation of his activities when Mahoney went to Amsterdam. While he was away, the Gardai took the opportunity to raid his mansion 'Somewhere in the South'. The place was ransacked, gutted of every moveable object. The hidden tapes of most of Mahoney's recent business deals were discovered, and all the police had to do was sit back and await his return. When the dishevelled and weary Mahoney landed at Dublin Airport in the morning of November 9 1974, he was immediately arrested.

Mahoney knew that he would be under threat from his suppliers and customers, he had even more to fear from them than from the police. For this reason, he said not one word throughout the whole of his trial. He was, of course, found guilty and sentenced to life imprisonment. On his way to his internment at Port Laoise prison, a bullet from a gun - some say it was Catholic, some say it was Protestant - entered his brain via his right eye and ended his existence.

Sally-Anne Bowker now lives permanently in Paris, in Neuilly, and is married. With this book, she reads the full story for the first time.

Michael Mouskos remained a 'troublesome priest' until the end. He died in 1977 of a heart attack... possibly genuine. He lies in the Kykko Monastery in Cyprus.

Christina Cascianis is now based in Athens and owns property in various parts of the Hellenic Mediterranean which she lucratively leases to holiday-makers. To this very day she visits Cyprus at least once a month and lays flowers on the joint grave of George and Stelios Grivas. Occasionally she works for the *Mossad*. She is an exceptional lady in every way. She meets Ilich Ramirov again in *The Windsor Secret*.

Ilich Ramirov, with a slight adjustment of his name and his South American cover strengthened, went on to become one of the most feared and famous terrorists (or freedom-fighters) of the nineteen seventies. The Press gave him the nickname 'Carlos The Jackal'.

Cast off by his Russian masters on the fall of the USSR, he became a freelance. At the turn of the twenty-first century he was supposedly spending the rest of his life in prison in France. But Ramirov had never been arrested by the French. Using the Makarios precedent, it was a double the French had unwittingly incarcerated.

Ramirov continued to live in freedom in Venezuela, foraging into the northern hemisphere when his special talents were required. He had gained a certain perverse respectability and was employed as necessary by governments and royal households. His more notable later successes included a car crash in Paris in August 1997 and a plane crash off Cape Cod in

July 1999. He meets Christina Cascianis again in *The Windsor Secret*.

Faisal Ibn Musaed had perhaps the most macabre fate of all. He was publicly decapitated with six hideously painful strokes of the executioner's sword in April 1975 after he had assassinated his uncle, King Faisal of Saudi Arabia, the previous month.

The Eye of Makarios never left the possession of Michael Mouskos. It was taken with him in the pocket of his pants when the British flew him out of Cyprus in July 1974. It stood to reason, after all, that Papadopoulos being a duplicate Makarios, the 'diamond' carried around his waist would be a duplicate as well. The item held in the hand of Chief Inspector Johann Versleas in Amsterdam on the night of November 8 1974 was indeed an opaque, roughly-cut chunk of glass...

The Star of Sierra Leone. It has never been conclusively proven that this and The Eye of Makarios were one and the same. It's fate is uncertain. Rumour has it that, after the death of Makarios, a Swiss jeweller spent three years supervising its cutting, and the stone was eventually cut to become the 170 carat *Star of Peace.* If this is true then it gives this story its final irony - for the person who bought the three million pound diamond in early 1981 was a prominent, and subsequently famous, member of an Arabian Royal Family.

Ψ

REFLECTION

At the time of writing, neither Black September nor any other body has yet exploded a nuclear device in Britain or, within these terms, anywhere else. However:

"We undertake not to drop it on anyone, but if someone is going to drop it on us or someone is going to threaten our existence and independence, even without the use of atomic weapons, we should drop it on them."

Colonel Muammar Qadhafi
in a televised lecture, June 1987

It was to take thirteen more years before Someone realised that they did not need to make their own nuclear devices. Objects that would create similar devastation and loss of life were already flying in and out of airports every day of the year in every country in the world... and they were their's for the taking.

Ψ

APPENDIX 1

CYPRUS

The Island

The island of Cyprus in the eastern Mediterranean is 805 kilometres from the Greek mainland and just 65 kilometres from the Turkish coast. It is one of the world's tiniest countries. In 1974 its population of 650,000 was composed of 78% ethnic Greeks, 18% ethnic Turks and 4% other.

Greek colonies were established in Cyprus over 3000 years ago, and the island later formed part of the Roman, Persian and Byzantine empires. It became a Frankish kingdom in 1193, a Venetian dependency in 1489 and was then conquered by the Turks in 1571.

Under a convention concluded with the Sultan of Constantinople on June 4 1878, the island was made over to England for administrative purposes. Great Britain annexed the island on November 5 1914, and it was given the status of a crown colony on May 1 1925.

Michael Mouskos

Michael Mouskos was born on August 13 1913 in Ayia Panayia, a village in the remote south-west of the Paphos District of

Cyprus. In 1926, at the age of 13, Michael became a novice at the famous Kykko Monastery, in the Paphos District. In 1942 he took his divinity degree at the University of Athens and then continued to live in Greece. He was ordained in 1946.

Two years were then spent on a scholarship in the United States, and while he was still there he was elected Bishop of Kitium (Larnaca). In 1950, at the age of 37, Michael was elected head of the Greek orthodox Church of Cyprus upon the death of Archbishop Makarios II (Makarios means 'blessed'), and, like his predecessors, he also assumed the role of Ethnarch, national leader.

On April 1 1955, a Greek Cypriot terrorist organisation known as EOKA began a campaign against the British in Cyprus. They wanted *Enosis*, complete union with Greece. Mouskos himself was suspected of being the instigator and real leader of EOKA.

Mouskos was arrested in March 1956 and deported to the Seychelles. He was released in 1957 with freedom to go anywhere but Cyprus. He chose Greece.

Although exiled from the island, Mouskos twice attended the General Assembly of the United Nations, and, although he initially demanded *Enosis* and nothing but, he was pressured into acceptance of a compromise solution guaranteeing independence for Cyprus. On February 19 1959, the London Agreement was signed, which meant that Mouskos and Cyprus had renounced *Enosis* forever. Once the Agreement was signed, Mouskos was allowed to return to the island.

Cyprus became an independent republic on August 16 1960 (although Greece, Britain and Turkey still maintained an interest). Mouskos had been elected President the previous December.

However, there were those who were opposed to the renouncement of *Enosis*. EOKA lived...

George Grivas

General George Grivas, a strong supporter of *Enosis* and a good friend of Makarios before the London Agreement, was in charge of all Greek Cypriot forces on the island. He was withdrawn by the Greek Colonels in 1967 at the urging of the Turkish government.

By 1971 Grivas, as head of EOKA, was in hiding. EOKA's terrorist attacks increased and occupied most of Makarios' time.

The Cypriot National Guard

The Cypriot National Guard was a force of about 12,000 conscripts led by some 650 officers on loan from Greece.

Ψ

APPENDIX 2

BLACK SEPTEMBER/*EL FATEH* IN 1974

El Fateh, the largest and strongest of the many Palestinian resistance organisations, was born out of the smouldering ashes of the Arabs' defeat in the battle for Palestine in 1948. One of the many lives lost in the fight was that of Sheikh Hassan Salameh, the legendary Palestinian leader and a hero to his followers both in life and in death. At the time, the entire Palestinian people mourned his untimely departure. Little notice was taken of his then young son, a son who was to become even more famous than his father, and who was to spread the word TERROR throughout the world - Ali Hassan Salameh, co-founder of Black September.

The word *Fateh* is based on the initials of the Palestinian Liberation Movement and means 'Victory'. The name 'Black September' is commemorative of the massacre in Jordan in September 1970 of *El Fateh* guerrillas. Not all died, and the survivors - headed by one Yasser Arafat - slipped across the northern borders of Jordan into Syria and Lebanon. The group was bent on revenge and on righting the injustice they considered to have been done to the Palestinian people.

They first came to the world's attention in Cairo, Egypt, on November 28 1971 when four gunmen shot dead Jordanian premier Wasfi Tell at the entrance to the Sheraton Hotel. One of the gunmen - as was seen on television screens throughout the world - bent down and licked the still-warm blood of his victim from the hotel steps. Although arrested for appearance's sake, the four gunmen were fêted as heroes, and they were eventually released by the Egyptians.

Black September flourished. Many idealists from other countries joined them or announced affiliation. The united groups performed acts of terror, spreading throughout the world, going from strength to strength, reaching an all-time high in atrocities in 1972 with the massacre of the Israeli athletes at the Munich Olympic Games.

However, in games with high stakes, tides easily turn. In the spring of 1973, an Israeli assassination squad raided a certain house in Beirut. Inside, a core of Black September's leaders and advisers had been planning a series of military spectaculars to take place in Europe that summer. Three of the top men died: Mohammed Yusuf Al Najjar, Kamal Adwan and Kamal Nasser (who went the way all men would wish - in bed with two naked girls). As well as this stinging blow, the Israelis also seized a vast amount of Black September/*El Fateh* documentation. Now it was Black September's turn to have its back to the wall.

It was because of this depletion that the remaining powers of the organisation had decided that a military act so grand, so spectacular, so *terrible* had to be committed within the next year. It would be designed to let the world know that their cause was not dead, and to raise them once again in the eyes of their Iraqi, Syrian, Libyan, Algerian and Russian backers.

It was this resolve that led to Black September's liaison man with the IRA, the Maoist Khalil al-Wazir (code-name Abu Jihad) arranging, through the Belgian, the meeting of Michael Mahoney and 'Akay' Al Khalifa.

Since the Israeli raid the previous spring, the core of Black September had kept themselves well hidden and protected from the jubilant *Mossad* (the Israeli Secret Service). No meetings had been held and no contacts made; no direct military act had been perpetrated at their instance. *[The incident at Rome's Leonardo da*

Vinci Airport on December 17 1973, when Arab terrorists killed 31 people, was not a direct action by Black September/PLO. Likewise the shoot-out at Athens Airport the previous August, when 5 people died, was committed by two young hot-heads without the official backing of Black September.]

It was seven months after the Israeli bloodbath that the remaining three core members had met in secret at Zahlé, near Lebanon's eastern border with Syria. There they formulated their plans for the ultimate military act.

The three persons who met in Zahlé were Ali Hassan Salameh, at that time controller of the intelligence and action arms, and who was feared even by Yasser Arafat; Salah Khalef (code-name Abu Ayad), co-founder of Black September and the group's *consiglière* (counsellor), and also second to Arafat on the central committee of *El Fateh*; and a gentleman who has never been positively identified but who is thought to have been the number two of the *Fateh* intelligence agency, Jihad-al-Razd.

These three persons were also present at the subsequent meeting on January 3 1974 (originally scheduled for October 1973 but delayed for three months because of the *Yom Kippur* war) which is related herein. Also in attendance were Abu Jihad, the IRA liaison man, and Faisal Ibn Musaed, a young Arab whose origins were uncertain but who had risen quite suddenly over the past year to become, effectively, a personal assistant to Hassan. Hassan held the young man in great esteem and it was thought by the other core members that Musaed was being groomed to take over should Hassan's demise come suddenly and unexpectedly - which was more than an even bet when you were the leader of the world's most prominent, if currently faltering, 'liberation army'.

Ψ

APPENDIX 3

A Summary of Events Leading Up To The Coup in Cyprus on July 15 1974

The coup was organised by Brigadier Dimitrios Ioannides, head of the Greek military police and on the outer circle of the Colonels who seized power in Athens in 1967. Through his own efforts, Ioannides assumed total power in Greece in 1973. He operated completely behind the scenes, and few people in Greece even knew what he looked like.

Stationed in Cyprus in the 1960s, Ioannides developed a hatred for 'The Red Priest'. Ioannides had under his control the 650 regular officers of the Cypriot National Guard and elements of the old EOKA (known to some as EOKA 'B') to whom Mouskos was a traitor for having abandoned *Enosis*. The intention of the coup was to rectify this.

When Ioannides gave the signal, the National Guard and EOKA brought down Makarios.

THE WINDSOR SECRET

by

DAVID CULLEN

‡

Wednesday August 6 1997

Troodos Mountains, Cyprus

"He iss gone, Stelios. At last, after all this time, he iss in hell where he belongs." Christina looked two metres to her right. "General, your son hass been avenged. *We* haf been avenged."

The sun beat down from the impossibly-blue sky. Even up here in the mountains – where it would start to snow in three months – it was hot. But the forty Celsius heat was well-tempered by the altitude. Down on the coast, the tourists would be sweltering and dropping.

The graves were in a sheltered clearing, in amongst the pine trees, well away from the main road. It was peaceful and naturally scented by the pines. Birds sang. Not many people now knew that there had once been a house on his spot. The house where the General had died on January 27 1974. Just two days after his death, the house had been razed by the Tactical Reserve Force of President Makarios. All but two people had died. At the time of the attack Christina and her lover, the General's son Stelios, had been higher up the mountain.

The summer Christina and Stelios had spent together had been... eventful. They had been on a quest, but they had been betrayed. Betrayed by the man whose death had been announced last week. By a man they knew then as Martinez. Only after Stelios' death had she discovered the true identity of the traitor: he was to become known to the world as Ilych Ramirez Sanchez, a Venezuelan idealist whom the Press would call Carlos The Jackal In fact he was a Russian called Ilich

Ramirov

By that time she had also discovered that Stelios, a Cypriot Greek half-Jew, was also an agent of Israeli Intelligence. She had begged *Mossad Aliyah Beth* to let her help them find Ramirov. Initially they had refused. But over the years they had tested and utilised her, starting with little 'errands' until, many years later, she was trusted enough.

Ramirov had dropped out of sight at the end if the 1980s (it was even reported by some that he had died), cast adrift by his true masters upon the collapse of the USSR.

But the Jews never forget.

Information was gathered, analysed, retained, *remembered*. Israeli agents all over the world watched and waited. Like with the Nazis, the Israeli patience was long.

When Ramirov was kicked out of Syria in 1994, the Israeli machine was kicked back into life. Ramirov went to the Sudan where he thought he would be given sanctuary. But he was not. An Israeli tip-off to the French, a French 'word' with the Sudanese, and Ramirov was arrested in Khartoum on August 14 1994.

And watching in Sudan when he was arrested, and again in Paris when he arrived under heavy security, twenty years after the betrayal in Cyprus, was Israeli agent Christina Cascianis.

Officially General George Grivas, Head of EOKA and sworn enemy of Archbishop Makarios III, still lay where he was originally buried in the grounds of his house in Limassol. To this day the grave was tended by EOKA supporters, not all of them old.

Only a handful of people knew that the General had occupied the grave for little under a year. Upon the death of his son, he had been moved to the joint grave up here in the mountains, *his* mountains.

Christina knelt between the unmarked graves in the small clearing. Leaning forward, she ran her hands simultaneously over both the rocks underneath which the dead father and son lay.

"It iss over," she said to them both, speaking in English for Stelios' sake, her accented Greek voice deep and mellow. "Now we can at last get on with our lifes." She turned to the rock on her left. "Stelios, iff only you had not left me. Think where we could haf been now. Think what Cyprus could haf been had you lived. The island would be united. We could haf had children..." Her eyes clouded.

Then she said briskly, "But, my dear, I yam too old for that now. And anyway you are nott here. And I never wanted children with any off the others."

She opened the small plastic bag she had brought with her and, as she did every month when she visited the graves, she upturned it and sprinkled flower petals over the two rocks. This month it was oleander, so she was careful not to touch the petals.

Then she stood up. It was time to go. "It iss over," she said again. "At last we can all rest in peace. I love you, my darling. I will see you next month." She turned and walked away.

Two metres underneath the rock on the left, the bones of Stelios Grivas began to scream.

DAVID CULLEN

THE MESRINE CONCLUSION

ONLY ONE MAN CAN RETRIEVE THE SECRET - IF HE CAN STAY ALIVE

THE MESRINE CONCLUSION

David Cullen

1978. Only two people still alive know the explosive dark secret of the British Royal House of Windsor.

One lies in her dotage in France, the other continues to rule the royal household in Britain as she has done for 40 years.

A robbery in Paris. The secret is stolen. It must be found at all costs. Police enquiries draw a blank. They need help. There is only one man with the skills to locate the secret – Jacques Mesrine, France's Public Enemy Number One.

But there are those that want the secret for themselves and others who will stop at nothing to ensure the secret remains hidden.

Can Mesrine find the secret before the hunters find him? Death, treachery and double-cross all lead to

THE MESRINE CONCLUSION

Available from *amazon, Lulu* and other online booksellers and thru all good bookshops.

DAVID CULLEN

THE WINDSOR SECRET

ANYONE WHO KNOWS THE SECRET, DIES - ANYONE

THE WINDSOR SECRET

David Cullen

1997. Three women are out for revenge.

In Greece, a lover discovers that justice has not been done.
In England, a princess seeks to humiliate her ex-husband.
In France, a daughter vows retribution after eighteen years.

A secret which they thought was buried forever comes back to
haunt the British Royal House of Windsor. And the deaths must
start again.

And this time to preserve the secret they will even kill the
mother of the future King of England…

Exactly what happened in Paris on August 30 1997?
Who really killed Princess Diana?
And what is

THE WINDSOR SECRET

Available from *amazon*, *Lulu* and other online booksellers and
thru all good bookshops.